# The Archer

✖✖✖

ALSO BY SHRUTI SWAMY

*A House Is a Body*

# The Archer

❌❌❌

*a novel by*

## SHRUTI ANNA SWAMY

ALGONQUIN BOOKS
OF CHAPEL HILL
2021

Published by
Algonquin Books of Chapel Hill
Post Office Box 2225
Chapel Hill, North Carolina 27515-2225

a division of
Workman Publishing
225 Varick Street
New York, New York 10014

*A Kitchen at the Corner of the House* by Ambai, © 2019 by Ambai,
translation from the Tamil by Lakshmi Holmström, published by
Archipelago Books. Used by permission.

This is a work of fiction. While, as in all fiction, the literary perceptions
and insights are based on experience, all names, characters, places, and
incidents either are products of the author's imagination or are used
fictitiously.

LIBRARY OF CONGRESS CATALOGING-IN-PUBLICATION DATA

Names: Swamy, Shruti, [date]–   author.
Title: The archer / a novel by Shruti Anna Swamy.
Description: First edition. | Chapel Hill, North Carolina : Algonquin
Books of Chapel Hill, 2021. | Summary: "Vidya, a rebellious young
dancer and motherless daughter, comes of age in 1960s and
1970s Bombay"— Provided by publisher.
Identifiers: LCCN 2021010464 | ISBN 9781616209902 (hardcover) |
ISBN 9781643752167 (ebook)
Classification: LCC PS3619.W3524 A73 2021 | DDC 813/.6–dc23
LC record available at https://lccn.loc.gov/2021010464

10 9 8 7 6 5 4 3 2 1
First Edition

For my mother,
and for her mother

I did battle for you once, then lost. Would I deny you music? I will be your guru and give you lessons every day. Let the music break out of the vinai and flow everywhere in the forest. Don't think of it as an ordinary musical instrument. Think of it as your life, and play on it.

—Ambai, "Forest"

# The Archer

✖✖✖

# 1

F or a time Vidya had not had a mother or a brother, she had only the idea of a mother and a brother: they were imaginary but real in the same way god was. For a time she had not had a mother but an aunt and not a brother but two cousins who had lived with her in the one room flat she shared with her father. The Cousins were girls, older than her, they were not cruel but it was clear they found her irrelevant. They did their schoolwork quietly in the kitchen, whispering to each other, glamorous secrets of movie stars and breasts. The Aunt had rough, worried hands, and yanked the comb through the girl's hair, which got snarled even in braids. When Father Sir came home from giving tuitions she had gone to sleep but heard the door open and shut.

There was a woman in a room they went to visit every month, a woman with no voice and a face that turned toward the window, but that was not a mother, mothers lived at home with their children. And sang to them.

Now the Aunt-Not-Mother had been put away with the Cousins-Not-Brother, and the Room-Not-Mother had come to live in the house and answered Vidya's question when is my mother coming home, which she asked out of habit more than hope, with the firm and sometimes angry response of *I am your mother*. The child put her hands curiously in the Room-Not-Mother's hair but the Room-Not-Mother brushed her away as though she were a fly. She asked Room-Not-Mother to sing a song to her at bedtime (Aunt-Not-Mother did not sing to her at bedtime, as was expected: she was a not-mother) and Room-Not-Mother did not sing a song and instructed her to close her eyes. She closed her eyes. In the dark she could hear Father Sir talking to Room-Not-Mother, who answered his questions very simply with yeses and nos. Was the heat making her feel ill. *No*. Had she heard from her sister. *No*. Would she write to her again? *Yes*. Then her mind flattened like a coin and she was asleep.

Now Vidya studied (Room-Not-)Mother as she wiped her face again and again with her sari. Earlier she had been in a frenzy of chopping and frying, but she seemed not to know anymore what motion to provide her restless body. Her eyes were keen and dark and hard, like the eyes of a man. She wore a pale green sari with a pretty gold border, cotton, but her best. Skin pulled taut against the drum of her body, in the strip between blouse and skirt: ribs, like that of an unhappy dog. Outside she wore strange shoes of

brown leather and real laces—shoes that made the neighbors whisper—inside her bare feet were big like Vidya's
were big, Vidya's already three sizes larger than the other
girls at school. Father Sir, emerging from his bath, gave a
sharp glance to Vidya sitting idle on the divan, swinging
her legs. "Are you helping your mother?"

She shook her head.

"Well?"

"I'm finished," said the Mother.

"Before you sit down you must always say, mother dear,
how may I be of service?"

"I said I'm finished," said the Mother. "I don't need help
now."

"The girl should learn."

The Mother turned away. She was preparing the puja
plate, and placed a whole laddu beside the tiny holy things
necessary for the rite: a pile of uncooked rice, an oil lamp
still unlit, kumkum and sandalwood paste to be smeared
wetly, and a small brass bell. Vidya was glad that she had
not been pressed into service in the kitchen, not because
she disliked chores (though she did) but because the sight
of so much food, so much food all at once, brought on a
kind of fright in her. It was not time to eat yet and she had
been scolded out of the kitchen several times—not even a
taste—and sat on the divan swinging her legs with anxiety.
Would there be enough? What would she eat first? What
would this brother be like—would she know him? What if

the Brother ate everything, and there was nothing left for her? Recently, the sight of food, food cooking in the stalls along the side of the road—jalebis, bhel, aloo tikki, sev puri—made her feel a wretchedness that was like falling ill. It was dulled only after the morning glass of milk, if she got the morning glass of milk, which, now that Aunt-Not-Mother and Cousins-Not-Brother's hungry mouths had vanished, she was given every morning, and some-times in the evening also. Father Sir left before she woke and returned after she was asleep, and on the weekends he would see her and say: well? This made her uncontrollably shy and she would mouse down into her dress and say yes sir.

"What time does the train get in?"

"One."

"So go, na? You don't want to make them wait."

"I won't make the train come any faster."

But she was nearly pushing him out the door. He put his shoes on in the hallway. He was laughing and said again, "I won't make the train come any faster." Then there he was downstairs, walking through the dusty courtyard, straight through a cricket game of the chaali's boys; they paused and watched him while he passed, in white, a dhoti and a clean kutra. When Father Sir was gone from the window, Vidya turned to watch the Mother again. She had forced herself down into stillness, sat with her hands folded and gripped hard on her lap. She was muttering something under her breath, barely audible, forbidding vowels. Then she fixed her eyes on her daughter and said, "Come here."

Vidya crossed the width of the apartment to the chair where the woman sat: a distance of no more than a few feet. The woman touched her daughter, fixing, smoothing what couldn't be fixed or smoothed, the wild puff of hair that fuzzed up the girl's neat braid, the wrinkles sweated into her good dress. "Do you love your brother?"

"Yes," said Vidya dutifully.

"Then you must tell him. You must say, welcome home, my dear brother."

Vidya nodded.

"And you must care for him like a mother."

No. No. *She* was to be a not-mother. She looked at the woman with panic.

"I thought you were the mother."

"Yes," she said, her tone quickening. "I am the mother. But what I mean is you'll have to help me take care of him."

"Why?"

"Because he is your brother."

"Will I be the mother?"

"No, no. I am the mother." Then, exasperated, she stopped speaking. The apartment was filled with the smell of food. It was like a dream—or a nightmare—so many smells. Vidya had dreams where she was eating everything, kulfi and handvo and rotis and dhal and kheer. She fell upon her knees and ate like a dog, crying out with pleasure and joy. But in these dreams the food never filled her, it was like eating fistfuls of air. Woke with that hard pain in her stomach, and couldn't sleep sometimes, until dawn.

Each minute ripened. It was incredible how much time could be contained in the increments measured by the clock. She thought she would ask again about the food but each time she looked at the Mother she was hushed by the look on her face—it was a terrible look. The Mother was folding herself inward and trying not to cry, and the effort to suppress this monumental emotion was making her eyes red. Vidya looked out the window. The cricket boys had resumed their game, they were calling to one another. Even the littlest ones would not play with her because she was a girl, and spoke to her, when they had to, with disdain. But brothers were different, she was confident of this. In fact, a brother could crack the world of the boys open, and invite her inside. They might never make her the batsman, but surely she could be a minor fielder until she proved her skill. They would rush her, chanting her, she would crow with them: king of the boys! But the Brother? The Brother was a blank, she had no notion of his face (there was a picture kept framed in the house of the Mother holding a baby, but the features were so indistinct it could have been any baby, including Vidya herself), yet she felt him in this moment looking up at her admiringly. King of the boys, she and her brother, but mostly she.

Then, there, on the far corner of her vision, a tonga

dropped three passengers off in the street. They were as tiny as toys: the tonga pulled by a toy-donkey, and the three passengers—a man dressed in white, a dark woman in a parti-colored sari, and a child, an almost baby, carried in the arms of the woman. The girl watched them quietly as they crossed the courtyard. The game had to be paused, but it was paused good-naturedly. Father Sir called something out to the boys as he passed, a greeting of some sort, and there was joy in the sound of his voice if not the words it carried. The Mother heard Father Sir's voice but remained where she was, as though calmed by it.

"Listen, now, when your mother's sister comes you must tell her how much you love the beautiful dress she sent you."

"But when should I kiss my brother?"

"After. Say my dress is very lovely auntie."

"My dress is very lovely auntie."

"Good, just like that."

The Mother was smiling and wiping her eyes. The three toys were moving up the stairs but neither woman nor girl rushed out to greet them. The woman took the girl's small hand and held it tightly, squeezing it. The feeling of being touched by the woman was so lovely, that the time that had moved for ages so slowly began, now, to quicken. Only moments, only seconds before she had a Brother, and her Mother touched her hair. The door opened. Slipping off their shoes in the hall—

THE LIGHT COMING from the doorway darkened them.
They were just shapes. Then Father Sir stepped through the
door and became himself, and the woman in the brightly
colored sari holding the boy became herself, and the boy
became himself. Who were they? Father Sir was self-evi-
dent, he was tall and thin with a high forehead and beady
glasses like Gandhiji. The woman who must be her aunt
had a dark face and was weeping. There was a stud of gold
in her nose. The sari was checked with green and yellow,
bordered in red, the colors that licked the eye. Before she got
to the boy who was her Brother she performed her task to
the weeping woman's knees. "MydressisverylovelyAuntie."

The Mother pulled Vidya away roughly. "Where is my
sister?"

"Her son fell ill, madam."

"So she sends a servant?" said the Mother.

"She didn't want to leave her son, madam." She had
managed to stop weeping, but was holding tightly to the
boy. The boy, the baby, the Brother. Vidya could see his little
feet dangling down, bare feet, but he had folded his face into
the chest of the woman and showed his sister only the back
of his dark head. Sister. She said, "Welcome home, my dear
brother," and then looked at the Mother, now doubtful, to
see if she had spoiled this task as she had spoiled the other
one, perhaps she had muddled up the words, the order—an
adult mystery. But the Mother did not seem to have heard
her and was looking now at the boy, hard at the boy. On her

face was a tightly concentrated fury. Fury at Vidya, at the Brother, at the other woman? Or, most unfathomably of all, at Father Sir? The Mother held out her arms. The expression on the other woman's face trembled for a moment and the boy, who had been sleeping, began to wake, transferred from mother to mother: Vidya caught his face, gathering red and splitting open into a cry. He was saying ammu, ammu, as the dark woman relinquished him, twisting away from the woman his mother, back to the arms of the woman who had brought him, who cast her gaze down and squeezed her hands together. The Mother's face became tender as she held the boy. She rocked him back and forth and whispered to him silly little rhymes, ones Vidya had never heard the Mother utter. He would not calm. He began to kick. Instead of setting him back in the other woman's arms, which were stretched out to receive him, he was set screaming on the divan. Immediately the boy was up, tottering on his skinny legs, toward the parti-colored woman, who touched him, his head, and began to speak to him gently in a language that no one but he could understand.

The Mother was standing clenched, so upright. Her keen dark man's eyes were full of red.

"Come, come, let's eat," said Father Sir. "We're all of us hungry."

Food! And Brother so small and fussy—he surely would not eat very much. But the Mother would not move from where she was standing to ready the meal and offer plates.

Father Sir said, "Wife!"

Fear—the room held it, that the Mother would crack. As she stood, holding her sari balled in each hand, so still, with only the vein at her temple flickering with pulse. Not a sound was made, even Vidya held her breath. And in an instant the room righted itself, an inexplicable shift in weather, the Mother said I forgot to do the puja, and the boy was held again by the woman, calm now, sucking his thumb, while his mother circled his face with the small flicker of light, ringing the small brass bell, then printing his brow center with a smear of red, and fragrant beige, and a single bead of rice, which fell off right away. She broke the laddu in two and pushed the sweet between the boy's lips—he chewed at it distractedly with nubbly teeth. The other half was given entire to the woman who held him. Laddus: the ferocity of yellow sugar. If Vidya was given a laddu she broke it in her palm and ate each grain. The boy ate his oppositely, fast and unthinking. He looked calm now and didn't seem to mind being at the center of so many's attention, tugging the ear of the woman who held him, tiny, a baby, with none of the plumpness of baby, with none of baby's glowing health. He looked yellow and somehow tough, his skin scaly with dryness.

"Are you hungry?" The Mother pointed her question at the other woman without seeming, exactly, to address her. Her voice was filled with a determined coolness, and she used the familiar, though not the most cuttingly familiar *you*.

The woman seemed to have trouble with the question and stood for some moments looking uncomfortably at the floor. Then she said, "No, no, please don't trouble yourself."

"Don't be silly," said Father Sir. "You've had a long journey. How many hours?"

"Thirteen."

"Thirteen hours. Come, wash up, we'll run some water for you. Then you can eat."

The woman was brought a towel, she parted from the Brother with reluctance, pulling shut the curtain that demarcated the washroom from the kitchen. He screamed, the Brother, his eyes outlined in kohl: kohl gave his eyes the burning quality of a saint. The woman began to talk to him from behind the curtain as she washed—at the sound of her voice he quieted. The Mother was loath to leave him, but she did, immersing herself in the kitchen to prepare the food while Father Sir seated himself on the floor and waited for the plates to be brought to him. Vidya, reminded, rose to follow the Mother into the terrifying kitchen, which was filled with the noise of food. "Go give this plate," and she carried it with care, heavy with food, sick with food, kadhi and raita and black chana, and shaak and rotis made fresh, one after the other, by the Mother who squatted by the stove with the shine of sweat across her brow and made them thin with the intelligence of her own fingers, thin as paper, puffed over the flame, fragrant of ripe wheat shined with ghee. Father Sir first, then Vidya was given her own plate, her own roti, while the Mother sat down by the boy and began to feed him with her own hand, food he accepted with a benign indifference. She was smiling now, the Mother, as the boy let her touch his face, though every once in a while he would turn away with an anxious look to the dark woman, who had emerged from behind the curtain and would smile at him, and then he would turn his face back toward the offered food.

Vidya was in an agony of indecision. Faced with so many dishes at once, she touched nothing on her plate, just stared at it—four little cups containing bright circles of food, the perfectly circular roti at the center, cooling. The smell of the food came up to her, it came into her, thrashed against her. Rice was brought out. But the food—her food. Her stomach hurt.

"Eat," said Father Sir, who had already finished his rice. She knew better than to cry or say I can't. She could see herself, her little brown hand, come quick down and tear the roti between her fingers, then dip into a dish—which dish, which food?—and bring the morsel into her mouth. But she could not will the hand to do it. She looked away from her plate, and then eagerly back at it, afraid that it had vanished. It was still there. She could not move.

"What's the matter?" said the Mother.

She shook her head.

"What's the matter, don't like?"

"No."

"Don't like? Don't eat," said the Mother, and lifted away the untouched plate.

The Mother did sing. Badly. But not *to* her. The notes felt curiously sour and wrong, even when there was no other music, and the voice that sang them was uncomfortably naked, like the voice one prayed with, or the body that one bared with honesty to the doctor. She practiced in the full light of day, loudly, after morning's breakfast, and took lessons on Sundays at the Kalā Sangam Bhavan Classical Music and Dance Complex, bringing the Brother and then Vidya to care for him.

Vidya discovered that the Brother was a good audience for jumping off the Bhavan's steps; to him, even a jump from the first step was impressive. Gaining confidence she would climb, watching him watch her with admiration as she leapt down the second and then the third step, he laughing in delight at her neat landings. But the fifth was tall, as tall as her, she looked down over the edge. She had jumped from there last week but had forgotten how it felt to be so brave. The sixth! There was a thing called death: you went to another place. You jumped off the highest step in the world and were thrilled into flying. No, death was a bad thing, a lonely thing. A stern grandma had died, you didn't see her anymore. The loved grandma remained. But death came for all, not only the very old. Death lived maybe on the tenth step.

Against the wall, half-dozing, a watchman in khakis and long wool jerked up and smiled at the Brother, and then at her. She didn't return the smile. They looked at you like you were the same as other children, they always smiled at you as if you were the same: silly, clowning, social, unserious, playing make-believe or, worse, becoming precious for them. Some of her cousins behaved like this when trying to win the love of Grandma during summer visits and it disgusted her. Her Mother would whisper to her, with delicious scorn, look at that little liar; Grandma was never swayed, but aunties were, which made them not worth loving.

She skipped the sixth step and went directly to the seventh, where she always stalled; she could climb no closer to death. She sat for a while with her feet over the edge. The Bhavan's courtyard seemed to exist outside the city, borrowing only its birds, which crossed in lazy flocks the rectangle of sky that capped the compound. Parrots showed green against the blue, but their scribbling noise was muted by the assonant chorus of music lessons, each individual lesson weaving into a new whole that contained an element of the Mother she could not quite hear, but still somehow sense. Through the door, she had seen the Mother's teacher wince at the sound of her voice, but the Mother had not noticed or cared, and plowed on, heedless.

Yes, though, there was another noise, a sense of rhythm, the shivering sound of rain. It was nearer, and then voices too, on the ground floor, and Vidya, now curious, followed the steps toward the sound: the level half underground and half above it, with windows that looked onto the court-yard and the street, letting in a dim yellow light:

there were girls moving with purpose in this new secret room; their movements were described twice, by the rhythm of finger and palm against drum (a man played the drums, pulling from it a range of tones both heavy and light, his fingers springing away from the dark cores) and by spoken voice (a woman recited the rhythm in a language of single syllables, mysterious, expressive words both odder and more familiar than English)—and a third time by the bells wound thickly around the ankles of the best girls, and thinly around the ankles of the younger girls, some almost as young as her, some teenagers or even young women, moving with varying grace and control, but all moving with purpose, their bodies taut with the effort of correctness, their feet speaking and their eyes driven inward. Vidya, in the doorway, was not seen, was only seeing, her body lifting unconsciously, straightening itself, wanting to stand and move correctly as she watched a girl at the front of the room moving in a whirling yellow kameez, with short, swift limbs, who made a phrase with her body and was scolded by the woman who had spoken it, who made the phrase again with her body, moving this time her arms in concert with her legs, her bells glistening with hard noise, and was scolded again by the woman, who, in the dim light, had the fierce, kohl-made eyes of a leader and a ferocious bearing, not unlike the Mother's, even while seated. This woman was beautiful, magnetically so. Her hair, striped with white, was parted down the middle and pinned into a low bun in a plain style so that her opulent face stood out in relief to it, pale and richly colored, her eyes a glinting black as though jeweled. Her hand slapped against her thigh, marking the same rhythm she spoke through that strange language of single syllables, and the moving girl again tried the phrase slightly refined and this time was not scolded by the woman—not praised, but her bearing became prouder, as if she had been praised. The room was incredibly hot: there was no fan, in the corner was a small shrine to Shiva with his foot lifted in destruction, a stick of incense burned to the nub for him and the room smelled of it, and loudly of sweat, the girls' and the percussionist's, whose hands seemed to take a precise effort regardless of how quickly or slowly the rhythm was that issued from them, and he held his arms very heavily in order to let his fingers be light. She could be tiny in the doorway: just eyes. Watching the girl move now made her want to be nothing. A thought came to her and it was like the first thought she had ever had: I am nothing. How long she stood there, fixed—moth: flame. Then suddenly coming out of a dream she remembered her Brother and ran up the steps.

Evening had deepened outside but the Mother was not

finished. The Brother was sitting by himself on the step she had abandoned, a cry starting to bubble into his face, and she snatched him up and stood in the courtyard listening now to the sounds coming from the building, trying to parse and understand them. What was the language the woman spoke? And to whom were they speaking, exactly? Not with that odd spoken language, not just. With their bodies that they made follow a set of grace rules.

"Ah, you must be a dancer," said the watchman.

"That was dancing?"

"Of course. What else would it be?"

She thought it was the clapping and swirling of Navaratri, exuberant and ordinary. She sat on the step. To be small was to be comfortable with the world being constantly upended: oh, but she wasn't. The sun was going and the sky began to bruise from its absence.

"Vidya!"

There she was, the Mother, so tall, in her funny outside shoes, men's shoes made of brown leather, with laces and too large, in her gray and red sari, descending the steps. The hour's music had left sweetness on her tongue. In the fading light the Mother looked familiar and fragile, and Vidya ran up the steps toward her, heedless of the trailing Brother: wanting the Mother, wanting no harm to come to her, wanting her hand. She took it, cool, in her hot palms.

"Here I am."

Sleeping, she thought about moving like the girls until she was dreaming. She was underwater where the gods drowned in the festival looked at her with their cracked wide-open eyes. Her movements were difficult and pure in the salt of the city's bay water. She woke when the Mother woke, in the small hour before dawn. The Mother made no sound as she woke, and the others slept on heedless, but Vidya was tugged out of sleep to watch her rise from her mat and walk to the kitchen and light with a match the small kerosene lamp they used in the evenings when the power was cut. Through the flickering light, Vidya watched the Mother draw out a notebook from the cupboard that housed schoolthings. The defensiveness with which the Mother held herself was entirely absent: it was as though she had walked straight into her notebook from her dreaming. She seemed to be leaning out of her body, reaching with her mind toward the notebook as her pencil moved over it. Her lips moved as though she were praying. What was she doing? In her face, in the eyes, there was that same quality of intention, of will. Holy eyes. The nature of the work, it was clear, was inscrutable but important.

Watching the Mother, Vidya was coming awake. She liked to come awake slowly, like this; it was difficult changing states, a night creature turning into an entirely different one that functioned during the day, and then had to turn back into the original creature once night fell. Father Sir and the Brother were unlike her: they were awake as soon as their eyes came open. Fresh pale light began to gather at the window, when it reached a certain density Father Sir sat up and stretched. Vidya went outside to clean her teeth, dreamy at this task, rubbing the bitter tooth powder with a lazy finger, then spitting over the railing (look first! shouted an angry neighbor—but she never did). She liked the feeling of her soul returning to her body the same way her arm came awake when she pressed the life out of it. In this time, she could see herself outside herself like when she watched the Mother, she could see her own smallness, the small holes where her eyes were and her tiny ears, and her tiny grasping hands and feet, her pink divided tongue with its flat tip: all the equipment she had to divine the world's moods and rules and strange events.

Bodies were secrets: not hers. She was a clean little egg, hunched in the bathing-room, she spread the lips of her susu and enjoyed the look of it, glossy before it was even wet, with a lush texture and the faintest most animal scent. But take too long at your bath and the Mother might pull you out and slap you. So she was careful. It was important to not be slapped in the morning to keep the feeling of dreaming on, until it dissipated, slowly, of its own accord, during the yellow hour of mother-chores. Then she was transformed into her day self, standing triumphant on the roof, dredging the washed clothes from their bucket and laying them on the railing so she could overturn the bucket to stand on as she hung them dripping from the line. From here, six stories up, the heat and noise of the city—the city's weight—was eased and softened. What lay before her seemed to her to be the whole of Bombay with its flapping laundry and water tanks, though she couldn't see the ocean, obscured by Malabar Hill, a green slope dotted with the white mansions and bungalows of the rich and the Saint Catherine's Nursing Home, where rich babies were born. Even white babies, though she had never seen one—only the white baby dolls in the window of the toy store in Colaba that shut their lovely blue eyes when they were laid on their backs for bed. The day self was strong enough to withstand it, to withstand chores, and school, and the evening hours before bed. But the night self was the true self, the one who dreamed.

The Mother didn't like to talk during the yellow hour. Sometimes she lay down on the divan with a look of pain on her face and would not be moved. Mi-grane, said Father Sir in English, who showed her to take a rag and dip it in cool water to spread across the haunted forehead. In a nightmare the Mother was moaning, her hands pressed against her ears. Her blood was too hot and needed to be cooled, Vidya understood, laying the rag against the Mother's skin: she understood the Mother's nightmare. Vidya would be standing at the window watching the dogs at the edge of the courtyard bunched in their bodies and dreaming, she would be sucking her finger to get its first tang of salt, and humming something to herself mindlessly, four or five repeated notes in a drowsy sequence, and would feel a flickering thing within her like a very very small flame, very very small, but if she could hold on to the thread of it she could say what it was and grow it, it was a good feeling, deeply good, but so shy and without any name—and then suddenly a dog would wake and snap its jaws, it would nose into itself to bite a wound that itched, only that, and the feeling would snuff out and she would feel wildly bad, as though she had been slapped.

The day would fall into a despairing mood, and turn so ugly, she would spend brown hours doing chores or her schoolwork, and there was nothing good in the world but the jar of honey kept on a high shelf in the kitchen, which, when held to the light, glowed gold like a lantern, and when licked had a terrible sweetness. But she was not allowed to hold it. She didn't even want to *eat* it, just to hold it. She was not allowed. She was in a rage and wanted to do something bad; when no one was looking, she broke Father Sir's red pencil in two, sorry as soon as she'd done it. The two broken halves looked as disturbing as the gecko split by her evil boy-cousins, and she put them trembling back in the case, leaving the nightmaring Mother with the Brother, and went to school with her slate wrapped in a cloth so it wouldn't be smudged. Mi-grane. The Mother was not well. Crossing the street carefully, Vidya walked quickly past the sweetshop not wanting to be flooded with itchy desire. All day all day she thought about the pencil, the way it snapped so easily in her hands, like time itself, separating between what could have been and what was. She was not ready with an answer when Schoolteacher called on her and she received a rap along her knuckles with the flat of a ruler. Stung! She felt ashamed before god and asked for his forgiveness, but she didn't receive a reply. What an evil girl she was, what bad deeds she was capable of! Walking home, she looked at herself in the jewelry store window, delighted, momentarily, by her wrongdoing. She would run away! She would lead a rebel army, like the Rani of Jhansi!

The Mother was up and cooking, the boy banging two cups together, adding his noise to the evening racket. The chaali was never quiet, but in the late afternoon it ran several channels of gossip and at least two fights, and all sorts of yelling from the kids downstairs, not to mention the Mehtas' radio with the sound turned up so the neighbors could enjoy the program. The sounds of water, washing, of work, bodies laughing and groaning and living. Stripped suddenly of her courage, she wanted to weep, she was so bad, so sorry. She imagined a mother who would look for a moment at her, with the eyes really looking at her not just her shape or dirtiness or bother, but at *her*, to the dreaming core, and say her name. For a moment that was all she wanted in the world, that the Mother would look up and say her name. A name would pin her back into the world, make her belong inside it again; a name bound one person to another, made them belong to each other. Then she would do anything, anything, without complaint. "Take him, will you?" said the Mother without looking up.

Dutifully she took the cups out of his hands and lifted him up. He was soiled and she changed him. He was worse than a doll, laughing at her. She would not kiss him, or give him any sweet thing. When she put him down he started to cry so she picked him up again. Why did you break that pencil? she whispered in his ear, placing the broken halves into his hands like toys.

Then it was summer, already too hot, and they took the train to Father Sir's father sir's home in the north, in a world built of brown dust. From the train window she saw the black mountain where the goddess lived, and where, each harvest, pilgrims climbed in the desperate heat to offer her their prayers. In Father Sir's father's sir's pale blue house Grandma sat in a room surrounded by Vidya's one hundred cousins, looking like a huge, amazing, loving, gentle beast. "Come, Vidya," she said, and lifted her onto her lap, heedless of the Brother. *Vidya* was favorite. In the sleeping hour, Grandma slept inside with the adults, and the children slept outside in the shaded courtyard. Vidya hated the sleeping hour, and would have preferred to wander, quiet, though the mud-cool rooms of the house, to sit quietly in the innermost room where the curd and milk and gods were kept, very quietly, she would not disturb anybody, but knew that if she were caught in this trespass her punishment would be severe, that the condition of Grandma's love for her was more exacting than Grandma's love for her wretched boy cousins. It was like god's love: it demanded absolute fealty. She had crossed Grandma once, and Grandma's face had turned startlingly violent, like a bull's. And then Grandma would not look at her. This went on for days. She remembered begging at Grandma's ankles. Low down she had the smell of soil in the folds of her sari, and the sweetish smell of the sandalwood and kumkum she used each morning in her prayers. When Grandma returned to her, Vidya was obedient to her every command. She sat charmed on her lap, tracing the tattoos that had been poked into Grandma's skin with song and ink, blue as the blood that showed at each wrist where the skin was thinnest. Wasp, goddess, crescent moon—Grandma said they made her body more beautiful, and more sacred, but smiled: you didn't even know I was beautiful, you wouldn't believe it. And it was true, the girl could not imagine a grandma who was different from the old woman whose folded legs she so proudly occupied. Vidya would never be old, as she would never be beautiful, just a girl, and shook her head. You will be too, my girl, said Grandma wickedly. You too, my girl, will be both soon enough.

She lay down now on her mat. Her body became itchy all over in the windless air and she looked with longing at the older cousins who lay close to each other, speaking softly and laughing, languid but not sleepy, occupying the sleeping hour like swimmers waist deep in cool water while their top halves still resided in air. She forced her eyes closed and thought about dancing. Dancing—a secret was passed along, something a body told a body. She could not steal it, so how would she acquire it? The Mother would say no! It required money. Perhaps she could steal it by standing quietly and looking. She thought of the movements she remembered, but already they were blurred. Something you did with the hands, flashing the palms? To submerge the eyes in absolute serenity. How could she sleep now, when the world persisted, filled with shattering movement?

The Brother, bathed and fed, had been taken in to sleep with the grown-ups; now, fussing, he was carried out by the Mother, who stood on the verandah with him still in her arms, her arms always reaching for him when they were not otherwise occupied, an apology of arms always reaching for him. She walked slowly across the verandah bouncing the boy in her arms. After a while the Brother stopped fussing and fell into a doze, his body sagging against the Mother's. But even then she did not stop walking back and forth across the verandah. She walked, rocking him, her lips were moving, her body gaining energy as it moved. She walked like this building fury until Father Sir came outside. Come inside, his body seemed to say, as he reached for the boy to put a hand on him but the Mother was too quick.

"He wakes when I stop moving."

"He's too old for this. You'll make yourself sick. Have Vidya take him."

The Mother clicked her tongue. "He's my boy."

"You didn't sleep at all on the train. Even my sister can help."

"Your sister who fed her children the milk that was meant for yours? And tell me this," said the Mother, not even whispering now. "If your mother loves you so much, why didn't she take him?"

"You know she couldn't. They can't take care of children."

"She's not an invalid."

"They're old." Father Sir's voice was unusually sharp; he was worried about being overheard.

"What nonsense. She carries on with the children all day."

"It wasn't up to her."

"Jackals, all of them," she said. "Everyone looking at me with their eyes like daggers. And this heat. It's worse here than in the city."

IN THE AFTERNOONS, the children went down to the river. She had been told the river was broad in the month following monsoon, big as the ocean it was named for, but whenever she was here it was flanked on both sides by hard, dry mud, with the same cracked fractals as elephant skin. Boys got to swim, but the girls of the family had been forbidden: long ago, a teenaged cousin had drowned. After chores, the girls made a doll of Vidya and practiced complex braids in the late afternoon shade. She enjoyed the feeling of their sudden attention and the feeling of so many hands in her hair as her head was tugged this way and that, listening equally to the distant shrieks of the splashing boys and the gentle voices of the girls who enjoyed singing the movie songs they had half-learned and embellished together the parts they didn't know. After a while they became bored with being kind and started to tug her hair and tease her and goad her, calling her a tribal person. She was too dark, Suchitra pointed out, presiding over the group of girls as regally as Grandma presided over all the cousins. She was too dark; the color of her arms darkened, it seemed, as soon as she arrived in the village, to something the color of river mud: wet. Of Father Sir's family, everyone seemed a light gold; it was the Mother's side who incubated the secret tendency toward darkness, visible on the faces of the Mother's elder brothers, whom Vidya had met long ago, as though in a dream, and of whose faces she remembered only this singular feature. Where do you belong, said Suchitra, with mud-people? You should go live in the forest with your tribe. Vidya ran away, her hair still loose, and so angry, rubbed herself in dirt, wanting to be dirt, living in her true family. If she knew how to move with purpose, nothing would wound her. But she had not considered the darkness of her skin. The neighbor girl was far fairer than she. Maybe she would not be allowed to dance, would be punished for stealing. Maybe she could not even steal!

Then she was in despair, returning to the house filthy and knotted like an animal, and like an animal, loping, alone. The Mother was sitting with the aunties preparing dinner, but all alone slicing doodhi against a curved black blade. It was sad to see her next to but still apart from all the aunties, her eyes narrowed to her task, shutting out all possibility for conversation as the aunties laughed and gossiped. In the presence of the aunties, the Mother looked shrunken down and incorrect. The Brother sat near her, holding fascinated in his hands three red coins of carrot.

"Vidya?" said the Mother, so astonished by her daughter's appearance that for a moment she didn't seem angry. In fact there was something else on her face, an almost-smile that quivered her lips for a second before it vanished. "You see," said Aunt-Not-Mother, "what I had to put up with? That girl is running wild."

The knife clattered from the Mother's grip, she lifted Vidya and spread her quick across her lap and smacked her hard, five times, all the mothers watching with their lips pursed in disgust, and before Vidya could make a sound the Brother did, letting out a wide wail, and the Mother stopped before her hand smacked the bottom for a sixth time, or, a seventh, or an eighth, as it seemed to want, growing as the blows were in intensity and speed. Unlike the Brother, Vidya knew better than to cry, her eyes looked for Grandma, who had not been cooking but directing and gossiping, and whose eyes now met hers with a gaze neither compassionate nor even tender but still seeing Vidya in her wretched state. But to glance back at the Mother, which Vidya did, quickly, was to see a red-eyed and confused creature, not a vengeful one.

"Vidya," Grandma said, still not tender, in a voice almost stern—the girl glanced back at the Mother again kneeling alone, oh, she was sorry—Grandma smelled strongly of coconut hair oil as she led her to the area of the courtyard where the women bathed. "Get some water," said Grandma, and Vidya drew up bathwater from the shallow well and heaved the bucket over to the old woman. Under Grandma's hands she knew herself to be a miracle. Naked now, bent beneath the cool stream of water, the dirt and sweat and black tears eased from her skin and she was clean. Grandma did sing when occupied in other tasks, a song came from her lips as unconsciously as breath. "Oh Grandma!" she said. "Why am I like this?"

"You have your mother's blood—too hot," Grandma said calmly.

"But what can I do?"

"I don't know, little one. Sometimes god puts a soul in the wrong body. You should have been a boy, with your nature."

"What is my nature?"

"You are restless, you are unsatisfied. You cannot reconcile yourself. A boy could find an outlet for all his restlessness. Not you."

"Why not?"

"Because you will get married, little one, and you will live in your mother-in-law's home. And you will have to do as she says."

"No, no. I won't get married."

"No," said Grandma, taking the girl's cheeks in her hands. Now a breeze licked against Vidya's wet skin and she shivered. "You wild thing. I don't know what's going to become of you."

LATER SHE WOKE violently to her Mother's voice in the dark. The Mother began to cry loudly, waking some of the other sleepers, the Mother saying, in the dim room, that Shanta-Kaki was a jackal. They were all jackals: she said it in English, jackals, jackals. She said a pox on both your houses. She was crying and someone lit a lamp so from the doorway Vidya could see the scene suddenly wild with light, the Mother with her long hair outspread, and her hands outspread, and her eyes red, her gray sari damp and rumpled, screaming at Shanta-Kaki who seemed to look around the room with a kind of vindication, an exaggerated shock. "She *spat* on me," said Shanta-Kaki, one of the prettiest, meanest aunts, "we were just talking—"

"None of this trouble if he'd married my sister," muttered the wife of Father Sir's eldest brother. Vidya was a mouse in the dark, unseen, unknown. Something had shattered, cracked open, things spilling outside of the Mother that should remain in. The wildness of the Mother's eyes imprinted on her. Could no one else see it, how afraid she was? She went to her. The Mother was kneeling down, and Vidya put a hand on either side of the Mother's hot face. Her eyes and the Mother's eyes looked at each other. A long sour exhale came through the Mother's lips. After that the Mother was calm, and let herself be led out of the room.

Early morning they left, waiting at the train station until afternoon. It was her fault, Vidya realized obliquely, though nobody had thought to scold her. If she could simply control herself, if she could behave better, more correctly—if she could love her mother-work, and cool her blood, and want to get married—all of it—things would not be this way. The Mother sat oddly on the bench with her hands clutching her suitcase, her head at a high tilt and her eyes hard and very angry. No one spoke to her, not Father Sir, not the children, as though they had all agreed without conference that any small slip could set the Mother off again into her wildness. They had not said goodbye. No one looked at them except Grandma. Grandma took the girl's chin in her hand and squeezed it, with love and warning. Vidya took the Brother, now fussing, to the candy-wallah to look at the chips and sweets. He chose, hypothetically, chocolate, she a fat samosa, both of which Father Sir bought for them after some time and which they both ate very quickly but somehow without relish. She leaned against the slim core of hunger to keep her from feeling bored and sorry. No, but she was sorry.

On the train she sat beside the Mother, her head growing heavy as sleep took it, and she willfully let her head rest against the Mother's shoulder. Up close the Mother smelled bleak, almost like blood: she hadn't bathed. She smelled bleak, of headache and anger and illness. But this was hers: the Mother's true smell. Vidya, half dozing, felt herself wanting to press in closer, to the source of the smell, to return to the smell, which was so achingly familiar she understood herself to be born from it. In a small red room she had waited, she felt herself remembering it now, seeing red all around instead of the black that closed eyes make, rocking back and forth in a regular rhythm as the train rocked the sleepers in the regular rhythm, her body driving deeper and deeper into its sleep.

Home again. The Brother was sweet in the damp evening. Milk plumped his cheeks and made his skin soft: sometimes Vidya stroked his face with curiosity and he allowed it, stoically. She whispered words into his ear but he didn't appear to notice—just random words, *tree, bell, stupid-idiot.* So deep was his silence it infected her, and the words felt soft and inert in her mouth. The words dropped into his ears and stayed there, like stones into silk. So calm, she wanted to rough him sometimes, she wanted to put the heavy weight of him down, the weight that made her arms ache. It was Saturday. The Mother was working on a small pile of papers Father Sir had left her.

"Don't pinch," said the Mother, without looking up.

But she hadn't done anything, she had only held each of his elbows to test the bend, and he still hadn't made a sound. "I only—"

"Do your schoolwork."

"I did it already."

"All of it?"

"Yes, all."

"Come here." The Mother put down the pen to slap the girl. Vidya lifted her hand to the hot cheek, her right: the Mother always slapped with her left hand. "This is what liars get."

But she was told, wasn't she, to love her Brother? She rubbed her cheek. She had done all her schoolwork except for her English, and she hated it the most, so had saved it for last. It was not English's fault: the teacher was the meanest. They sat in rows and recited nonsensical sylla-bles, He-lo-tich-er-howyare-oo? The smartest girls got their hands rapped with rulers with absolutely no provocation, for they had all quickly learned not to ask questions. No such thing as a smart girl, her English teacher had said, but of course Vidya didn't believe her, and had said so, and had been punished. Stubborn girl, the same as a bad girl, but she had not changed her mind.

"What is it, English?"

Vidya said yes.

"What are you writing?"

She brought the slate over to the Mother, and the textbook she copied the words from. "What is this?"

She shrugged. It was about Jane, Jane who was invited to a party—that is, something for English children, and wanted to bring a—cake—everyone wanted to eat, but it looked frilly and pretty, like a thing you would only look at—but on the way to the party, the cake—

"Bapre, what garbage. This is what they're teaching you?"

Garbage? Didn't the Mother love English? Was it a test, she wondered, and looked up at the Mother silently.

"Listen," said the Mother, closing her eyes. As she spoke, Vidya strained to listen, knowing it was English, wanting to find in the lush jungle of sound some trees or even branches she could grasp, but found nothing: not *cake*, not *Jane*, not *tich-er*. Why didn't the Mother sing like this, loose and soft and graceful? Why did she not move through the world like this, a lion?

"You see?"

Vidya nodded: she didn't.

"You know what that was?"

"No."

"Ask your teacher about Tennyson."

She nodded: wouldn't, but. "Mother?"

"What."

"What work do you do in the mornings, before everyone is awake?"

"Work?" the Mother said.

"Yes, with your notebook."

"I'm practicing my music."

"But you don't sing."

"I don't want to sing. I wanted to learn tabla but they won't let me."

"Why not?"

"Women can't play tabla."

"Why not?"

"Oh, don't ask why not why not—you'll always be unhappy."

"I want to learn dancing," said Vidya. Blurted—it could no longer be held in. Want and want and want, the condition of living: sweets, dolls, milk, toys—dance. "Like they do at your school."

"Dancing," the Mother said very sharply, a strange look passing over her face, "dancing, why dancing?"

"I saw a girl—I saw them dancing—when you were at your lesson."

"Is that all, you want to be like the other girls you saw?"

"No."

"Then—"

"I don't know why. I *want* to."

The strange look on the Mother's face—was pleasure. Her mouth stayed stern but her eyes were smiling. "You do, don't you. You know I named you after a kathak dancer. I saw her picture in the newspaper. I never thought . . . she looked like she—understood something."

The Mother's voice, dreamy? Her arms relaxed against her knees. She brushed her fingers against her daughter's cheek. "If you want to learn, you have to be serious about it. It's not playing. You have to have discipline and practice."

"I will."

"Do you promise?"

"Yes."

"If you make a promise, you must obey it. Do you know the story of Eklavya?"

"No."

The Mother said: "Once there was a Nishada boy named Eklavya. Eklavya was a gifted archer, and he sought out Drona, the greatest teacher of archery, to train him. Drona was already employed to teach the king's sons, so he turned Eklavya away. Not deterred, Eklavya made a clay idol of Drona and took him as his guru, and practiced before the idol until his skill was as fine as the sharpest arrow.

"One day, Drona was walking in the forest and came

across a sight that intrigued him. There was a dog whose mouth was muzzled with arrows—muzzled shut—but the arrows had been so skillfully deployed that the skin was not even pierced. Drona followed the dog through the forest: the dog led him to Eklavya. Eklavya was delighted to see his teacher. He explained that the dog had disturbed his daily practice by barking, so he had peacefully silenced him. Drona, stunned by the skill of this archer, asked for his identity. Eklavya pointed to the statue and said that he was his, Drona's, student. 'If I am your guru, you must give me dakshina.' Eklavya said he would give Drona anything he wished. Drona asked for the boy's right thumb, so that he would never be a better archer than his beloved student, Arjun. Eklavya took a knife out of his pocket and sliced off his thumb."

"But why did Drona ask for something so cruel?"

"It was his dharma to ask, and for Eklavya to give it. See, no matter what the promise is, you must not break it."

"But why—"

There was a crash. The Brother, unobserved, had been climbing in the kitchen, up the shelves, and jumped. He lay on the floor, unharmed but squalling in a scatter of pots. At the sound of him, the face of the Mother seemed to remember itself, like the pain catching up to a burned finger; it seemed to look out of its own eyes again at the small, dim flat, at the pile of papers before her, and her child, her children, each a gruesome weight, and her face began to close, swiftly, like wings drawing shut against the back. "Do your English," she said, and went to scoop up the crying child and rock him in her arms.

Before she can even move like the other girls she must stand at the back of the class, just stand, with her back very straight, her neck fully extended, her shoulders relaxed, her arms raised in front of her, hands clasping each other like small hooks, only standing, because she can't quite get the body right, the shoulders too high, the hurting arms sagging, the chin distracted by the dancing girls, whose movements are a rebuke to her stillness, even if they are clumsy, or bad. But Teacherji barely looks at her, beginner, after issuing stern instructions to the Mother in Hindi, which the Mother translates to their mother tongue: still for the first day, just standing with the spine straight, and watching the others moving until she understands what is expected of her body, watching Teacherji, who is no less beautiful today in the dim, rainy light coming through the windows, looking magnificent as she speaks the bols and the dancing girls' feet answer and answer.

If she moves suddenly Teacherji's quick eyes move to her and she barks a command that doesn't need to be translated by the Mother, who nonetheless adds on her own, punishing embellishments in Gujarati. Slowly Vidya gets restless, then hungry, then angry, holding the stupid pose, her body becoming stiff and boring. She is smallest in the room, and she feels her mistake piercingly, and feels alone in her small foolish body that is occupied in the stupidest of tasks, of trying to become nothing. What had she wanted? She can't even remember. It is only fear that keeps her still: Mother, Teacherji, with their whipping eyes.

But she will go back: she will go back. She had made a terrible promise. Shame sends her back. In the second class she is allowed only to move her feet very slowly in one two three four one two three four, the four a tak marked by the heel instead of the ball of the foot and the second count of four arcing back in the other direction, a loop of four and four forever and boring but so difficult to keep a steady rhythm like the soft breathing of a sleeping person, a person in deep sleep breathing a pattern of soft regular breaths without any effort, it should be like this: without any effort, and the body must be kept still but for the moving feet, the torso and shoulders should not betray the movement of the feet, not go galumphing from side to side like her body does as it shifts its weight. Teacherji becomes aware of her only to correct this error again and again, mocking her with her shoulders huffing from side to side, pointing to the star-girl and saying look, like her, are you even looking? But after this the eyes and face should be kept still fixed at a point straight ahead and not looking! At the end of this lesson she feels the rocking movement of her feet and body for hours after. She twitches her feet in the arc of fours as she falls asleep and in the morning, knowing that practice is expected by the Mother, she adopts the pose and forces the rhythm into her feet again like tight shoes.

The third lesson she is again mocked by Teacherji, who calls her a monkey. Close your mouth! the Mother snaps. This time the humiliation makes her hot and angry and she forces her body straighter, leaning against her anger, sinking all her focus and energy down into her stubborn feet. The feet drive hard again and again into the earth as she promised. At first, anger drives the feet: still, no matter her motives, in the mornings space is cleared for practice. They cannot hire a tabla player, so as the girl dances the Mother calls the bols, marking the taal against her thigh. It is the dreaming Mother who says the bols, the early-morning Mother. The voice that leads the feet is steady and full of its own music.

He was four; she was seven. She walked with him to school, taking, when they crossed the street, his hand—she still waited for a nearby adult to cross as well, not trusting her smallness and his to survive alone against the snarling traffic. Still, his presence protected her in other ways: men felt ashamed and gave her berth until she was joined by her schoolfriends. Also, she liked the silent, watchful way he was with her, as trusting, wordless, as an animal. In two years, he had become lush, beautiful and golden. And his small voice, when he spoke, was measured and serious, so small, but he thought before he spoke, a fact she alone seemed to find, with her own kind of pride, remarkable.

School was school; she didn't suffer. But the day had a tomorrow-feeling, Vidya thought, as she entered the flat. As usual, she looked to the Mother, but the flat was empty. Was she hiding? Of course not: that possibility would be even odder than the one she was facing, she and the Brother, who held her hand. They were both hungry so she climbed up on a stool and pulled the bhakhari tin off from the top shelf. The Brother was all scuffed up from rough play, but looked somehow clean because of his eyes, his large wet eyes that never seemed to blink, as though he didn't want to miss a second of the world, so awful and astonishing. Sometimes when he looked at her with those eyes she felt like slapping him, to hurt him first.

Perhaps an hour passed. The tomorrow-feeling squirreled around in her gut. She wiped their plates, and washed the boy's hands and face. What was he up to at school? The neighbor boys had little interest in him: he was still too little and they had no time for babies. There was the hope that he would grow up to be charming. For her it was too late, she was not charming, but it was irrelevant: she was not a boy. He could be smart, smarter than her, or good, better. He seemed good. He did everything he was told to. He let himself be kissed and petted but didn't seem to enjoy it, or at least, if he enjoyed it he didn't let it show. For a baby it was difficult to read his face.

Not a baby. He looked like one—plump and soft like a baby with his large features, his large eyes. Her friends from school cooed over him. She understood the pain of being a doll but would have made him into one anyway if he had been a girl, and she could have combed his hair very sharply and mocked him. Still, there were games they could play together. It was easy to say, "I'm Rani of Jhansi and you are my soldier," though it had been a little time since she had taken up such a game with him; she was getting too old. He looked up with surprise from the playthings in his hands—the knotted rag doll that had once been hers, a long wooden spoon the Mother allowed him when she was not cooking. He was so small—did he too notice the tomorrow-feeling?

"I'm Rani of Jhansi," she said. "Come, soldier! We depart for battle."

He followed her around the empty flat, brandishing his wooden spoon. After a while, she began to forget the tomorrow-feeling: they came into a nonsense world, inarticulable to outsiders, even to herself when she came out of it like a dream. It was beautiful, this place they walked through, she described it as they walked: the divan a shining lake, and beside it, the almirah growing the branches of an incredible tree thick with flowers they feasted on. She watched the Brother reach up to pluck the flowers, unable to reach—she lifted him to the higher boughs where the flowers grew thickly, smelling of rasmalai, and creamy—they tasted together. "It's sweet!" said the Brother, licking his fingers. Sap ran down the branch: pure milk. They lost their human aspects and became wild things, crouching, snarling, living wildly but privately. They seemed almost not to be with each other, deep in this forest, so wreathed in their own imagination: she saw so many things and described them to him, narrating it like a story: the gods she saw and walked with, swimming with them, and dancing.

"A tiger," said the Brother, pointing, "there—" and they followed it down the hill, until the Brother caught its neck in his arms and Vidya came astride it, lifted him up. They were not children anymore as they rode the tiger. Being alive together in the invisible world made them kings. And so steeped in each-other-ness that they would never be alone.

The Mother's face, when she arrived, was flushed with heat. From the moment the screen door whined open on its hinges, they were children again, thrust back into the visible world. They knew better than to speak, just watching her. She drew a cup of water from the clay pot and drank it, and then another, with movements that were blurry and slightly uncontrolled. The Mother and her face were full into tomorrow, but she wore it differently—tomorrow was calm upon her. She offered no explanation of her whereabouts and was not asked to provide one. Instead she asked, "Have you done your work?"

"No," Vidya answered. The tone of her voice had not been scolding, and this unnerved the girl.

"You'll do it, won't you?"

Vidya nodded.

"Tell me all your promises."

She couldn't remember.

"One," said the Mother, "you promised to take care of your brother. Remember?"

"No. I promised to take care of you."

"You promised to care for him like a mother."

Instead of arguing, she nodded.

"Two, you promised to do your dance."

The need for the promise had broken now, even as the promise held fast. She practiced every morning, though she was not improving. She could feel her limbs gaining some control but for all the control she developed, her body revealed infinite capacities for rebellion: her limbs were not strong enough to hold their stillness, her fingers too inflexible to curl slightly up as she held them in their kissing mudra, her feet unable to separate the beats fully into distinct phrases. She was still at the back of the class, but knew enough Hindi now that the Mother didn't need to translate, and no longer sat in the room to watch her. She walked home by herself.

"Three?"

She had promised Suneeta to help with her maths, in exchange Suneeta would do her sewing. She didn't tell this to the Mother. Two promises seemed terrible enough. "Only two."

"What happens when you break a promise?"

"Punishment."

"That's right," said the Mother. "Punishment from god. Come, let's rest."

"Rest?"

The Mother was already unrolling the bedtime mats, pulling the shutters hard across the window's eyes. The Brother lay down and shut his eyes immediately, but Vidya lay down with her eyes open, looking at the Mother. The Mother, heedless, undressed in the room and stood nude for a moment near her astonished daughter, who looked at her: the gaunt body, the rough black hair of her sex, and her heavy breasts, loosed of their blouse, tear-shaped and capped in dark loose nipples. Even unbound, her grooved hair held the ancient structure of its braid. She disappeared into the washroom, then, she was clean, returned, dressing in her best sari—the best of the best, her wedding sari—the red border woven with true gold. Late afternoon—with the windows closed the room was filling with a brown heat. Was she beautiful, the Mother? Was she beautiful? Yes, she was very beautiful, she was immense and terrible in her beauty, braiding her wet hair with its new strands of white. Yes, very beautiful, fragrant in that shabby apartment in that strange dark light. Her hands made careful movements, straightening the flat and touching all its objects with admiring fingers. Vidya kept still so as to not banish the beauty. Tomorrow was here but she was not ready.

"Are you tired?"

She didn't move.

"I went to the sea today."

"The sea?"

"I wanted to go in. But I didn't. I wanted to swim."

"Why?"

"The water is so warm, Vidya."

"Can you swim?"

"We never went to see beautiful things. To go look at beautiful things just because they were beautiful."

"Dance is beautiful."

"Yes," she said, "dance is beautiful. Sleep now. Shut your eyes."

The woman of tomorrow had a gentle voice. Vidya kept her eyes open. The heat pressed on her. There was the sound of the Brother breathing, breathing easily, already asleep. How can you sleep if tomorrow is here?

"Will you stay here?" she asked like a baby would. This mother said yes. "Until you fall asleep."

"Then I'll never fall asleep."

The Mother smiled. Her face was large in the girl's vision, shining in the dark. She smelled of beige soap and again of sweat, not bitterly of it, only honestly, and the coconut hair oil that glistened in her part. She could watch the face forever, the face that looked back at her, without anger or indifference, reaching out toward her from the hard eyes, the eyes that had softened in the dim light until they were as young as a girl's eyes, they were Vidya's own eyes looking out from the Mother's face with lightness and openness. The eyes of today and tomorrow both.

BUT THE BODY—WAS slipping—into the heat—slipping, as the eyes grew heavy, and the thoughts started running—and she was on a wide, flat, hot, blank plane—running—and she tried to lift her eyes and open her body—but she could feel it separate from the dream body, which ran forward—heedless—and tripped and fell down a well—and shouted—

Mother!

# 11

✖✖✖

Were you always "I"? For there was a day I arrived to myself, when I became I. And when I arrived into that moment I remembered, dimly, that there had been several before it, each preceding time more distant, more eerily felt, for I could not remember the circumstances, only the barest trace of feeling, like the perfume of a person who has just stepped off the lift. I am speaking abstractly, perhaps because as a dancer I have little faith in words to convey the meaning the body so effortlessly conveys. Perhaps you have never arrived to yourself, perhaps you have always remained "she," looking out of your eyes at the world you know exists outside you, whose lights and shapes and sounds and smells and colors create specific but random configurations that only appear to be stories, stories happening outside you and only seeming to happen *to* you. More likely, you have never needed to arrive to yourself, you have always been "I"; the story that organized itself had you as its protagonist, your remembered moments a strong, smooth, infinite bridge, the small and large humiliations of bullies and your own mistakes and the warm hours of pride and pleasure serving to polish and strengthen it, so you are able to walk across this bridge of self untroubled through all of your days.

I know this: one minute I was a girl dancing, a girl who watched carefully through her own eyes the world outside them, glancing down at the position of her hands, focusing all her effort on the movement of her hands and her feet both at once: impossible: the hands moved up and down as though gathering flowers, and the troublesome feet just managed to ride on the edge of their rhythm without falling out of place: then, suddenly, the feet began to gather the rhythm into them, to understand it, and the world flared open. The feet danced themselves: no, I danced them. The practice, the care, the worry, the observation, fell away and I felt my soul stretching taut in my body, or expanding within it, I smelled the sweat of myself through my cotton and thought *mine*; I felt my soul or my awareness driving through me, through my hands and eyes and most powerfully through the violent cadence of my feet, each moving separately from the other, leaping away from me even as my body remained on earth. It was through this "I" that the room remade itself in wild clarity: I was in it, smelling its thick stinking air, dancing along with the other girls even as I fell away from them, moving deeper into my body as the world became sharper, Amrita the closest, whose feet were a little off, though her arms moved precisely, and the light fell across her oiled hair and the line-true part in her scalp, and now the music, the tabla and the bol, spoken by my teacher, but which felt spoken by my own body: so many times had I practiced this composition that my body knew the next phrase before it was uttered, and sought to create it unbidden by the conscious part that commanded it. When Sita stood in the fire, perhaps it felt like this, a wild, nearly unbearable pleasure in which a voice shouted—I! and the voice, both spoken and heard by the body, answered again I! and the body heard I! and I! and I!

When the composition ended I was glad because I don't think I could have borne it for any longer. I squatted at the back of the room and closed my eyes: still burning. Until my heart slowed I was frightened. Perhaps if you lived your whole life in "I" it didn't burst out of you in one scary dazzle. Slowly the I was receding: I felt it leaving, the aperture of the world closing slowly. Class had ended and I went outside. What had happened, was I mad? I was not dying, I thought. I was still there. But I could see myself, dimly, still through the eyes of myself: the body of a girl, sweating, drenched, foolish in the broad heat, grateful for a breeze when it came and slowed her heart back to rest.

This girl, the Vidya, back inside to gather her things, could feel her teacher looking. She had been dancing in a group of twelve other girls and forgot she herself could be observed as the world gaped open, she still in her amateur back-of-the-class position. "Come here, child," said Teacherji and Vidya came with the reluctance of one about to be scolded. Teacherji lifted Vidya's chin and examined her with the steady concentration of a jeweler.

"What happened today?"

"Today? Nothing, Teacherji." Her heart was beating. Something had been seen, a private thing. But private was not the same as shameful: not always, maybe.

"Do you practice?"

"Yes."

"When."

"Every morning, Teacherji. And I do the steps in my mind when I walk home so I remember them. And on the bus. And sometimes . . ."

"Sometimes?"

"At school."

"Ah," said the teacher. "That's very good. But don't let it get in the way of your studies or your mother won't let you come here." The teacher's face faltered with her mistake, naming the gone Mother. "Your father won't let you come here."

"Yes, teacher. Teacherji."

"Are you vegetarian?"

"Yes, Teacherji."

"No eggs?"

"No."

"You need to eat more. You have to be strong to dance well. Can you get some eggs?"

"I don't know," she said. "I don't know what to do with them."

"Crack them open and put them in sabzi." Then she asked. "Tell me, do you love god?"

Vidya hesitated, wanting but unwilling to lie. It was the teacher, exacting. The voice that spoke the bols spoke them loosely, almost as a question. And the voice that asked the questions was the opposite, spoke the questions as a command.

"No," said Vidya, waiting for her slap. The teacher looked at her, but not with reproach. There was no emotion on the teacher's face that she didn't will there: you danced long enough and your body became yours: a hard-won instrument. Severe.

"I want you to come on Tuesdays and Thursdays also."

"I can't—"

"I'll talk to him." Him meaning her father, or god. Or both. She knelt down to take her blessing from the dust of Teacherji's elegant feet. Walked home. It was always dusk when she left and the dusk today deepened against the sea. She watched it for a moment pausing on the pedestrian bridge to see the queen's necklace glinting against the salty neck, diamonds in one direction, rubies in the other. Farther down, curved out of sight, was the nightly carnival at Chowpatty Beach, where you could buy bhel puri and stand eating it from its newspaper cone: the slight taste of ink, released from the paper by moisture and oil, was an essential ingredient, as was the salt air you ate it in, sharpening the other flavors and the alternately crunchy and soft textures as you stood in the dirty sand watching the stupid children who wasted their parents' money on rides upon the rickety Ferris wheel. She had wanted a ride, once. And the Brother too, before he had learned disdain from her. She could remember how he had reached for the wheel with his two small hands, with his whole body, and she had leaned down to him and said, "We're not like those empty-heads, are we?" And he had nodded, watching her, pressing the desire out. Who are we like then? he could have asked, but didn't. No one, she might have said. Or, each other.

Something had happened today. Now the feeling was gone, it was like remembering pain—impossible—just the trace of it left, some feeling of alteration. Now she felt calm enough to wonder at it. What had happened? Would she miss it, now that she had tasted it? Had she been marked, changed? Would it come back? If so, how would she bear it? And yet the thought that she could return now, just like this, with only the memory of the change, seemed less bearable still. She wanted to be marked, altered, changed. Split open.

Downstairs, in the courtyard, it was the Brother who ran now between the wickets, staining his bare legs with dust. If she could not join him, well then, she didn't want to: her wants had changed direction. Skinny now, the Brother, he lengthened from baby to boy, she loved him most watching him run the courtyard or off the bus from school. Where this joy came from she had no idea. The fact he didn't have to manage the washing or prepare dinner each night, she guessed. But watch him run. He was all legs and arms whirling in dust, a smile parting his lips as he ran, quite fast, unconscious like a dog with a dog's subtle grace. She left the window. The bai who came to chop the vegetables was finished; Vidya squatted over the cookstove to make the rotis. Never quite as thin as the Mother's golden circles puffed so elegantly with heat, and she had never shown Vidya the correct proportion of the spices: Father Sir said so sometimes, but ate, the Brother ate, not complaining, then she ate last, in the kitchen, after everything was put away.

After dinner she switched from wife to daughter doing her studies, her books and notebooks outspread on the floor. Father Sir, no matter how exhausted, sat down with them both to practice their sums, she correcting the Brother's work, and then Father Sir correcting her maths before she turned it in the next morning. He was intolerant of error, but he was not, in this context, severe. He wanted them to understand not just the sum that lay before them but the animating concept behind the sum, behind the formula: he wanted their sums to be immaculate for it was an essential punctuation, but he was less concerned with the right answer than how they arrived there. When he spoke, his voice lost its commanding tone, it rose and fell in an almost musical cadence, and behind his beady glasses his eyes lifted: she loved him, this version, and what he offered her, which was to structure her mind pristinely, to make it logical and unceasing, the way dance made her feet logical and unceasing. The world could be perfect: it was her mind and her body that failed its perfection.

She washed her face before bed. The dull mirror held only her head and the top of her shoulders if she stood as tall as possible on her toes. She knew how to check for signs of incipient prettiness from the girls at school (big eyes, soft lips, small nose, round face), of which she found none. The mirror didn't give her accurate color, but this she could glean easily enough from an arm outstretched in sun: the arm replied sin-dark as coffee though her secret belly and her thighs revealed themselves more muted in the bath: there was no sun in the bath in the city so the color was damp and unconfirmed, not gold, but still, beauty might later visit these parts. If only she'd plump. So skinny, like the Mother, her feet big already like the Mother's.

The Mother's shoes had sat empty with the other shoes of the family by the doorway for several weeks after the tomorrow-afternoon, though the rest of her things had vanished along with her, and Vidya had slid her foot in one—the left—several times when no one was looking, always withdrawing her foot as though burned. They were smooth, they didn't feel like shoes, like rubber sandals that slapped against the soles as she walked them. They felt base and dirty and elegant, soft with wear and sweat. There was more room than foot in the shoe, but even the Mother's feet had not been large enough to fill them. Vidya would squat down to study them: they smelled beautifully sour, their toes were scuffed bare of polish, the laces gray from sun and dust, and inside the shoe the clear imprint of a sole in black: if you pulled away the tongue and exposed the inside to light it was the foot entire three inches short of its rounded end. One day the shoes were gone. Someone must have sent them to the Mother. What happened to my ammi, the Brother asked and asked, and Vidya, with the supreme confidence of a liar said:

You were misbehaving. So she left.

I was?

He began to cry and she picked him up. She didn't feel like crying any more than the dog licking an itchy wound would feel like crying, nor did she feel particularly sorry for hurting him. He was easy to hurt. He put his hot face against her neck and bit it—hard enough to cause pain without breaking the skin—but she didn't put him down: she liked his hot weight in her arms, and her ability to be cruel. She could feel the grooves his gapped teeth had left. She was a little sorry. No, I was misbehaving, she said. She left me. The boy rubbed her neck with his small hand. That was years ago. Now, some girls in her class had breasts.

She had won a scholarship to an English-medium school, where the girls were rich and sophisticated. They snuck around with imported lipstick, the rich girls who always knew how to show you they were rich. They came to school with their hair in bob-cuts and their skulls bound with ribbons of any color they desired, not just the uniform blue: jade green, gulabi, or the pale yellow of the star flowers that littered the schoolyard. They were dropped off by chauffeurs in cream or black Ambassadors, and those same cars idled along the road as school ended, each vying for a place closest to the school gates as the girls began to stream from them.

She was nothing more than a mouse to them. She didn't mind. She didn't want anything from them, not even someone to loop their arm around her small shoulders, as all the girls did with their friends, putting their lips close to the ear of the friend to speak wild secrets. They told each other, they must, how to be a girl. And since she had no friends she didn't know how. Each day she arrived focused, tensed, sitting straight up in her chair, neat, combed, bathed, her clothes pressed, her schoolwork so tidy she won a prize for handwriting, a small volume of English verse she loved only as a won object, and slept with the book beside her head like a doll. But it was not her studiousness that repelled them, for there were other girls even more serious. Part of being a girl was feeling utterly sweet, having the charm to smile and laugh and make jokes with other girls.

Part of a girl was being lovely, with high, clear, shining eyes. She could not be lovely. Perhaps the Mother's absence had left a smell on her. No one spoke of it. What did they speak about to each other? A breath hot in a whispered ear. Or a hand holding a hand. Or two bodies, sisters, curled together in sleep.

She walked home. If she was alone she wanted to be alone, she wanted to stand in the city alone and feel it around her. There were paths she always walked: home to school, school to the Bhavan: Bhavan to home, stopping at the stall of the vegetable vendor. What of the cove where the fishermen pushed their curved wood boats into the water? The boats were painted with eyes at the prow, and their dock stank of the fish and shrimp that lay in shining piles, squatted over by the women who must smell of it always, even after the day's work. There were the hills and bungalows of the rich, of politicians and movie stars whose lives were as mysterious as they were glamorous, unfolding wholly in the luxury of their privacy, their walled gardens rimmed with crushed glass and fallen flowers from the trees that stretched their branches over the gate. And the reaches of the city's south, the foreign stone buildings warring with tropical heat, carved with a foreign queen's name. And so many places she had not yet seen out of the bus window or walked around on her own two feet, so many secrets the city held, tightly. She lived in the city as the Mother had lived in the village, with no firsthand

knowledge of the greater world. The Mother had wanted
to visit London-England and also New-York-New-York to
speak properly her English. Perhaps she was there now, in
London-England, sitting in the back of a darkened auditorium as Shakespeare brightened the stage. No: she had
gone back to her room, of course, her head sopping with
headaches. She couldn't speak for the moaning, she was
too weak to lift her head up, she would take years to get
better. Maybe there were medicines now so that she didn't
suffer so, she needed only rest, good rest. Vidya thought. A
look from Father Sir stilled the questions on her lips; the
look said: you know, don't ask me. Still. She would have
liked a letter from the Mother, just a word, even if she was
not allowed to visit the Mother's room. *Her* mother, well
then yes, hers. A thought can cause pain, worse pain than a
headache. So, she could think of the Mother her mother in
little sips only. Mother coming up the stairs. Mother cooking dinner. Mother slapping each of Vidya's hands. Mother
sleeping calmly. Mother descending the stairs. Mother
hailing a rickshaw. Mother going far away—

The Irani baker also sold eggs. He came by the chaali
three times a week bearing an aluminum trunk that
wore the sun brilliantly all over, and the cart alone was
enough to excite the wild hunger of the chaali children, who
came clamoring down from the flats and running across the
courtyard to meet him. He sold from it Irani sweets and,

most deliciously, khari biscuits, so coveted by Vidya that in the years she took the bus to school she would often walk the hot kilometers instead, her hunger sharpened by the walk and the clink of saved paisa in her pocket. They never quite knew when he was coming, and when he arrived he would call them all to him in a voice that had an element of the honey-soaked sweets he sold them. She did not run down—she had more dignity, and bought her khari biscuit with the grace and indifference of an adult—but would run up the stairs to halve the biscuit with the Brother, who had sacrificed nothing for it, but looked at her so pathetically as she ate she could not help it. From her he learned to eat slowly, to measure each morsel with delight, and they could sit together very quietly for a long time eating a khari biscuit layer by flakey layer in the time it took the other children to eat three or four. Khari biscuits were not difficult to buy from unspent bus fare, but eggs were expensive, and it took a while to save for them. For this purchase she had to go to the Irani baker's shop. He recognized her, standing furtively with the money clutched in her palm. Her voice was so abashed she had to repeat herself twice, and when he finally understood her he could not help but tease her, rubbing his bearded chin as he laughed. The eggs he gave her were small, blueish, and weighted coolly in the palm, but she didn't know how to open them when she brought them back to her kitchen. She crushed one with her hand as though wringing it, blood from a stone, over the pan and it shattered and hissed, whitened as it touched the hot metal. There was a spot of blood in the bleeding yellow that made her want to retch. When it was cooked nearly to black, she took the pan off the stove.

"What are you cooking?"

"Nothing," she said, covering her sin with her body, but her voice betrayed her. The Brother leaned in the doorway, confident as a cricket star.

"It smells awful in here."

"Oh, go play. What are you even doing in here?"

"I was thirsty."

"Well have some water and leave me alone."

He walked to the clay pot and dipped a steel cup into the water. He was sweating, so skinny, with his growing-boy gait. His hair was long, falling into his eyes, she'd have to cut it, along with his long filthy fingernails: no matter how many times she showed him with the knife he would not do it himself. But she liked cutting her own nails right down to the quick, and actually, his too, like slicing fruit. Now he could see the blackened pan. "What are you cooking?

"Get out of here, you pest."

"I'll tell Father Sir."

"Go ahead, tell him."

But from her voice she knew he knew she was bluffing; he came closer and said, "Are you going to eat that?"

"Yes," she said.

"Well, I want some too."

"No you don't. It's not delicious."

All evidence pointed to the truth of her statement, yet he persisted, perhaps thinking of the bitter fried karela that he so loved even though he had received a similar warning. "If you're going to eat it I want some too, otherwise I'm going to tell Father Sir."

"Tell him what."

"You're cooking lamb."

"It's not lamb, it's—oh, fine. Have some."

They had to pry the egg loose from the pan with a knife. It flaked and crunched between their teeth, tasting of singed rubber. They squatted beside the pan and pulled up the loose shards with their fingers.

"You like this?"

"Yes," he said, unable to fully erase the grimace.

"It's eggs."

"I thought eggs were round."

"They're round before you cook them. You have to open them."

"Are we still Brahmins?" He was having his thread ceremony in three weeks, and studied the shlokas seriously. Only boys got the sacred thread: she studied with him when Father Sir was gone, wanting to know the ancient secrets: she didn't care about the thread. She didn't want to be fussed and smeared and tested and strung like a bow, not her. What did girls get? Marriage, but boys got that too. What did girls get? Babies. She would never be a mother.

"Yes, if you don't tell Father Sir."

"I'd never tell on you."

He looked small again as he said it, her boy. She loved him in a rush, taking his chin in her hands. "You used to be so chubby."

"Stop it." But there was pleasure in his voice.

"Pappu has a girlfriend."

"No he doesn't. He's eleven years old."

"He says he does."

"He doesn't even know what a girlfriend is. Anyway, Pappu is a thug." Pappu's father was a drunk, his elder brother was a drunk. How it worked, exactly, stinking liquid in illicit bottles—alcohol too was banned from the chaali—she didn't know.

"Pappu has a mustache already."

"You'll have one too."

"When?"

"Do you play marbles with them?"

"No." He said it reflexively.

"I've seen you."

"So what, it's just marbles."

"You shouldn't play with them."

"Why not?"

"It's trouble. It's gambling."

"It's not gambling. It's just playing."

"Later it will be gambling."

"They're my friends."

"They shouldn't be."

"What would you know anyway," he spat suddenly, "you're just a girl, an ugly girl, you're darker than anyone in the whole chaali."

He was sorry: it passed across his face, then was gone, slipping from her, back into his boy world, the dusty afternoon. It wasn't the worst he had ever said to her, but the desire to wound unnerved her. She'd keep her khari biscuits to herself. The eggs had left a foreign taste in the mouth, a brownish-blacking taste, and the shards pricked as they went down. She scrubbed the pan for a long time, not leaving it to the bai. Was she stronger now? She felt the same, only a little dirtier. Maybe it took more eggs.

Vidya started to come to the Bhavan early, not dawdling from school to the complex but going there directly many times a week. When she arrived, the star-girl, Puja, was finishing her private lesson: she occupied the room alone, but for the teacher and the tabla player who was the teacher's son, and who was, it turned out, handsome. It was like watching three horses racing forward, each keeping pace with the others, each turning to the others to say keep up, keep up, though the teacher's hand against her thigh almost lazy, and her mouth shaping the syllables softly, like it was easy. Her eyes stayed fixed on the star-girl's every mistake, and she yelled them out with great disdain: Mooh-bandh! ungli band! bhago mat! Puja's body registered the harsh voice but didn't falter. The girl watched the star-girl as the others in the class hung around and gossiped. She watched avidly. Puja was good, yes, but kathak was not just a matter of precision and control. Some beauty was lacking. When you watched her, you wanted your heart to fly up into your throat, so dazzled. But it didn't. Why? Maybe it had to do with that feeling Vidya had sometimes when she danced: Puja didn't feel it, so nothing came into her eyes as she danced, they remained flat and blank. Now and then the feeling returned to Vidya as she danced, more gentle, and so less frightening, slower, briefer, warmer.

Even still, Vidya's body tried to follow the movements of the star-girl's, and couldn't, even the swift uprightness of Puja's spine shamed her. She counted along with the beats. There were so many ways to break time into smaller parts, and from this regularity you could build a lavish pattern. At times the steps were demonstrated by the teacher, having no one more senior to call upon, her body passing from stillness into motion as she unfolded herself from her seated pose, and then the beauty came suddenly into the room: she took it all: it shone out of her. Even bell-less, her legs and feet made the movements dense, perfect. See? she would say. And then Puja would try it. Perhaps it wasn't fair to see them against each other, the star-girl sweating, the teacher cool as silver.

The group lesson never began at a set time. Puja finished, and the girls started to take the space she had left, but not purposefully, not waiting for instruction, but idly, still chatting. Puja brought a metal tumbler of fridge water to Teacherji, kneeling as she presented it so Teacherji could bless the top of her head. But she was already blessed: she was to be married to the tabla player, Teacherji's son, next year when she was seventeen.

Mothers wound the bells around their daughter's ankles. The girls tied their dupattas across their chests like soldier's sashes. Sometimes an hour would pass like this, and even the eager Vidya appreciated the slow transition from one thing to the next, which allowed her to pass, slowly, from human to dancer, though she did not gossip with the other girls and wound her own bells around her ankles, not yet the full strand, just beginner's brass, separated from her skin by old cotton. Not just *bells*, for "bell" could denote many things—temple bell, school bell, a bell rung to summon a servant. These, small brass, stranded with clean cotton thread, were ghungroos, their mouths split open lengthways and crossways so that the tiny brass tongue could be seen wagging. Singly, the sound was highish and dull, unimpressive, but threaded around the dancer's legs—beginners were allowed only a single strand for each ankle, but experienced dancers bore the weight from the ankle bone midway up the calf—the sound was multiplied into a kind of shimmering, the bells rung by their own tongues and by the bodies of the other bells, marking, with their own heavy inertia, the lightness and quickness of the dancer's step, her victory.

Then the tabla player, having rested his arms, tapped a few high notes into the drum, and these three notes caught the attention of the chatting girls and they began to take their places in the room, embracing the room with their arms, taking dust from the feet of their teacher, and then touching the ground with their fingers to ask its forgiveness for the day's pounding.

"You, girl," said Teacherji, pointing at her. "Vidya. You come up."

Up to the front? She flushed, with neither pride nor pleasure, but with the strangeness of being seen, first by Teacherji, then by the surprised students, then by even the handsome tabla player who offered a wink with his smile. She took an edge, not center. She stood up straight. Her movements took on a new meaning at the front of the class. If they were incorrect they were a horror: if they were correct they could be more so. In her years of practice she had learned to halve her body, to put the rhythm in the legs and feet without moving or using the rest; passing the beat steadily between the two feet could not take conscious effort, because so much else required it, the arms and fingers, the expression of the face. If the beat sped up, the feet heard the tabla without the mind interceding: should. And stand up straighter. Could she be a star-girl—*the* star-girl? No, *better*.

Where was the I? Today it had not come. She was focused, sweating, ordinary, even in her new position.

"Child, you said you didn't love god," Teacherji said to Vidya after class. The other dancers had turned back into girls, gathering their things, chatting again, but not her. From the time she left class to the time she returned home dance fell from her slowly, like a dress dripping rain.

"Yes," she whispered, panting still, kneeling.

"How will you dance Krishna if you don't love him?"

"I'm dancing as Krishna?"

Teacherji smiled. Oh, she was kind suddenly, her face unfolding a new aspect. Her queen's smile was regal but not distant, it was warm. "Tell me."

"Neelima Azim is Muslim."

"She loves her god."

"I could love Krishna."

"Will you?"

"I'll try."

"And what about your studies?"

"I won't fall behind. I'm at the top of my class."

"Good, good," said the teacher. "We'll begin on Thursday."

Dance had fallen from her all at once. She left the Bhavan, parting, with her dark body, the dark city. No, never dark: lights were winking on everywhere, the city waking to its second day, the yellow-sulfur municipal lights of the streets, flickering from hijacked electricity, and the warm-bulb light of the ground-level shops, and the thin blue light of the tin-shack kerosene. If men called to her she barely heard them. So this was joy. She felt like racing home, but forced herself into measured steps. Sweat cooled on her brow. In her mind joy followed joy: she made a plan. She would write to the Mother, she would say, look, I've kept my promise. She would say *write anything back*.

She made dinner sloppily, badly. She was so excited. When Father Sir came home he saw her grinning. "What is it?"

"I'm dancing a solo in the recital. The Krishna-story with the snake."

"Ah, very good."

"It's tenth-December, will you come?"

"Tenth-December? We'll see."

He left the flat for the shared toilet, shutting the door. He was so blunt, so calm and private. Some days weary, some days stern, though he never raised his voice, he didn't need to: measured, and cool with anger, his voice could be chilling. A voice you bowed before to seek forgiveness. When he gave it, you never quite felt better, you felt almost restored but slightly less. And some days Father Sir was just like this, passing through each day with just a slight resistance to it, with an almost amused kind of objection to it, as though encountering the second final price offered by the vegetable vendor—not satisfactory, but not absurd. He returned from the toilet clean, smelling of talcum powder.

"Is dinner cooked?" he asked in admonishment of Vidya's idleness.

"Yes," she said.

"Go call your brother, then."

She did, standing out on the shared balcony. She could see him, a dark shape, wild-boy, but boys could be forgiven for being wild. He didn't hesitate, called in parting to his friends, hunched over their marble game, all still in their white uniforms streaked now with dust that some mothers or washerwomen would have to scrub. He must be hungry for the way he took the stairs, but she didn't stand there to watch him do it, instead going back into the kitchen to heat the food and serve Father Sir, who ate quickly, as he always did, finishing before the boy had washed his hands and face. She served the boy too. She could never seem to keep him full, he was always hungry. After Father Sir had washed his hands but before he spread his newspaper out over the divan she said, "Father Sir, would you be able to write to Mother and tell her about my performance?"

He looked at her. She so rarely saw him surprised that it took her a minute to place the expression: she had thought, at first, anger. "Or, I could write to her. You could just write the address on the envelope."

"Write to your mother?"

"Yes, sir. If it's not too much trouble."

"Your mother is dead, girl."

She looked at the Brother, whose right hand dropped loosely in its plate. He did not, actually, seem surprised— only startled by the word *dead*. He pressed his lids together and then opened his eyes, shaking his head as though to clear it, and began eating again.

"But we didn't do the rites."

"Of course we did." Now surprise softened to pity behind the round glasses, which was worse. "Don't you remember those pujas we did?"

"What pujas?"

"Girls can't come to the burning, you know that. But we did those pujas, remember? Two-three pujas the week after she died."

"Where?"

"Right here. Right here in this flat."

"But who did the final rites?"

"Your cousin Manu."

"Oh." Oh. Oh. Oh. Dimly, she remembered sitting in the hot room, full of people in white. Only dimly . . . it was confusing, no one had told her why. She held her Brother on her lap, his hair shorn—he had just had his haircutting ceremony, late, she had thought, but at least he had had it. Her hair was untouched, perhaps if they had shaved her head too she would have understood. Now, of course, the truth was as obvious as furniture, and she felt embarrassed that she had not known it all along. Her question to Father Sir had been a child's question. She went to the washroom and slid shut the new door. She peeked up into the blunt mirror. It didn't look like someone capable of Krishna, only a girl, a small girl. There was a heat behind her eyes and prickling at their outer corners. No tears, but the breath shifted quickly in her lungs. The look that the neighbor women gave her made sense, *poor motherless*, and why they sometimes brought over the food they made, saying it was extra. The extra was not an accident, it was an offering to ward off similar misfortune. As though she was a god of it: and she was a god: Krishna. Straighten the spine. She watched as she posed in the mirror and something in her face began to shift, angle up. Her eyes became pointed, narrow. Her face looked thrillingly angry. She could do this? And then she let it drop and tried another aspect, one of sweet tolerance, of forgiveness. Suddenly her face was lush, her cheeks and lips ripe. Sorrow, and her face became one of suffering, her eyes spangled with tears. Mask after mask. She was good. The star-girl could not do this. A lover, her eyes looked flushed, not dreamy but focused with desire. Ah, she returned to anger. Anger was the most beautiful. Anger slightly parted her lips. Anger bent her brows into arrows. Anger made her eyes black and hard, capable of driving the feet against the earth without mercy.

Two hours before the performance, she was dressed by Teacherji and sent off to the studio around the corner for her portrait. The outfit she wore was unprecedented and magnificent: an orange silk half-sari wrapped around her legs into pants; a gold blouse, fitted, itchy, tamped around her torso and the tops of her arms; and jewelry, including a gold-plated necklace with an ornate pendant that slapped against her chest as she tried a few experimental turns. The jewelry was Teacherji's own, the silk the teacher's own, though Father Sir had paid for the fitted blouse, which was hers to keep, extra fabric sewn in for eventual expansion, and the two small darts at her chest pointing hopefully outward where there were no breasts but might someday be.

Teacherji draped the fabric around the bare legs of her student, Vidya feeling a dark pleasure to see her teacher kneeling at her feet to fix the edges of the silk so that the gold border striped the legs perfectly. Teacherji smelled of sandalwood and faintly of hair oil; from this vantage, she seemed small and fallible. She handled Vidya's body with a professional detachment, still, to be dressed by a woman was to be regarded with even some measure of tenderness. It seemed to cause satisfaction each time Teacherji draped or pinned a new element into place. She painted a new face onto Vidya's plain one: deep red lips that tasted of clay and rubber and eyes outlined in thick pencil so they could be seen from far away, and a little powder for the skin to make it paler. Teacherji pinned Vidya's braid into a thick knot and then wound it with flowers, harsh with the bobby pins: tears smarted in the girl's eyes. She was so proud. She felt neither girl nor woman, but like a marvelous other thing: like the half-man, half-tiger that broke from the pillar at dusk to kill the evil father of Prahlada. At the photographer's studio she was stood under hot lights and told to pose. Vidya, tensile, a star: ready. She looked down the muzzle of the camera and smiled, baring her teeth.

Before the recital they prayed to Ganesh and to Saraswati, and she privately and atheistically to Krishna. The girls were dressed extraordinary but none were as spectacular as her—none but the star-girl, whose limber frame was clothed in violent red silk and a fitted gold vest that gave suggestion of curves. The mouth was the same color as the silk, the same red. She wore her own jewels. She was easy, laughing with the others; she did not hold herself separately from them as Vidya did, she did not need to gather her focus as they waited in their practice room for the audience to arrive in the auditorium, there being no backstage and the dancers not wanting to be seen until the event, like brides. They glittered and rustled in the dim light, the ghungroos on their ankles sparkled with sound at their slightest movements. She was threading her own calves with ghungroos now, looping the end of the strand around her big toe. Sometimes when she took off the full set she felt too light: unsteady, as though a breeze could pick her up and lift her away. Tying the brass to the body was like tying the body to earth. She knotted them firmly.

"And who will you marry, Vidya," Lanka called, "if the Teacherji's son is taken?"

"Careful, Puja." Sonal was laughing. "You better marry him quick, before she gets better than you."

"She won't," said Puja, not with hostility. With only a little hostility. In makeup her face looked garish, radiant. "There's too much effort in her dancing."

More girls laughed. "Yes, and anyway she's too dark," said Amrita, who had previously been the darkest. They all looked whole, loved god. Vidya pitied them. She moved away from them in her mind, saying her steps to herself silently, bringing her mind through all the movements of her body. If she missed a step! All those eyes! She had never practiced in her costume and now it occurred to her to worry. If she missed a step or the blouse arms ripped. And suddenly she was folded in worry, wanting to throw the whole thing away. Her stomach hurt. When all she had wanted to be was nothing! She remembered standing in the doorway watching Puja. A turn and a turn and a turn, like she would now do, her eyes whipping forward to brace against a spot in the room so her body would not falter. Shine like that. She wouldn't.

Teacherji came and led them to the auditorium, and the sound of their ghungroos as they walked across the courtyard corrected their casual footsteps into something deliberate, the sound of their ringing steps coalesced into a single sound, a single step, laughing out of nervousness and out of pleasure at the spontaneity of their shared step, as though young unbattled soldiers marching through a loving crowd. All but her. In her head there was nothing but white panic. It was a force like a train or a headache. It

was an invasion of nausea. Father Sir had come because she
had asked him several times. Even now he was there sitting
in one of the velvet seats. As they passed into the auditorium the wide light that their eyes had grown accustomed
to dropped away, then the auditorium revealed itself slowly,
formally, the tapered, lily-shaped light fixtures that graced
the walls, the threadbare velvet seats now occupied: a mass
of eyes fixed on the entrance of the girls from the back of the
room to the front, climbing up the stairs to the lit stage. The
musicians were already seated there, and the teacher took
her place beside them and accepted the reverence of the girls
as they all bowed toward her, to the musicians, the Bhavan's
music teachers pressed into service for this task; to the small
altar erected at the front of the stage; to the earth, and then
took their places, similar to their positions they danced in
the room, senior students up front and the junior behind,
Vidya in her customary position just left of center, just left
of the star-girl, whose body was pristine in the wonderful
light, but whose eyes—yes, were still flat, absent, in a way
that Vidya could sense even beside her.

It was alright to absent her body and look out at the
room. The noise of the music and the ghungroos and the
movements of the body were comforting; she could feel her
panic ebbing from her body like an illness. The automatic
movements caused her, as they sometimes did, to float out-
wards, letting the cool mind observe the room with little
feeling. In the false dark of the auditorium, it took her a

while to find them, but she found them: Father Sir upright and expressionless three rows back, with the Brother, bored, beside him, still in his white schoolboy's uniform, where his day's errors were already visible. He was picking his nose and then flicking his findings at the girl—Kusum's sister—seated in front of him. Kusum's sister in the second row was watching Kusum, whose perfectly round moon face was replicated on each sister, and could be beheld in full original upon Kusum's round mother, who sat beside her younger daughter, keeping the beat with her fingers and nodding. Vidya was better than Kusum, a second-row dancer, but their eyes stayed on her, Kusum, while Father Sir's moved from girl to girl with the face of a patient man trying to occupy himself while he waited for the bus to arrive. Beside Father Sir was an empty seat like a missing tooth. The girls cleared the stage.

Then the star-girl took it. Through her eloquent feet many sentences were spoken. The light burned her dress more red, her gold more gold. Despite herself, watching from the wings, Vidya was lifted. And the star-girl too, her face shifting under her makeup. At the apex of her composition, her feet moved so quickly she was not touching earth, but vibrating just slightly above it with perfect noise. Wah! someone cried. And the audience was on their feet applauding.

Now she—Vidya—was next! No, no, a nightmare as she strode onto the stage. The mass of eyes fully fixed on her, because there was no other to be fixed on. Between skin and powder there was sweat at her forehead and her cheeks. Eyes and eyes! There was Father Sir, looking at her with a mild expression, the one on his face when he asked to check her sums. No, more, looking at her deeper. Had he ever really looked at her like this? The tabla player tapped the first beats of the drum and she almost couldn't move. She just nodded. Teacherji clicked her tongue, as though angry. The tabla player tapped out the same notes again, calling to the body. The body knew the voice of the tabla. There were no bols to be called, only music, a singer to articulate the story and lend meaning to the theatrical movements. And a tambura to add sweetness to the singer's voice. What a little clown she must look like, a child. Skinny, stock still, no-breasts, with a clown's face painted atop her own.

But the body remembered. It began to move again boyly; boyly she smiled. She could rid herself of her girl's body if she wanted, and climb into another. Turning her head at the gopis she saw in her mind's eye—they, bathing in the lake, smiling and shouting with laughter under her gaze, covering their large beautiful bodies provocatively with their hands. Now she was all play, splashing water at them. Through the screen of this story she could still feel the eyes on her but they made her brave, they thrust her more deeply into the story unfurling in her body because a story needs a listener. Listen: there was a blue god, young, a child, beloved. There was a small god who was taken from his princely life and given another one, the humble life of a cowherd, he was taken from his mother and given another mother, and he played in this new life like a game, never forgetting himself and so living with delight in this toy-world full of gopis, who looked always at him with half mother-love and half desire. In the lake in which these girls bathed there was a snake-demon-king: the child-god would have to kill it. Her body lost its play, hardening to the task. She would have to kill it. Ah, she had them too, the audience, she could feel now without looking, the feeling of them leaning forward, not singularly—she had lost that awareness—just the mass of them. Their interest in the story and in her movements gilded her body with purpose. Here, though the dance was still narrative, a clever pocket of nritta, pure-dance, was hidden within it; the teacher had composed a dark, whirling pattern to fell the serpent, in which the feet, now weapons, moved faster and faster upon the serpent's head. Yet, even as Vidya danced the pure-dance, she had to dance it with the fury of a god, she had to bring that into her face and body: Krishna's serene fury, killing it harder and harder with her feet, until a delight arose in her cheeks from the sureness of victory, until she spun, and spun, and spun without pause, and finished with a final, triumphant stamp, from movement to stillness in the space of a second, her hands thrown up and her head tilted up and a winner's smile on her lips.

Oh, she loved it, the breath forcing itself in and out of her chest, heavy, as she bowed to the crowd, again to the musicians, again to the teacher, again to the altar, and strode, still half-god, off stage. Oh she loved it—and the I? Yes. I remember an aperture opening again, that the body was given an odd feeling as the I flared in; it was a feeling I found later in pregnancy, as I lay awake, on my side, the enormous belly just a few weeks away from bursting—at least it felt like that, though I didn't burst, only died, and came back to myself having touched death to expel out of me life—and I could feel that though I was ready for sleep my child was awake, and I could feel this not from her movements inside me kicking and whirling, or sweeping a limb across my belly, my belly her sky, but from the wide-openness of her eyes, black, and lashed, lidded, open inside me. Looking. I was being looked *through*, and because the seeing was so deep I looked in and out of myself at once: the body out of the dancer, and then the body out of the mother: and the observation married so oddly and exquisitely the look of the body and the feel of it, its weight and presence, it gave it meaning. Instead of ecstasy it was an animal calm, like those dreams where you remember you can fly.

# 111

✕✕✕

I was in college, dancing every day. The college was in the north of the city, which was at that time the "edge" of the city, and the campus had an "edge" feeling, the buildings outposts in a strange jungle, with a large flat lake on either end—man-made, they were reservoirs for the city—yet people used them like any other body of water, swimming and bathing and even rowing small boats across. Since there were so few women in the college, we each had our own room, and against the window of mine an ancient mango tree routinely tapped its leaves and branches, scattering the glass with rain during monsoon, and touching dust onto its surface in the summer, as though several fingers touching and brushing affectionately at the glass, as if a friend's hand. I studied at a small desk that I set against that window and watched a spike of flower produce a single hard green bud: I watched that bud swell, still green, and smooth as a stone outside my window, each day growing bigger. If I opened the window and leaned over the desk I could brush my fingers against it, and I did this often, obscured from view and ridicule by the branches of the tree and the leaves, whose bulk and motion over the months had taken on a presence to me. Truly I felt the tree living and I felt it to be my friend, in a profound way I never felt before or since.

Which is not to say that I was lonely. I was not lonely. I lived in a house full of women. But the tree was quiet, many decades old. It had a strong, rough bark of golden wood. Under my fingers, the fruit-bud was warm from the dappled sun, warm as human skin. Then one day when the fruit had grown to the size of my fist—which, I have since learned, is the size exactly of my heart, and a similar shape—a blush came over it, red-yellow, as though all these months it had been quietly ingesting sunlight, and had finally decided to reveal its solar nature. The orange-red spread, it softened. Should I pluck it, and eat it? I fretted over this question. From below, the tree's transformation was evident, it had hung itself gaily with yellow ornament, as though with a hundred golden earrings, but from my window, it seemed like this small fruit was the tree's single expression, that it had used all of itself to make it. Silly as it sounds I could not bear to eat it and could not bear to think that anyone else would. I felt tenderly toward it and possessive over it, the way one never is over possessions one feels one truly owns, and can do with as one likes. I suspect that my possessiveness would have been the same if someone had plucked that beautiful wheat-haired doll from the window of the toy store in Colaba and placed it into my desirous hands. I would have felt pain, I think.

Each day, the afternoons grew hotter and the mango grew more ripe. I spent days studying for my final exams, studying alone, mostly alone, because I was the only woman in my batch in my major, which was Electrical Engineering— normally popular, but this year the other women had all opted for Chemical or Mechanical. I would glance up at the fruit. It was a miracle that a bird had not pierced it with its sugar-seeking beak, as I would have, had I been a bird, or a monkey had not snatched it in the evening raids they conducted, raining their wild feet over the roof. Three more days, I thought, and it would fall and rot. I imagined it rotting, its beautiful skin blacking. Red and black ants would come and defile it, leaving a sticky trail. Worms would bore into the heart. This was why we burned our dead, so that our flesh would not have to suffer such mutilation. Yet, I could not bear the thought of plucking that fruit.

It was the gardener that decided me, his torso lost in the branches of another tree, while his bare feet gripped the ladder that leaned against the tree's trunk, and whose hand held a small knife that dipped at the air at times before disappearing back into the branches, and whose other hand held sometimes air and sometimes the full golden fruit of that tree: my tree was next, Farnaz told me, she said *our* tree, as her room too looked out onto its branches, and she was amused at my dismay. The gardener's ladder would not reach the upper floors of our hostel, but if he reached for it he could grasp it, my fruit. If he grasped it, if he touched it—I leaned out the window. I could touch the fruit but not pluck it from this position and so climbed onto my desk and kneeled, reaching my arms and torso quite absurdly out the window. It was evening, but the air in my room was already cool, shaded by the tree. To reach the fruit I had to assume a posture of supplication, then one of desperation, like a thirsty man reaching violently for water, one hand gripping the window edge, the other thrust out into space. Thank god for my long limbs, my mother's. I grasped the fruit in my right hand, gently. It pulled easily from the stem. It was as though it had made itself ready to be plucked at that very moment by my hand. It was a pleasure to hold in my hands, leaning out the window, like a creature of two worlds, and before I retracted my body back into the shell of its room, I cast my eyes downward, and saw that from this position, my face and chest and waist and the trailing edge of my sari were in fact visible through a gap in the branches to anyone who would happen to pass under that spot, and where in fact a meandering path led around our building and out to the lake, used only occasionally by the girls of the hostel and their suitors, though even they preferred a different path, one that looped around Hostel Seven and kept the girls away from the disapproving gaze of the Assistant Warden.

When I looked down I saw two men looking up at me: one I knew from my physics lab, and who had often been very friendly to me and once even asked if I would like to take a walk around the lake, which I declined, intuiting a code for something more illicit, though at that point, I didn't know what. He had taken this refusal with good humor and continued to be kind to me, he even asked to study with me a few times though he was a terrible study partner, his buzzing mind leaping from subject to subject and then growing bored, a confident boy, not quite handsome, but rich, whose interest in me I correctly assumed was due to my rarity as a female and my proximity. And indeed, he soon found a more receptive target for his affection at the ladies' college where women were more plentiful. The other man I had not seen before. He was tall and fair, almost pale, and wore an appealingly moody look, though at the moment we caught each other's eyes we lit with a mutual surprise, a warm, mutual surprise that took the embarrassment I might have felt from being so exposed and turned it into laughter. The man I knew gave a little wave. The man I didn't offered a bow. I pulled myself into my room, my heart beating very quickly.

The fruit, when I ate it, was very sweet.

As I said, in those days in college I danced every day. But not long after I began my classes at the college, I left my teacher. At times, and especially as I improved, I could feel a tension in her—or at least, I thought I could—a desire to meet my hunger to move more correctly, and a withholding of the means to do so, as though she were stopping herself from offering further instruction, or more complex movements. Because, I wondered, of Puja—had she been chosen as the sole inheritor of our teacher's skill and knowledge? Was I—my dark skin, my poverty—so unworthy? I felt restless, returning again and again to the site of my childhood, to the ghost of my earlier self. For weeks, I determined to speak with her, and when I finally mustered the courage to do so, it was she who told me it was time to find someone new to learn from. In all my years with her, not one crumb of compliment had ever passed through her lips, nor any encouraging expression crossed her face. I had outgrown her, she said, a kind of praise at last, and I felt it like a slap.

Still, I was used to her voice. It was her voice I heard speaking the bols to me as I practiced. I was used to her stern face, the narrow precision of her eyes that watched me like a predator, detecting flaws in the slightest movements, which I understood to be a kind of love. It was love, wasn't it, to look? When I practiced at home, I would think of her looking, her eyes in my mind becoming ever more seeing than they were in life, and I would make myself perfect, looking at myself and through myself as I danced to anticipate the flaws that she would see and correct them. I would go to the Bhavan with my body barely able to contain the steps I had practiced, wanting to lay them out at her feet like gems before a queen, but under her true gaze, one of distracted or conflicted indifference, something would begin to slip: the bend in my fingers losing their symmetry, my face sliding into the wrong expression as I concentrated, showing the effort of my quick steps, or, horribly, missing a step or falling slightly off the beat as I sometimes did, the sequence correct but the rhythm lagging, slightly lagging: it was as though you held a palmful of water as you danced for her, desperate not to spill a drop from your palm but the movement of your body demanding some water spilling or slipping, something always slipping. I had grown used to dancing this way.

Around this time, a movie was released that contained a sequence of kathak danced by a Bombay dancer. This sequence so impressed me, so moved me, I went to see the movie many times, sitting impatiently in the dark for the dancer's feet to appear in a shimmer of sound. At first glance the dance seemed light, almost girlish: the feet matched the voice of the tabla, each phrase beginning slow and ending quick, and a series of her beautiful chakkars was followed by turns even more feminine, in which she leaned back as she turned, dipping or swirling herself through low air, catching as though by accident her skirt with her arm so it flared around her, burning white. As the rhythm picked up, the contrast between the lightness, the girlishness, and the intensity of the movement deepened: there was something clever in this contrast, I thought, almost subversive, to tuck such power into such lightness: smiling fire.

There was nothing not traditional, not classical about this dancing—yet I could see in it the thing I wanted, the thing I would chase after foolishly, desperately, until it was mine. The kind of awareness that I could manage to sustain for only a few moments, she lived in, so much so that even the watcher took on the feeling of that ability as she watched. All your life you walked around going about your daily tasks, and then you watched her dancing and remembered you had a soul.

I wrote her many letters begging for a meeting. She lived in Versova, two buses and easily two hours away from the college, and she was from a different lineage than my old teacher, who, for this reason, would be unable to make a convincing introduction. Despite these obstacles I persisted. Four of my letters were unanswered, but my fifth letter received a terse reply, communicating the date, time, and address of our first meeting. I was at least an hour early, maybe more, as the buses were unreliable and I had not wanted to be late. Pausing at her doorstep after checking it several times against the address she had written in a lovely looping script and finding it to be correct I rang the doorbell. During the long silence that followed I considered ringing the doorbell again. She answered the door herself. "So, you're Vidya?"

"Yes, ji." I was crushed by shyness as she looked at me, then, in defiance of my own shyness, I lifted my chin. Her face, whose beauty I might have been inoculated against from the many times I had seen it onscreen, was actually more astonishing in life, where it appeared more complex, though the film had not robbed her face of its limber quality, its natural expressiveness. In the flesh, her face was living, simply that. It had its own heat and light. It was bare today: no kohl lined the wide-set eyes, no lipstick reddened her dark lips, no bindi anointed her brow.

"Early."

"I can come back."

"That's quite alright. Come in. I was just finishing my own practice."

"I can come back."

She was smiling. "I didn't expect you to be shy."

"Ji?"

"Come in," she said again, and I followed her. In that bungalow the windows were always open, and the door to the verdant patio was also kept open in every kind of weather but the stormiest. I had never been in a house before that had been arranged for pleasure, that had offered pleasure through its simplicity: for though the house was mostly free of decoration, the objects she had gathered, small pieces of pottery and palm-sized brass statues of several gods, the dark carved wood divan upon which sat some cream-colored cushions, or even just the facets of the house itself, like the sea-facing window, offered pleasure not just for the eye, but somehow for the lungs, the body, which lightened in the lovely space, freed of some weight.

"Get us some water, Vidya," she said. "The kitchen is just over there."

In the kitchen I found a clay-pot and ladled the water into three tumblers, holding one in each hand and the third in the crook of my arm. The tabla player accepted the water without acknowledgment, the teacher—she was not yet mine—said, "Next time, use the tray."

"Next time?" I said.

"Sit."

I sat on the floor, blushing. The water had the delicious taste of clay. She beat upon her thigh the theka she desired, the tabla player repeated it, and she began to dance. What I had seen only on-screen I now saw in person. She had found within the movements a looseness and ease I had never seen before, and this ease did not seem at war with the rigor of the postures; rather, these two qualities were sliding against each other, in a way that was intriguing and joyful, even in the simplest movements, for, though she was working on a composition herself, she spent time on her basic footwork, keeping her arms clasped in front, as I had as a beginner, and passing the rhythm back from foot to foot steadily: this seemed to be a lesson: her home and her dress, both of which were simple, almost plain, with no extra ornament; her hair in a clean braid down her back; her clothes white; her walls empty except for its small, lovely window; her beginner's steps that she practiced with steady grace and concentration, until I saw they too were lovely, they were the pit of the dance, the hard, lacquered center. Every once in a while she would stop to speak to the tabla player, offering corrections or refinements to the rhythms he was playing that she demonstrated both with her feet and the clapping of her hands. He accepted these comments seriously, amending the cadence of his fingers—his fingers were quicker and surer than Ravi, the tabla player of my former teacher, and his patrician face so fully inexpressive it was easiest to tell his mood, I found later, by the lightness or heaviness of his hands against the drum.

After her practice she wiped her face with a hankie, made some chai for all of us, and began to interrogate me.

"Will you leave your dancing when you get married?"

"I'm not even engaged," I said.

"If not now, then soon."

"My father wants me to finish my studies."

"And then?"

And then? It felt unreasonable for her to question me like this, as though it were under my control.

"I'm tired of teaching girls who only want to add dancing to their list of accomplishments. Then once they've secured a husband, they leave it."

"Not me."

"Not you? Why not?"

"If I couldn't perform I would dance every day in the kitchen even if no one saw me. If I was injured I would dance every day in my mind."

"Oofo, very serious. I remember this from your letters. But when you dance I hope you remember to smile."

When the tabla player was finished with his tea, I showed her. I followed the beats the tabla offered me easily, working through a composition of my teacher's that I knew suited me. When I was finished she said, "It will take a lot of work to scrub out all the Lucknow affectations. No disrespect to your teacher. You've worked so long in this style, why would you want to move on to another? You cannot do both."

"I will give up everything and start over."

"Will you leave me so easily one day?"

"It is not easy. But I want it. More than anything."

"Want what?"

What could I say that would not make me sound crazy? "To be perfect."

"Yes, I can see it in your dancing," she said, "this arrogance."

"Me?" I said, genuinely surprised.

She had a warm laugh. Behind the shame of being called arrogant there was a small pride: the only people I knew who were arrogant were men.

"A little is good," she said, "it gets you through your inexperience. But too much and you won't learn anything."

Twice a week I went, for I could not afford to come more often, nor did my school schedule allow me, though I would have come every day if I could. Some days the bus was not running because the rains were too bad, and those days I stayed home and practiced, or sometimes, when the buses were running but the rain was bad I still walked the two miles between the bus station and her house, arriving warm and wet, soaked to the bone. The outdoors saturated the indoors: sometimes a little rain blew in through the screen and pearled the leaves of the potted plants that sat on the marble sill, various herbs she grew and ground into a paste to enhance the radiance of her skin. In her plain house there was one outlier: a pair of jade and lime colored lovebirds that perched in a circular brass cage. When it rained, she placed this cage also near the open window, so that they could smell the rain as they loved to, she said, and indeed they were quiet in their cage by the window, their beaks pointed toward the rain. Drenched, I'd arrive, dripping wet on the soft concrete floor, enjoying the performance of my devotion to her and to dance, and she, I think, enjoying it too, being in every way a natural performer. She'd give me her own sari to wear and spread mine out in front of the fan so that it dried by the time I was finished with my lesson (hers somehow just as simple as my own, but finer spun, more elegant, and in her sari, surrounded by her powdery scent, I felt called into the elegance of her body and danced better). Then she would, after a pause, resume her own practice, allowing me to watch her. I watched her with real hunger, a hunger for her movements and the possibilities they offered, for her compositions, which, though in fact quite traditional, seemed also particular to her and therefore new, for her body danced them easily and brightly and with much pleasure.

She knew drama: she knew oddness: she was unmarried, not widowed, a single woman living alone. She knew oddness: shame: gossip. So I think we spent time together in those morning hours, working with each other in a kind of intimacy unlike that I had had with my previous teacher, one that came not from the formality of our bond, but rather from our surprising ease within its confines. When we spoke, it was never about biography or emotion; we spoke just enough to work more. But I think we spoke through work, through our bodies that learned to understand the other, mine always following hers, curved as a temple carving, and bright with its lazy quickness, as she often leapt to her feet to correct me or demonstrate a new way of moving. Though the tabla player was present at all our lessons, his presence had a different quality from Ravi's, and our time together felt nothing like that of the star-girl's and my former teacher. Where they were three, all separate, urging one another all along further, we were often one, an extension of my teacher, whose essence seemed perfectly expressed by the tabla's unceasing rhythms, and imperfectly expressed by my own body.

My former teacher had not taught me the gliding step by which gods crossed the stage, or people moved through rivers, or demons traveled in flying chariots, and my new teacher taught this to me first. You must swivel your feet, turning them by their ankles, open and closed while the rest of your body remains still. It was a feeling unlike the rest of kathak, of smoothness rather than sharpness and precision. Then for many afternoons I went back and forth across my small room, crossing it again and again in silence, as the other girls had complained it was too noisy when I practiced with my ghungroos. Anyone who looked through my open window might have seen a girl through it, moving without friction and in the kind of fashion, I thought, that people might use to occupy heaven.

In those days I felt more like a child than I had during my childhood, when there were always meals to prepare, and a boy to care for, laundry to wash, and all the small pinpricks of household chores that I did daily, each little chore a tiny needle at the surface of my thoughts, which, so pricked through, could never fully grow. Here I lived in the college hostel. I had only one person to care for: myself. There was a cleaner who came to sweep out the hostel halls and scrub the bathrooms so we were only responsible for the tidiness of our own rooms, which though they collected dust very easily and required regular upkeep, were each left to our personal tastes and so I kept mine neat for my own pleasure alone, never for the expectation of someone else. Likewise, while I did not have the money to have my clothes washed, and while I had so few clothes that I had to do the washing daily, I found this task to be a mild delight, as there was running water at all times of day. The mess hall served our four meals, including tiffin, which I had never been able to afford, and where there was always an urn of plain hot chai, very strong. Our food was very good: better than the boys', because the students of each hostel helped manage the kitchen, but the other girls often supplemented these meals with home-food they brought back with them to share after weekend visits—or sometimes home-food would be sent with some relative or visitor if the girls were from farther away. I alone was never the direct recipient of these snacks and meals, for I never visited my home, and there was no one to send me food from it: I and another girl, Radha, a tailor's daughter from Bihar. Radha was a legend by the time I arrived at the college. She was in her last year, and alone in her major— that is, there were no other girls—not because it was the best but because it was the least useful: Aeronautics, there were few jobs in that field in India, and those pursuing the degree would have to go abroad or find another field once they graduated. Because of this, at least in part, Radha's intelligence—brilliance—had gone undetected for several months before the boys in her classes had uncovered the top scorer in each of their exams by ruling out every other possibility and then seating themselves strategically nearby when the tests were handed back, and verifying with their own eyes her perfect marks. Her limber mind: from then on there was no doubt, how rigorously she trained it, more rigorously, I think, than I trained my body; how she drove herself with a kind of violence forward, far beyond any of her peers, male and female, and coming first in every exam.

Radha studied alone, her door locked against the noise the other girls made, teasing and chatty as they studied together. My door was often locked against the other girls too, often but not always, because there were days when my solitary room, a solitude which I had so coveted, became dark and oppressive, the few objects in my room acquired an almost sinister quality and the tree outside felt far away. This feeling squeezed me in a familiar way, from the inside. And I couldn't bring my mind back, I couldn't offer it anything. I almost couldn't breathe. I didn't want to. After a while I would unlock my door and find some pretense to join the room in which all the girls gathered, the common room downstairs, or more often it was Saheli's on the first floor, hers being the most spacious and the most central, and she being the most popular of the girls. When I came in to the room, they accepted me within it without remarking upon my previous absence, the circle broke to gather me, then re-formed to include me, and the talk continued undisturbed. We were seventeen and eighteen; the older girls were twenty-one. Serious, all of us serious, but in that room the talk was light and full of teasing laughter, a kind of talk that could fortify against the male world we had barged into.

Radha never gave in the way I did: her discipline was holy. When she left her small room to visit the bathroom those evenings the girls all gathered they would call out to her the way men would call out to us to get us to turn and look—but not with malice, only the affectionate envy sisters have for one another, for with brothers the envy is felt in a different place: the envy you feel for one who has what you will never have, rather than the envy you feel for one who has what you could. She was our most precious fighter, valiant in our war, though she gave no acknowledgment she fought for anyone other than herself. She proved again and again her worth, and so ours too, and the calls subsided with deference, as soon as her serious, half-absent gaze crossed the doorway. Did she even see us there, sitting on the bed or cross-legged on the floor, or leaning against the wall or against one another's knees? She made no indication that she heard us. The room was just outside of the reach of the mango tree that shaded so many other of the rooms, and if one stood at the window one could be seen by all passersby, and many passed by to sing up at this window, sometimes on their knees, sometimes drunk, sometimes shouting, to one particular girl or to the nameless several as we stood, laughing or irritated or shouting back, taunting, or once pelting down rose petals to a particularly love-sick young man. They were always chased away, eventually, by the scowling watchman, equally angered by the gall of the boys and the need to rise from his post, expressing his anger in a bewildered aside to himself in Hindi, Marathi, English, and Panjabi, calling upon all the languages he knew to express his disapproval, diminishing him into a bumbling, comic figure, which gave an added pleasure to the boys who howled with laughter as they ran.

Yes, the black feeling passed. Yes, if it was loneliness, it abated. But the other girls were easy with one another in a way I was not, the silent one. I had almost nothing to offer into their quick-moving conversation. Where had they learned such ease? Watching myself beside them, I felt an oddness that would never subside, same as the oddness with my girl-cousins, and my childhood schoolmates. I sat upright, never leaning against anyone's knees, or even against the wall, sitting very rigidly in my body, alert, in my freshly pressed clothes, sitting upright the way a monk would sit in prayer. These girls tolerated my oddness, being glad freaks themselves in at least this one, shared regard: not the swiftness and sharpness of their minds, which many girls possessed, but from the frank prideful ambition that led them to race their minds against the minds of the boys, to prove against the minds of the boys the worth of their own, instead of locking them immediately away in motherhood and household chores.

And yet I missed my family. I missed unrolling the cotton mattress before I lay down to sleep. I missed my brother, not how he was now nearly grown but how he had been as a child, when he had been mine, though I had not fully wanted him. For many months I did not visit them, pretending to be busy with my studies. I wrote them several letters over the months that they never responded to, not out of anger or hurt, I knew; I knew it never even occurred to them to reply. I pictured them often in the flat. It was no more silent than when I had lived there: the noise in the apartment was generated almost completely by the world outside it. My father had hired a bai to do the work I had absented, and though I had never seen her I could imagine her squatting on the floor, cutting vegetables. If a thought causes pain you can move your mind away. This was true of almost any thought in the whole world. I thought then of Radha.

The day after our first semester exams I had woken early, very early, as was my habit from my childhood, which I had no desire to break. I loved those morning hours: loved them even more deeply here because the quality of silence at the college was deep and vivid, it was a village-quiet or even a jungle-quiet instead of the rudeness of city-quiet which was not quiet at all. Only birds: wind: sometimes the faint prayers from the temple by the lake edge, the ringing of the big brass bell that hung in the archway, whose grooved tongue you reached up to slap against the belly and wake up god. Hardly anyone else was awake at this hour, except during exams when the other girls kept odd hours, and a few doors wore a band of light under them, proclaiming its dedicated occupant was awake and studying. This disturbed my sense of quiet: it didn't matter that at this hour the girls made no noise. So perhaps it was not quiet I sought but a sense of solitude like those morning hours as my mother prayed over her English, reaching for something. The day after the exams, only one door showed a strip of light underneath: Radha's. On my way from the bathroom as I stood in the hall watching the door. Every once in a while I could see her shadow move across the light or hear her footsteps on the linoleum. Then she opened the door.

She was dressed in a yellow sari, and there were flowers in her hair. Chameli, bright against her dark neck. When she saw me standing there she smiled and it was such a surprising look on her face I realized I had never seen it before. Her shoulders were loose. "You're awake?"

"Yes," I said. No one really thought she was beautiful. I had heard them say her brow was too heavy, her lips too thick. Her face at rest appeared to have a slight frown on it. But I suddenly thought she was beautiful.

"Well, come on then," she said. "We're going to the temple to give thanks for our exams."

"We don't know how we did yet. They're only posting the marks next week."

"I know how I did."

Certainly, and she was right, always right, always first. I was still in the sari I slept in, mussed, and hadn't bathed.

But I was worried that if I asked for a little time to get ready she would leave without me. She carried a plate with sweets on it. All the buildings were dark still, the boys were sleeping, even the Assistant Warden was gone from her post. The world was ours. We took the path the lovers took, that looped behind the hostel and led to the lake—no men to call after us; even the cows we passed seemed occupied by their own thoughts, some kneeling, though not asleep, their dim eyes only half-open, as though rehearsing their dreams. I had been to this temple only once before but had not stepped inside it, feeling that it marred the edge of the lake, man-made but otherwise pristine, but today I felt more warmly toward it. It was a simple, almost humble structure, white walls reflecting the opening light. A flock of parrots laughing as they passed overhead. Radha might have liked this too. This was a girl I had never seen: she seemed so easy in her skin. I was irritated when the priest stepped out and greeted her by name, he bare-chested in the coolness of morning, and hairy. We went into the temple and he blessed us, pressing a thumbprint of kumkum on her forehead, then mine, and letting her hands pass over the sacred light, and I took it too, smearing it up over my eyes. She prayed and offered the sweets, and I sat there, looking at the small idol, pitch-black with white eyes, sitting in repose with her veena, her body studded with fresh marigolds, between her bent legs and her arms and even the crease between her breasts, and then looking at Radha, so small, so slight, folded up into herself, pointing the knife of her mind at her prayer. She was older than me, smarter than me, but at that moment she seemed to me like a small child, fierce but small, defenseless.

"Here," she said, and offered me a sweet from the plate. And then, without waiting for me to take one, she pressed it to my lips.

As I said, I felt like a child in those days, a second childhood, though really it was my first, and I admit I enjoyed playing this innocent role, even when I truly had a little more worldly knowledge than I let on, enjoying the surprise of a friend crying with alarmed delight—but you *do* know what married people do together, don't you? (I did, or thought I did, though later, it turned out I was mistaken, or, if not mistaken, then at least not completely correct.) Conversely, I took much pleasure in uttering crude things like a child would with great innocence, something illicit she has overheard without understanding the exact meaning, but understood enough to intuit its dirty nature, and using her innocence for impunity, like the time I used the words "blue film" in a rare conversation with a group of boys in which I was the only woman and therefore cast in the double role of innocence; this group turned raucous by my use of the phrase and my insistence that I knew what it meant. "Alright then, what?" they said and I answered "those art films that Satyajit Ray makes," and the group burst into laughter, thinking the joke was at my expense,

but I knew that I had played the joke for them, I had
stepped into the role and played it for my own pleasure,
liking, as a child likes, to be in the center of the room,
demanding special attention and care; it's almost deference
that the precocious child demands, especially a boy-child
whose gentle antics are always rewarded with smiles and
laughter and the affectionate stroking of his chin.

Radha's innocence, though, was wholly genuine, and
carefully protected: not an act but a choice. Because she
held herself in the strict isolation of her own mind; because
she rarely, if ever, came into the room where the women
gathered, and rarely, if ever, spoke to the men outside of
her classes (this indifference seemed to be mutual, and at
times boiled over into plain hostility: but they wore this,
we knew and she knew, to mask their fear of her, fear born
of love and reverence for her luminous, untouchable mind,
a mind so knifely focused it was like Sita's body in the
ashoka grove, utterly impervious and even serene), she
kept the innocence of a young girl easily, and wore this
innocence protectively around her. Their attitude toward
her didn't seem to wound her. She had learned from somewhere the dancer's bearing and stood upright. Innocence
straightened her back. It was like this when she placed the
sweet in my mouth. Her mouth opened as mine opened,
the way you feed a child, unconsciously parting your lips
so that the child will part his, and in the sweetness of this
gesture I felt like I glimpsed the thing inside her that she so

closely guarded—her slender, vulnerable core. Because of this I wanted to cover her mouth with my hand. I didn't. Her bright fingers pushed the sweet into my mouth: it was terribly sweet, not from jaggery, which would have stained it brown, but from pure white sugar, which was very expensive, and gave the food a singular, focused sweetness, cut only by the black scent of elaichi and the flecks of pistachio, whose skins had been roasted with salt, but which nonetheless had a tacit green softness when they met with the tongue.

"Oh, it's heavenly."

"It's just from the sweet shop down the street. I can make better."

"Why don't you show me how? Now that exams are over, we can think of other things."

She shook her head. "Last night I came home and fetched the sweet, and after that I went to sleep. In my sleep I could dream about whatever I wanted to, and this morning too, I could think about whatever I wanted to. But now that I've made my offering I will go back to work."

"Back to work? But exams are over."

"This semester's exams. What about next?"

"Classes haven't started yet."

She didn't reply, just shook her head again.

"What do you dream, if you can't dream what you want to?"

"I solve my equations."

"Bap re, Radha. And last night?"

"It was also equations," she said. I understood. Not with my studies, of course, but dance. Unlike Radha my marks were not exceptional; they were not bad but they were not the best, which, for us girls, was almost the same. But I was not troubled by my marks. Some days it was as though the world had burst open into a fully bloomed flower I wanted to stuff whole into my mouth.

"You should be more serious. You should study more," said Radha, not unkindly.

"I think you should study less. Why can't you one night dream about walking across the sea, or flying over our forest?"

"It doesn't interest me."

"Do you have bad dreams?"

"Yes. Sometimes the numbers don't make sense."

Though she had not meant it as a joke, I couldn't help but laugh. It was true that for years I had been the most serious girl in the room, though I had not thought of myself as serious, just someone who enjoyed her own thoughts. Against Radha I was playful. We had begun to walk back, stopping first to ring the bell. The note that sounded once, then twice, as each of our hands reached to stun the tongue against the belly was fast, acidic, like a spray of lime. The air was warmer, the sky coming open, a slight pink.

"When you're married, you won't dream of equations." This is something I would have never said to anyone but

Radha. It was like something that someone would have said to me.

"Not you too," she said. "The other girls are always teasing me."

"Everyone admires you. That's why. They see you so quiet for weeks and weeks, every class you're quiet and then suddenly look. You're on top."

She made a small, pained noise.

"I'm not going to marry. There are too many girls in the family and I'm youngest." Then she said, "I don't want to marry anyway. I don't want to go back to my village. I want to go to space."

Space? Her major now made sense, and, at the same time, became ever more absurd. Sometimes god puts a soul in the wrong body. I took her arm, cool, almost hairless, where three perfect moles in a line marked the place her limb folded into elbow. It had been weeks or years since I had touched someone, it felt to me at that moment, and the same for her the way she let me have her arm. We walked home like this, in silence.

From this time onward, I became friends with Radha. "Don't even ask her, she won't help you," Farnaz said when first she saw me standing at the door with my work in my hand, hoping for Radha to answer. But Radha did open the door for me, perhaps to rebuke Farnaz's warning. After that, instead of going to the room with the other girls, I would walk down the corridor and knock quietly on her door. As often as not, she would not answer, she would not even move from where she sat, which was on the floor, surrounded by her open books and her notes, and several grubby sheets of paper where she made soft notes with a pencil and worked the complex differential equations that also populated her dreams. I didn't feel rebuffed. I understood the space she needed for her studies and for her mind to grow, to grow like a tree with its roots moving downward and its branches moving upward and outward. That was work the tree did alone, and in silence. If she did not open the door I would sometimes return to my room, or sometimes, craving a human voice, I would go to the room of the women with the same question I had taken to Radha, asking one of the older girls for help—freely given, with gentleness but with haste. But Radha was a patient teacher, like my father had been, carefully guiding me from one step to the next. It was years later when I realized that this ability, seemingly as ordinary as water, was another facet of her intelligence, for her mind allowed her not just the vital leaps from one plane of knowledge to the next, but also the capacity to move down to the mind she spoke to and sought to instruct. What had once been a pretext for company now became a need; or if not a need, then a pleasure, because I loved the warmth her voice took on when she discussed the problem, I loved being able to use the sharpness of her mind to cut through my work; though

I did not exactly wield it, I understood what it might be like to. If when we finished, she turned back to her work, I left, though she never asked me to: as she returned to her chaotic pile of books and papers I felt as though I were witnessing something so private that I left of my own accord.

After a while I began to visit her later in the evening. She put away her studying neatly before she began to talk though the day's problem, and after we solved it, she offered me some of the biscuits she kept to eat in her room, as she often missed the mess hall meal. Knowing her poverty to be even greater than my own, I would break a biscuit and eat the half; she herself did not eat more than one or two. We didn't eat together in the mess hall, but I started to watch for her at dinner: if she did not appear, I would save some food to share with her later in the night.

"I don't mind being hungry," she said.

"Neither do I."

Still, she accepted the chapati I had folded in a handkerchief for her, then tore it and ate half. The other half was for me. As we ate, we sat in a silence we had grown between the two of us. I got the feeling that Radha was surveying the things she had planted in her mind earlier in the evening, to make sure they had taken root, or perhaps just for the pleasure of seeing them alive inside her.

"What is it today?"

"What do you mean?"

"Something's the matter, no?"

Yes, but I hadn't wanted to tell her. We all collected these small injustices, the professor who never called on us though we were the only one with a raised hand, the mistake that the professor deducted points for, but had let a similar one slide on our male neighbor's test. Radha got it the worst. A rumor circulated that she did favors for the physics professor; her "mannish" looks were discussed just out of her earshot; they mocked her English; once, a boy had confronted her, humiliated to the point of tears at his failing grade, humiliated by *her*, and her eyes flickered with something like pity. These insults, against others and ourselves, were the kind of thing we shared in Saheli's room along with the consoling teasing and the gossip, but since she never visited we never heard her version.

"When Prof. Sundaram gave me back my test today, he asked me in front of everyone if I was ashamed of myself."

"What was your mark?" asked Radha.

"Eighty-nine."

She didn't say anything, but her eyes widened.

"What?" I said. "It's not bad."

"It's not good."

"You're taking his side? Others did much worse."

"Boys."

"Yes, boys. He said, 'Aren't you ashamed of yourself? Made such a big fuss to be allowed in. Now here you are, taking some chap's spot, some chap who needs this degree that you're obtaining as timepass. Ruining some poor fellow's life for your timepass.' And of course, no one else said anything. They agreed with him."

"What did you say?"

"What could I say? I was worried I would start crying."

"Did you?"

"No." Not then. I had held my tears in until I reached my room, and then cried into the creased pallu of my sari.

"Why don't you give up dance? Why are you trying to do both?"

"Does it bother you that I dance?"

"No, of course not. But you can't do both well."

"I can do one well," I said.

"So you've already chosen dance. Why don't you give up your studies?" I understood her question: I was not like the other girls in our college, I had not bothered to make myself exceptional. Why come here, then, she must have wondered, if not to be exceptional? But it was simple. There might have been easier ways to find a quiet room for myself, to live, for a time, alone, not with my father and brother or with my husband's family, keeping my mind and body free of all but the responsibilities I gave them, that of my dancing, and to a lesser extent my studies, but if there was I had not found it. In this room, so private and singular, my life was full of dance, for if there was any inclination I would spring into movement, I would utter the bols or rhythmic sums under my breath as I worked— and if I did neither, then there was always the possibility of movement, of rhythm, as though, by virtue of my interest the space had become charged with it. After my studies, I thought I might find an engineering job that would allow me to live alone, but I thought this vaguely, with none of its difficult particulars.

"Do you too think I'm ruining the life of some poor chap?"

"No, not that—your life and this imaginary boy's have nothing to do with each other. Only, you should work harder, Vidya. You know they're waiting for you to fail, so why should you listen to what they say about you?"

"It's so easy for you!" To my shame, I cried this out like a child.

"Easy?" she said quietly. "Do you know what people say about me?"

I shouldn't have been, but I was startled. She had wrapped her arms around her knees, her gaze cast down. How alone she was. How far away from home. Other girls had come from just as far, but they had made a home in Saheli's room, mothered one another and let themselves be mothered, as Radha had not. She had no one but herself, her mind, her textbooks, her studies, her ambition—and, I thought proudly, me.

It was late, very late at night. Our curfew had long passed. But I had a strong desire to be outside with Radha and to walk where we had walked before to the small temple in the dark. I thought perhaps our arms would brush against each other in the dark. I don't know why I felt this way. The day's heat had been so intense that it had almost made me sick, I had begun to get the first pains of a bad headache, but in the evening I took a bath and felt cured. Some breaths of evening air came in through Radha's open window, and I went to stand beside it, smelling the air, which was freshened by evening as though by rain. A feeling was coming into my body that I had no name for. It had a kind of wideness, a good feeling, that moved up and outward from my center.

"Radha," I said.

"Yes."

"Do you ever miss your home?"

"No," she said, and then, "I miss my sisters. Not all of them, just my eldest."

"What about your mother?"

"No, I don't miss my mother."

"Why not?"

"She's a tired woman." For a moment she was silent. "Anyway, if you miss your home, go visit, you can take the bus there and see your mother tomorrow."

"Yes." I hadn't gone home once since I'd started staying in the college.

"I'll come see you dance," she said suddenly. "But after exams are finished. Will you have a performance then? Or, maybe you can make a special performance just for us."

"Us?"

"The other girls would like it too," she said.

I wanted to dance for *her*.

When I parted from Radha that night we were both half asleep. We were sitting on her floor so drowsy speaking of the rivers of our childhoods, mine the "ocean" I had not returned to since the summer my mother had, with her swinging anger, broken the ties between my father and his family, Radha's the silt-silver Bagmati, which she had believed infinite until she had arrived in Bombay and seen for the first time the true infinity of the sea. She was allowed to swim freely, a safe distance away from the higher-caste ghat, and she looked at me with surprise when I told her I'd been forbidden. What did it feel like? "Oh," she said, "quite lovely, cool and weightless. If you let your body go limp you could float on the surface but I could never quite understand how to do this. My legs were always dipping under, or my head." I walked down the dark hall, half asleep, thinking of this. I lay in bed until my bed seemed to be a boat on water, rocking side to side. It was a river I moved on, alone, a shining flat of water that made me squint my eyes if I kneeled to look. If I lay back there was blue forever, just sky. But then the scene changed. Instead of lying on my back looking up, I was standing at a window looking down at myself bent and prone on the ground. I was very far away from myself, looking down, but I could see my eyes staring open and one of my legs twisted back at an unnatural angle. I was standing and looking at myself in horror, yet I felt I must look. Look! I shouted to myself from the ground, though my lips did not move. Look! I woke with a cry and it was morning, though only a few hours had passed since I lay down to sleep. Still, I had no desire to return to sleep and pulled myself out of bed. I sat at the edge of it, taking in deep breaths of morning, until dawn came.

After many months I did go home. I dressed myself carefully in my dearest item of clothing, indeed, my most prized possession: a yellow dress given to me by an elder girl who had noticed my admiration of it—my desire, which I could not disguise, though it embarrassed me— and given it to me as a birthday gift several weeks later, like a mother would. The dress was not made of cheap cotton but a lush and silky polyester. It pained me to accept it, and after putting it on at the urging of the girl I folded it carefully and placed it on one of the many shelves of the dressing table each room came equipped with, glass shelves that in my room remained mostly empty: my paltry possessions occupied just one. I had a couple saris, with their petticoats and blouses, one old blue fit-frock that had once held a tiny bit of glamour, but had become thin with age, almost transparent, and the skirt of it now too short anyway, as it was several years old. And my books, carefully covered in newspaper, and my ghungroos. Atop the dressing table I kept a single decoration, a branch from a tree I did not recognize, upon which had grown many rows of neat yellow berries that had dried into dull gold, resembling the brass of my bells. This branch had been presented to me by Radha, and I was impressed by the eye that had first found its beauty, which arose from the straight orderly nature of the berries, and the wild dark curves of the wood, a beauty I surely would have missed.

Absent from my room was a picture of my mother. I did not keep one in my room—that is to say, I did not hang one on the wall, where she would have gazed benevolently under a pane of clean glass, glass cleaned by me and garlanded by me, and marked with a smear of kumkum and sandalwood paste after the pujas I performed to honor my dead. With no such picture my room was the room of a mothered girl, and so they did not look at me with pity. I was as ordinary to them as they were to each other: for the joy of being ordinary I gladly sacrificed the memory of my mother: only in private did I pull out a small photograph of her that I had found some years before, and measure my face against it as I often did, noting, as I grew, our faces parting, though once they had been alike: my nose grew, my lips stretched, my cheeks plumped over her glamorous hollows. In secret I imbibed this image; almost compulsively I took out the photograph when I was alone, looking at it so long it would print itself on the backs of my eyelids in reverse when I closed them. Too late, I realized that a static image would replace the living ones

I had tried to salvage from the years, but they could not be consulted like a photograph, and so degraded quickly, her final face, the one that loomed large over my own and smiling with that strange kindness, was replaced by the face in the photograph, whose eyes, reaching out through the screen of years were so powerful they seemed to overshoot the viewer—looking past her into something unseen, unknown, and unspeakably far.

I put on my new dress. In it I felt so different from the girl who had left home, a village girl though she lived in a city, unsophisticated and unwise, and in the mirror in the bathroom I beheld a shy, slender grown-up in perfect lemon yellow; no matter how dark, the reflection pleased me more deeply than it ever had before. The same girl who had given me the dress had also waxed my legs for me, taking each foot in her soft hand as she ripped the hot cloth from my calves, and though the pain was quick and real, it was the efficient tenderness with which she held each foot in turn that pricked my eyes with tears. When she was finished my legs were dull and gleaming, like an object made of brass.

I wanted to show myself to Radha. The other girls had seen me and teased me in a way that had heightened my embarrassment and my pleasure, but it was Radha's reaction to my transformation that would solidify it: if she laughed at me, I would feel foolish and abandon it, but if she admired me, well, it would be *me* then, truly, the city sophisticate who had slumbered so long inside the village bumpkin. But on this day, Radha was not in her room; possibly she was at the temple, as she had also been absent on the day they had waxed my legs and I had put on the dress and twirled in front of them, the other girls, so she did not have this image of me and perhaps never would.

From where I boarded the bus it was almost empty and I was able to find a seat. As the bus moved through the city it began to gather bodies, then more. The seats were quickly filled and then the aisles, then a bouquet of people bloomed from each door, front and back. The bus passed through a posh part of the city where the streets were wide and leafy, and where there was a large park with grass where children played, then as the bus moved farther on the streets became more and more crowded, mimicking the bus, crowded not just with bodies but by vehicles of all sorts, cars and motorcycles and rickshaws and bicycles, and vendors dragging their carts to more optimal locations, and children begging at the stopped and stalled vehicles, shooed away by their occupants. Here the streets began to take on the texture of home, like a well-worn garment one has cast away, and then, after many months, decided to put back on. It didn't quite fit now: it was constricting: and you looked at yourself in the garment and wondered how you had suffered for so many years in such an ill-fitting thing, but even still, there was a sweet feeling, one of pain to see yourself in it again. New saffron unfolded

in windows at the corners of buildings, wide cotton flags
that were already beginning to dirty at their edges with the
soot and grime of the city. Beyond this, it seemed that little
had changed. I elbowed my way off the bus, leaping from
the crowded door as the vehicle slowed but didn't fully
stop, and walked down the familiar street to the chaali.
The vegetable vendor called out to me, sounding offended
that I had not stopped to say hello, and when I did stop
and offer an apology he smiled and sold me a few karelas
for supper, admiring my grown-up air, which he couldn't
help but take at least some credit for; he had, after all, fed
me for so many years with his vegetables, of which, he said,
he had always saved for me the very best and at the fairest
prices. It was late afternoon and the Manekji chaali was
flush in a rich light, the neighbors' laundry slung across its
shoulders, brightly colored and flapping, some deep in borrowed wet colors, some already dry in the heat. Boys were
playing in the courtyard, and, lifting my eyes to the fourth
floor, I could see the black square of our doorway, though
not quite through it, the door propped open to let in the
scant breeze. The sight of the open door struck within me a
feeling of joy and dread. Someone, then, was inside.

As I climbed the stairs I passed two neighbor aunties, en
route to a kitty-party at a third's; the two lived in flats on
the top floor, with the nicest views and bathrooms that were
equipped with private toilets, though the third lived a floor
below, in a darker flat that nonetheless was more expensive

because it had more rooms. I remembered this now, though I could not remember who told me, if I had ever been told. The women were dressed nicely, wearing their real mangalsutras with the full gold. They seemed surprised to see me—Look at you! How you've grown! And your lovely dress, we almost didn't recognize you—echoing the same feeling I myself had, that of a bride returned for the first time to her natal village. These women, fierce and critical gossips, under whose gaze I had many times been uncomfortably caught after my actions proved me more and more strange, took my hands in theirs gladly, clucking over me as though a daughter, and the warmth of their reception, though it was given automatically—they greeted me as they would have greeted any girl returned home, no matter how distant or prodigal—moved me so much I had to will myself not to cry. Each was old enough to be my mother, and both had known her—but even she wouldn't have greeted me like this. They stroked the polyester admiringly, taking the skirt of the dress between their fingers. "Your father and brother are living like two bachelors up there," they said. "You must come home more often, they need a girl's presence—they need a feminine presence to soften their lives. And your brother still too young to be married. And what are you doing over there, studying what? Child, someone must tell you, you'll ruin yourself this way, no one wants a daughter-in-law who has so much education, someone must explain to your *father*—"

But then they stopped, perhaps remembering how my father himself had made me unmarriageable by making it known he would refuse to pay the bride-price. That man— they almost said, they would say it to each other when I was just out of earshot—that man is impossible, he needs a sensible wife to help him make good decisions for his daughter. And just remember her mother—and touched my chin and cheeks with something like pity, and with gratitude that I was not their problem. "Well, well, go up, I'm sure your father will be overjoyed to see you."

My father, overjoyed? I almost laughed, thinking of him leaping to his feet as I walked through the door. In fact, the flat was empty when I arrived, but for the bai my father had hired and who squatted in the kitchen, sorting through the dry dhal. I greeted her, first in Hindi, then in Marathi, though I knew only little of this language, hers, and she greeted me in return, not pausing her work, neither happy nor bothered by my arrival. She was a tiny woman, taking up so little space in the flat as she rested on her haunches, her thin white hair was pulled into a knot at the base of her skull. Her sari was a lush, eggplant brown undimmed by at least a decade of hard use. Fatherji was out, she told me, but he would be back soon. The boy that rascal was out too. She didn't know when he'd be back or where he'd gone. The flat looked very tidy: her doing. I felt tugged, guilty, watching her curved back, her efficient fingers. "I brought some karela."

"You can fry it when I'm finished. Ah, here's your father."

And there he was, bending to take his shoes off at the door, the old man, my father. He was nearly bald—no balder than when I had left, but I saw it anew—his pate a lovely, even bronze, and shiny with the day's sweat. I took the dust from his feet quickly, and he put a distracted blessing upon my head, walking into the house with an uneven gait, a limp in his right leg, and sat down heavily on the divan. And suddenly I remembered the old feeling I had as a child reaching up for someone, reaching for the gaze of my father or more often my mother, just to be seen though blushing hard in it if I ever received it whether for my goodness or for my evil.

"So?" he said, and then, when I said nothing, "Your studies?"

"Good," I said.

"Are you working hard?"

"Yes," I said. "What happened to your leg?"

"My leg?" he said, and then, "Ah, my leg, it's nothing. I was getting off the bus a few months ago and some rascal pushed me off and I fell on it. It's not so bad now."

"Have you seen a doctor?"

"I'm fine," he said, and then to the bai he asked, "Have you made any tea?"

She hadn't. She started to put down her work to take up this task, but I stopped her; I would make it. The thoughtless series of actions, so practiced in this kitchen for so many years, was as familiar as a dance. But the placement of things had changed: the pots on a new shelf that had been built in my absence, ground elaichi in a small bowl was offered to me by the bai, and my body moved with a half-grace, interrupted from its thoughtless rhythm by the new, unlearned steps. When the tea was foaming up the sides I clicked the stove off and brought my father the steel cup.

"The Mehtas have a refrigerator now, do you know that?"

"Yes, they got it before I left."

"Yes, that's right, isn't it. But they have a television too. The whole chaali crams in there when there's a cricket match on."

"I'm surprised Mrs. Mehta lets anyone walk on her freshly washed floors."

"She's so proud. She sits right in front and narrates the game for the people in the back who can't see it." He blew on the tea, and then slurped it down, not waiting for it to cool. If he had his way, I would never marry. I would come home and be my father's wife; make his tea every day, supervise the bai, and do the final stages of cooking myself. There would be no child to raise—my brother was already grown—but my father's body was showing age, and would age further and need care. I could occupy myself in my dance when I wasn't needed for the household duties; some freedom, but I felt something inside me shrinking. I took his cup and washed it. When he was in his bath I sliced the karela and pressed the juice out of it with my palms. I caught the juice in a cup to give to my father to drink to cool his blood and keep his heart strong. Then I fried the rounds of karela in oil. When my father came out of the bath the bai and I had made dinner and I served it for him. I couldn't tell if my presence gave him pleasure but he did enjoy the karela.

"Where is Rishi? The food will be cold."

My father looked wan. "He stays out late. He doesn't listen to me. He's doing badly in his studies."

This was not surprising. In the months before I left for college something had been brewing in the boy. He stayed out late with his friends and sometimes I saw him smoking a bidi like a taxi driver in the evenings on the street just outside the chaali, in a half-attempt at brazenness. Or so it had seemed to me. The other boys, fourteen or fifteen, were smoking too. They looked to me like boys who were courting a scolding, who wanted to be witnessed and punished for their brazenness. I could tell my father, or I could issue the scolding myself instead, but I did neither. Let him make his choices on his own, I thought, passing them with a cold look.

"Maybe you can talk to him, maybe he'll listen to you."

"Maybe."

"He used to listen to you," my father said.

"He listened to you." He listened to the flat of father's hand, at least, or, later, the sting of his belt.

"He is running headfirst into ruin."

In fact, it was long after dark that my brother returned home. My father was tired and went to sleep not long after dinner, but I stayed up sitting by the window, back in my old sari, not wanting to spoil the dress with overuse now that its effect had been noted (as much as it would be anyway, for my father had barely glanced at me, not remarking at all on my changed appearance, and the small compliment offered to me by the neighbors seemed to mark the limits of the dress, though I distinctly remember two years before how Mrs. Mehta's daughter left the chaali for her college wearing a similar frock, at that time so spectacularly rare that all the neighbors came out of their houses to watch her go), with my book angled toward the lights from the other apartments, since father had shut off ours, and the new streetlight that shone proudly from the opposite side of the street. Now and then my eyes cast downward to the empty courtyard: I wanted to see him coming. At this hour of evening the cats began to emerge, slender as shadows, and I would catch their darting movements from the corner of my eye and turn to look, but I could never quite get them in the center of my vision, only its edges. The noise from the chaali was lulling—the Mehtas' TV turned up to its highest volume for the benefit of the neighbors, the nightly news broadcast, two siblings bickering over a loved toy (when I left the younger had been a baby; now look, both of them walked and spoke, had grown impossibly taller in the months I had been away), a wife shouting at a husband, another husband shouting at a wife, someone singing, loudly and off key, with a cigarette-roughened voice. I began to doze with my cheek pressed against the open slats. Then I woke suddenly. A figure moved across the courtyard, stooped and wavering, not struggling, but walking with an altered gait. He was taller than I remembered. Up the stairs he carried the round, bitter smell, his sweat colored by it: whiskey, I learned, a vast golden liquid that charmed and lulled you and then spat you out after you'd made bad decisions. As he kicked off his shoes the alteration in his movements struck me again—it was as though he were the shadow and alcohol the body that cast him, alcohol oddly beautiful in its clumsiness, finding obstacles where the body would find none. In the dark I could see only the length of him, and the slurred grace of his limbs, but not his face, not his eyes, but for the crescents of light they caught from the window. He walked to the clay water-pot in the dark and drank many cups of water, and I watched him, silent: he was so focused on his task he didn't seem to register my presence at all. It was a bright hurt to watch him, for I had allowed myself to imagine him and miss him while I had been away, but I had not imagined him like this. It was only after he was finished drinking water, his eyes sharpened to the dark, that he saw me and let out a yelp of surprise, which, though loud, did nothing to disturb my father.

"What are you doing here?" And even his voice was lower, pitched nearer to the register of a man's. How much had changed in the span of a few months, like the months of babyhood, when if separated from the child even by weeks you would return to find the body altered, the mouth smiling and able to form new words.

"Do you never read my letters?"

He put a hand over his heart. "I thought you were my mother."

"Where have you been?" I said. "Have you eaten?"

He was silent, so I continued, "Dinner's cold now. I kept some for you. Go sit, I'll bring it to you."

We went both to the kitchen. I stood on my tiptoes at the high shelf and found a clay lamp and matches, struck one and it lit, giving off the mild smell of sulfur. By this small light I could look at him: fair, skinny, narrow-faced, sooty-eyed, with still the soft skin of a child, bare cheeks and upper lip; I could see the face of the boy stretching and deepening like the voice—he was handsome. He looked nothing like our father. It was our mother who unfolded in his face. "What?" he said, brushing his hand in front of his face as though waving away a mosquito—it was my searching gaze he was trying to brush away.

"You're drunk."

"So?" And he cast his eyes downward suddenly bashful. "What's wrong with it. You eat eggs."

"That's not the same." I put the cold rotis on the plate, with the sabzi, dhal, and bitter vegetable. He took it. Even drunk he ate carefully, just like I had taught him, as though he weren't famished, though the food was quickly gone from the plate.

"You like it?" I put more food on his plate without waiting for an answer.

"I thought you were my mother," he said again, shaking his head as though at his own foolishness.

"Why is it you say *my*? She was mine too."

"I don't know," he said. "I'm not used to talking about her."

I saw the two of us as though in a movie, and felt unprepared for the movie role that I had been cast in, the virtuous sister to the stumbling drunk, I pure and clean in my sari, he falling down in his stinking clothes. In the movie, she would drag him to a temple, weeping; she would fall down at the feet of god and beg him to save her brother; she would beg her brother to listen to reason, to fear and love god and give up drink, and he, moved by her purity, and by her love for him, would repent, and a god-promised miracle would occur. No. We were too small and plain, our flat too ugly, the light too dull for such a scene.

"What are you doing?" I said.

"Nothing," he said. And then he said, "It feels good."

"What does it feel like?"

He thought for a minute. He wanted to explain it to me. "Like all day you've been waiting to be happy. And then suddenly you are." He thought again. "Like those carnival rides at Juhu. The ones that take you up and down the wheel."

"We never went on those rides."

He became silent, eating his food. When he was finished I offered him more, but this time he refused it. I was disgusted and I understood. I think I understood wanting to be happy. And then this thing made you happy. Looking at him, I thought, I've already had a child, and he came out spoilt. Yet he was perfect in the light, all but his ruined teeth. The brown, jagged teeth of an old man, that had come in crookedly after his sorry milk had fallen, and had become rotten down with bad habits and bad luck.

"You go watch cricket at the Mehtas'?"

"No," he said, thinking it was what I wanted to hear, but when he saw indifference in my face he said, "Sometimes."

When he looked at me again his eyes were red and I could feel his desire. He wanted me to say something; no, worse, to slap him hard across the face, to call him a dog and accuse him of darkening the family honor; he wanted me to reason with him in sweet words, to beg him, in the style of the movie-role; he wanted me to touch his face with tears in my eyes until I exacted from him a promise to mend himself and mind our father until I finished my studies or he found a wife, a promise he would break, and break again, if another and another was garnered as violently or lovingly as the last. But I couldn't. I felt, suddenly, quite tired, as though I had been walking all day through sand. Oh, the voice, the boy, didn't fool me, it was a child that sat before me, his face stripped bare.

"Let's sleep now, it's late," I said, and blew out the lamp.

I practiced my dance daily, even on the days I went to see my teacher. Previously I had not worn my ghungroos when I practiced in my room, not wanting to disturb others with the noise. But now that I was not going almost daily to my teacher's house where I wore the ghungroos for hours, my legs were getting used to their bare lightness and weakening, so I received permission to practice in the auditorium on campus that occasionally hosted cultural events, but more often larger lectures and sometimes religious services. Needless to say, this space was unlovely—it had been constructed with no thought for aesthetics, acoustics, or even airflow, windowless, bunker-like, I entered clean and dry and left dripping with sweat, and hurried back to my room, hoping not to be seen in such a filthy state.

But I liked dancing upon a stage. I imagined myself watched, looking out at the empty chairs in the auditorium, imagined them sweetly filled by all my enemies, the professors who were dismissive of me, the schoolgirls of my youth, and all the men who ever teased me on the street or tried on the bus to grope my breasts. If I danced well, I thought, they would all be sorry. I forced myself to focus on my task and not let my mind drift up and away, but remain tethered to its posture, its feet, its expression, its eyes, and its core, the tall weird column I felt inside me like a whirling fire lifting as I moved, and which I fed as

I would a fire with the fuel of my attention. As I danced I could feel the air heat around me. Sometimes. Less. I was entering a restless period with my dance. My teacher had gotten stuck on my chakkars, the whirling turns that I loved to perform at great speed, and which I had mastered many years ago with my previous teacher. My new teacher, coming from a different gharana than the old, took issue with the way I had been previously taught to blend my turns together into one continuous motion, spinning like the earth on its axis, day fading to night brightening to day, marking within each turn no particular moment where day became night or night became day, one being only a shade of the other. My teacher disagreed. She wanted each turn punctuated by a point of stillness, however brief, a pose so precise even the eyes had to point in a certain direction when the body came to pause. The stillness was a cord that kept me from whirling out into infinity. I simply could not satisfy her. She slowed me down to a beginner's pace; we worked together and I worked alone, glumly, for I had not given my heart over to her way of doing things, and I think she could sense it. To pause between movements, for the space of a breath or a blink, was to blunt the delicious force of the movement, pleasing neither to the dancer's body nor the watcher's eye. I practiced so that she would let me move on, but still she didn't. I'd spend my whole life like this, slowly turning, never with enough speed to feel dizzy.

After class one day I was approached by the boy I had seen out the window that afternoon of the mango harvest, Anand, one of the pair. The other I had not seen since, not on campus or in class, though I had not quite been looking for him. For some reason I thought that if I saw him, even unconsciously, I would notice, since he seemed so moody and odd. Anand's hostel was putting together a play for the Dramatic Society's annual production, and he said that someone had told him I dance. Did I dance?

"Yes," I said.

Well, would I join them? They were making a play out of Tennyson's "The Lotos-eaters" and there was a section in which they needed a girl. Did I know the poem?

I did. "There aren't any girls in it."

"All the wives of the sailors left at home."

"Oh yes, the wife and the child and the slave?" I said this sarcastically, but he said, "Exactly!"

"Who will play the slave?"

"We just need one girl for the wife," he said. "She'll symbolize all three. I asked Sushmita," (this made sense, she was the prettiest of the hostel, and boys were constantly manufacturing questions to ask her) "but she said I should ask you, because you're a dancer and used to performing."

This information flattered and insulted me at once, and I paused, not knowing if I should accept. I was conscious that the whole interaction was being watched by a group of girls who were walking back to the hostel, too far away to glean what we were actually discussing and therefore misinterpreting it completely. Radha, though, would have her performance.

"Okay," I said.

"You will? You will?" He was so pleased he gripped me in a quick, impulsive hug, which shocked my whole system but was over before I could wriggle free.

So I started attending their rehearsals. They took place in the same airless auditorium where I practiced my dance, but the presence of the men's bodies in the seats gave the space a charge that never fully left it, even when I was again alone in it, perhaps because, after I had finished my training routines, I was also working on my element of the play, which was thoroughly self-contained within the play, so much so that there was almost no practical need for me to come to rehearsals at all. The men that gathered there were for the most part not the men I remembered from my classes, though there was some overlap: people like Anand and the director, who were semi-serious students, relying on their intelligence to bridge the gap between the requirements of their studies and the hard work needed to fulfill them (these students were satisfied with merely fulfilling the requirements, rather than wildly exceeding them, their fathers having already lined up jobs for them once they completed their studies). Stranger was the small sub-group of boys I was sure I had never come across at all, for they sat in the back of the class while I sat in the front, nor were they ever seen at the library or studying in the small groups that sometimes informally arose. Among the vigorous strivers of our college, this was a small contingent of vigorous non-strivers, rich boys who grew their hair long, sometimes binding their foreheads with kerchiefs in the manner of American hippies, and who spent many afternoons and evenings, I was told, drinking or smoking dope and listening to the records of Joni Mitchell and Ravi Shankar. These boys were, in the theater's parlance, technicians, or so they said, for I could not discern a single useful thing they did, technical or otherwise, sitting in the back of the auditorium and making noise, slipping out to return glassy-eyed and even more rambunctious, giggling at nothing until they were kicked out by a growling Anand.

There were just three of these boys, sometimes five. Among other things, they were supposed to be in charge of the lights. The cast was nearly just as small: three shipwrecked sailors, four lotus-eaters, and me. They seemed always to be arguing about something—the positioning of the bodies on the stage, or the inflection of the lines, or the meaning of the play and of the poem, arguments that thrilled me, the whole thing thrilled me at first, as I positioned myself in my seat among them. It was a beginning, I felt: here I was in the company of artists, their arguments proof of their commitment to the stage. Here were people who, like me, felt their lives on the stage to be more vivid than their ones on land. None of them were strictly handsome, but they all had their moments, their angles—they all knew their angles. I could have fallen in love with any one of them, I thought, if I needed to.

Yet: often my ideas went unheeded. I would raise my hand shyly, as though I were still in class, and when I was noticed, if I was noticed, my suggestions were not met with the same argumentative fervor of the men but with the tolerant deference reserved for sisters-in-law. Anand would "take it into consideration," but of course, I knew very little of the stage, while all of them had had so much experience with theater, and how it was done. Of course. I understood then why they had asked me, and why Sushmita had refused. They wanted an audience, not just for the finished product, but for the entire process: they wanted someone to see and revere them as artists. It was only in front of me—a girl—that they became artists—men—and they left this part of themselves as soon as they left the auditorium, and they would leave it here permanently, moldering in this college, when they finished their studies.

Against this I studied my own interest. Was I, after all, any better? I felt scorn when I thought about their futures, how they would so easily abandon the thing they seemed to care about above all else, getting jobs as engineers or managers, or a degree in business, acquiring a wife and children and other fine objects, supporting, too, their parents, an unmarried sister. It wasn't just greed or cowardice that would cause them to abandon their calling; I knew this as surely as I too would be pressured into abandoning mine—but this knowledge created in them a fervor, I think, to convince one another and themselves of its impossibility. And perhaps I too had performed my fervor, to the audience of my teacher, and then just to myself. I liked the guise of artist as much as they did, it gave me clarity, meaning, and pride. I was different from them in one regard: I was sure I would succeed where they were so ready— even willing—to fail, and this made me even more prideful, increased my scorn, and gave me a sense of loneliness that both pleased and saddened me. So while at first the play had served to lift my spirits and my esteem, it ultimately drove them down, and I stopped going to rehearsals.

Still, I took pleasure in the composition. I poached sections from other pieces, but since none of them fit the situation whole-cloth, I was forced to invent what I sought to convey: longing, distance, love, femininity, and a terrible beauty—none of which, strictly speaking, was in the text, but seemed apparent as I thought about the wives sitting at home, lonely, or strolling at evening beside the sea, looking for life on the horizon or even trying to look past it, into the dark, faraway corners of the earth where their husbands were hidden, or underneath the folds of the very sea where they lay dead. I felt the anger the women might have had, staring off into the vast horizon, which had offered everything to their husbands and withheld everything from them, the wives. The fact that I too felt like this when I looked at the sea, even then, as I composed, simply looking at the sea through my mind's eye was inexplicable, for I was not the widow of a sailor nor had I lost anyone to its depths. Yet the sight of it, especially blazing with the last light of afternoon, would fill me utterly with this feeling that no other body of water inspired, not the lakes that bordered the campus nor the glittering pools at the British-built clubs or the homes of the rich, where years later my husband took me to parties.

The evenings for others had turned romantic, the path outside my window into the forest showed an increase in traffic in the dusk hours, and, leaning out as I sometimes did to watch these couples pass beyond my sight, I felt chaste and benevolent, a goddess who had no consort of her own, but blessed women's wombs and assured them joy. The boys from my college strolled with the girls from my hostel, but also with girls I had never seen before, borrowed, I think, from the Ladies' College where the choice was more plentiful, and the girls were prettier and more feminine, at least so we were told sometimes by the men whose advances we had spurned (a more feminine girl than Sushmita, for example, seemed difficult to imagine, but I accepted these comments, applied generally to the ladies of our hostel, and once or twice, specifically to me, with the same shamed pride that I felt when my teacher called me arrogant.)

I was often leaning out my window then, watching these

couples with curiosity. What did they talk about, what did they feel, when they let their hands brush but not clasp, just brush against each other as though by accident, until they were under the cover of the trees? What did they do then? For it was true that I knew what married people did with each other, and also true I did not know, did not fully know until my wedding night, though I had seen a grown man's thing between his legs because he had wanted me to see, a girl alone, and dark; men started calling to me and whistling even when I was young. The thing sitting in the hand of the stranger had not provoked fear or even revulsion, only a mild dislike, almost a feeling of embarrassment for him, whose want was so naked on his face that I had to pity him: it had given me a kind of power to see the want on his face, reversing the hot-shame feeling of powerlessness all the other eve-teasing had roused. Chi! I said and spat at him, and then I ran.

To want it? I would have liked to talk about it with someone, with Radha. Even with her I felt too shy to say the puzzled words aloud. And of course, she would know less than me. You ask a girl like Farnaz, who passed many times beneath my window, and not always with the same man. What I had was a sweet, undefined feeling. I could not picture myself walking on the path with any man, brushing his hand with my hand and laughing. I could not picture a man waiting for me at the top of the stairs with a bouquet of roses in his fist. I could only feel a soft feeling that came at night, and alone, it was almost an unbearably tender feeling, provoked by no one person but by a moon-like presence, and the feeling would wash over my body like moonlight, very softly, it would part my lips, and on the edge of my mouth I could almost taste the flavor of a sweet I had once eaten, a memory so strong it left the barest trace of taste along my tongue. If I pushed against this feeling, the calm in me would start to fade, and I would start to feel something delicious and akin to panic in a way that scared me, so I would stay there, in the soft calm my body had created, without pushing further. It was in those sweet evenings or deep in the night when I understood it was not really a punishment to be a girl, for what I felt was a girl-feeling, I knew, though I had no name for it beyond that. In those moments I was glad to be a girl, and I was glad to be alive.

While I was working on my composition I had not seen my teacher; she had been away for a performance in Paris and one in Lyons and when she answered the door she looked neither happy nor displeased to see me, though I was bursting to see her, having worked on my composition for weeks I was very eager to show her. In truth she looked a little distracted, and her cottage, when I stepped inside, offered a few discordant notes: a black line of ants trailing the pristine kitchen; the divan, mussed, slept in, instead of neatened for its daytime use. She was

straight-backed and neat as always, almost severe today
in her neatness, with her hair pulled back sharply and her
sari so pressed. Within the harsh lines of her clothing her
body looked soft. "Subramaniamji has not yet arrived;
still, we should get started. Without the tabla you can still
show me your turns." I put on my ghungroos as she put
the bedclothes away and straightened the room. The way
she moved moved me, even when she was not dancing. Her
movements in both were neither showily graceful nor were
they stiff, rather, the grace came from their inherent econ-
omy, their purposefulness, and an innate pleasure: when
her hand passed over the divan's cover to smooth it, her
body communicated the feel of the cotton under her palm
and even the pleasure of its color: a spotless ivory. She
saw me looking. Her face at that moment was unguarded,
open, likely because she was tired. She had been hurt—I
could see it from the slight redness of her eyes and the way
she pressed her lips together. The hurt I could see, but not
its source. And I think because she loved me, she didn't
immediately break her gaze from me to conceal it, she let
me see: brave, and plain.

"How was your trip?"

"My trip was not good."

"Why not?"

She shook her head. Her face came back into the present moment. "Come, let's see your chakkars."

Not bad, I thought, each time I brought down my foot;

surely I had improved, though I still had not reconciled my body to the new way of moving, and my body rejected it, blurring, yes, I could feel it, the stillness with imprecise movement. After a moment she stopped me by waving a distracted hand in front of her face. "Are you practicing every day?"

"Of course," I said, trying not to sound too indignant, but she said, "How? Do you do the steps until they are perfect? Or do you just thunk thunk thunk mindlessly until your time is up?"

I didn't know how to answer. I looked down at my feet. The wide tiles held a trace of my reflection, foreshortened and squat.

"Well?"

"Well, yes, I suppose I have, if you say I have. If I'm not getting better."

She ignored my tone and said, "Shall I show you again?"

"No, I remember."

"So let's see it."

"Again?"

"Yes, again. Again again again until you've got it right."

"But—didi, we've been doing this for weeks, for almost two *months* and—"

"And?" Her voice was cool, almost amused. "Have you got it yet?"

So, again. And again. It was a terrible way to pass time. She would not let me speed up past a beginner's pace. After a while—hours?—it began to feel as though the room was spinning and I was still within it, lifting and bringing down, from time to time, my one foot, aiming my arms as one might aim a bow and arrow. The ball of my left foot felt raw, the heel felt light, my arms ached, my fingernails dull, and there was a queasy feeling in my gut. I cannot exactly call this pleasure, but after weeks I was finally losing the twitch of irritation and becoming curious about the new movement, almost despite myself. To thrust stillness into the heart of a turn now seemed decadent, like a sudden draft of cool air as the door of the jeweler opens when you're standing on the hot street. I remembered, in the film of her, the way the dense skirt of my teacher's dancing costume would continue moving around her hips when she paused, the hips that went, in an instant, from living to stone.

"Ah," she said, "finally you've lost it."

"What?"

"Your resistance."

"So can we move on?"

"That is just the first part of learning and it took you weeks—months, as you said. There's still more work to do but it will come quicker now. Anyway, Subramaniamji has still not reached—he must have gotten stuck somewhere. It's enough for today."

"Didi, what was Paris like?"

"Paris?" She sighed, but her mood had changed since my chakkars had smoothed out. Dance could do this to me, but I found it remarkable that just teaching me had done it for her, for as boring as I had found it to turn, how much more infinitely boring it must have been to watch me, and yet she had, sitting up very straight, her attention never flagging. It made sense she would like her turns this way. To do the turns in her style was to declare that stillness was underneath everything—any whirling motion, any violent emotion, joy, irritation, anger, grief—and so to offer both dancer and watcher a way out of their pain. "Clean. Gleaming. I performed in a very beautiful theater, as though I was a jewel in a box of velvet. All the white people watched very politely and clapped quietly when I was finished."

"Do you always perform solo?"

She smiled at me, amused. "I know what you're asking."

I blushed. "I wasn't asking . . ."

"Two years past I staged a dance drama with several dancers, my students and friends. But I only travel alone; it is more difficult with a troupe, more expensive. Two, though—"

"One dancer, one assistant—"

"Two dancers. But not now, you're not ready. You have not proven your worth to me, only your desire."

Had not yet—? Or she was teasing me for my naked ambition—for what is ambition if not desire—which did not embarrass me and which I made only little effort to disguise. For when she looked at me, it was never enough.

I wanted her always to be looking at me. "Oh, didi, I want to show you—"

"What?"

"I'll just show."

This I know, I presented pristine, for I had polished it with my feet and my mind, like a rubbed piece of marble growing ever more smooth: my lotos dance. I had taken from everything I knew and made a new whole thing, and as I danced I felt the smoothness and sureness of my composition, nearly forgetting my teacher in the joy of my movement. I was at the sea, I looked against the shore, walking for a better look: through the window of the bungalow I could hear it rushing, the real sea, the real making the imagined more strong in my mind, allowing me to vanish, almost, into the dance I was making. I could feel her looking, though I did not watch her face, keeping my eyes fixed on the wall behind her as my body kept the rhythm of my steps against the beat of my heart. Stop. Stop! "Stop!" She clapped her hands together one time, and the dance washed from my body all at once, like a spell breaking. As I gazed at her face, I wondered what I had possibly expected from her, pleasure, or respect, or even amusement, for there was none. Her face, so lovely and open and easy, one that glowed with fairness and health, was transformed with her anger: her lips folded, her brow bent, and a cast came over her face and made it terrible, almost ugly. "This is what you have been doing while I was away?"

"Yes," I said, thinking her anger was simply a mistake, and so still proud, "there's a talent show, you see, didi, and they asked me—"

"I can think of nothing, *nothing* more disrespectful to your guru or your gharana than what you have done. You think you can just play with this, with kathak like this, for your own amusement? What do you do when I'm not around? You wear your ghungroo into the toilet with you because you're too lazy to take it off after practice? You go and spit in your father's face for fun?"

"But you compose, your dancing—"

"Are you comparing yourself," she said, "to me?"

"Well," I said, "we dance, we both love dance . . ."

She took a deep breath, trying to calm herself. My body was alarmed by her anger, flushed and in a state that felt similar to joy, and because of this, I found myself on the verge of confused tears. Who else had ever scolded me with such passionate fury? And so, how could I be sorry for my error? No one but my mother.

"I warned you about your arrogance, didn't I?"

"Yes."

"Well, you'll simply have to discard your dance and do something else. Some other composition you've already learned from me or from your previous teacher. And seek forgiveness from god."

"You don't believe in god."

So shocking was my comment, that I heard a catch in

her breath. I too was surprised. It was small, but with it I had pushed us past the bounds of our relationship, that of disciple and guru, whose god-like words were taken as command, and into the uncharted and unnatural territory of false equals. Though my teacher had never enforced the boundary between us the way most others would, with her manner, her criticism, or even her bearing, still there were rules that governed our relationship and gave it its structure no matter how informal it appeared. My own rebelliousness frightened me, yet I was also thrilled by it, long dormant, hidden even from myself, and now flaring up at this unlikely and undeserving target.

"I don't believe in *your* god," she said.

"I won't."

"You won't."

"Yes. I made it, my dance. And anyway they're expecting me to perform it."

"To make the dance in ignorance—though it is difficult for me to believe your ignorance, I will allow you it—that is one thing. But to know, now, that it is an insult for a novice like you, an arrogant novice, to take a centuries old tradition and break the rules of it—like a *child*, playing with a precious vase, smashing it—"

"Don't you too do this? Bend and play with dance?"

"I *know* the rules to bend them. From years upon years, and with the blessing of my guru."

"Still, I won't discard it. I'll perform it." The joy was

leaving my body as my heart slowed, and my tears traveled up into the sockets of my eyes. Now I was fully sorry,
for I would have to leave her. My teacher's face was calm,
the hurt of the morning returned to it, and fresh hurt:
mine.

"Ah," she said again, but softly, almost tenderly. "You've
disappointed me, Vidya."

"I know," I said, because I could not say sorry. I did not
look behind me as I closed the door.

"In space? It's so cold, isn't it?"

"I think so," Radha said.

"Have you ever been cold? Truly cold?"

"The river's cold. Not the surface but deeper. That part's
cold." We were side by side on Radha's narrow bed in the
hottest part of the afternoon. As was often true about the
time we spent together, this was a secret part of the day,
now that the heat of the year had almost reached its apex,
so hot that most people took to their rooms, pulled the
shades down, and draped cool wet rags across their foreheads, not so much drifting into sleep as hurled into it
by the afternoon's unbearable temperature. Radha's skin
and blouse were damp, even the edges of her hair where
it touched her neck. Mine too. The weight of the heat
pushed all but the most dreamy thoughts out of my mind,
which was a relief, for since my argument with my teacher
I had spent many days unsettled, walking from one end of

my room to the other, just thinking of her. The pain felt
called up from a deep place, a black place, though I did not
regret my words, I did not feel shame for *them*. The pain
gave my dance a strange intensity, almost an urgency, that
left me breathless, even the simplest todas. I practiced her
chakkars. It was not regret.

"Like ice, though? Ice cold?"

"I've held a piece of ice in my hands."

"Me too. But that just makes your hands cold and the
sun is still beating on your neck."

"I can't remember. I think in the river I was cold. But
not for long. I came back up and it was hot again."

"What did it feel like?"

"How can I tell you? Have you never not once been
cold?"

"No," I said. Reading all those years about snow and
ice in my English textbooks, I would feel a longing for it
without knowing quite what I was longing for. To be cold,
it seemed to me, was to rid oneself of one's animal stink
and therefore one's animal tendencies: it was to be clean,
pale, and godlike and free of pain.

"Well," she said, and these words we spoke slowly and
thickly through the heat. "It touches your skin the same
way heat does. Or when your skin prickles up when you
see something beautiful. You gasp, it's like surprise. And
when you come back to the heat you feel grateful."

"Who taught you how to swim?"

"No one," she said. "It's easy if you just watch and pay attention."

"But girls drown."

"Yes, girls drown. That has nothing to do with swimming."

"What do you mean?"

"They do it on purpose," she said.

We fell asleep. It was a wonderful abundant sleep together as I had never had, I felt *with* Radha, somehow, as I slept. In my sleep as though in a dream I heard her tell me a secret. It was so dark in the room with the blind shut, stifling hot with the fan going on and on and the quality of the quiet different from early morning or evening: a crushed velvet quality, like bare feet walking against moss. The secret she told me required her to lift her sari to her thighs, she did this without sitting up, tugging the fabric up to bare her thighs, smooth and softly furred, but marred, each leg, by several scars that described a deep pain. They were yellow and pink, slick as though wet, and irregular, the largest the size though not the shape of my palm, the smallest the butt of a pencil. In fact there was more scar than skin across her legs like a burst of wild, horrible art.

What happened?

Hot oil, she said.

How?

It doesn't hurt anymore, she said. It's from long ago.

Very, very lightly, I touched the largest of the scars with
my index finger. Heat came through the stripped skin in a
different way, and the finger I laid upon it was damp with
sweat. I thought I could feel her pulse beneath my finger,
not quick, but long and steady.

I didn't make a sound, not at first, Radha murmured.
But later I did, I screamed.

Are there more?

No, just these.

I don't know why, but I felt compelled to kiss her on the
scar I was stroking. Had we not been in the dream-dark,
we both might have acted differently, but she received the
kiss with a calm that was almost indifferent. No, I could
hear her breath shift, slightly, to quicken. My lips tasted the
salt my fingers had left there. I wanted to look at her entire
body, to see what was damaged and what was whole. Each
quality enhanced the other, the scars on her skin making her
legs more beautiful instead of less. Save for the three small
moles in the crease of her elbow, her arms were unmarred;
her waist too, so small, it could be encircled easily by my
outstretched arm—almost, it seemed, by my hands themselves. There was a moment that passed between us that
felt too sweet, too soft, tender the way a bruise is tender
on the ripest fruit. Yet I could see no confusion nor pain in
Radha's face. Her expression was innocent and joyful, like
the time she pushed the sweet between my lips. I fell down
beside her and slept. When I woke up it was dark outside.

She was sitting beside me with her knees gathered up in her arms and her cheek against her knees, looking at me. My mouth was filled with sourness so I knew I had slept deeply.

"What time is it?"

"I don't know," she said. Her voice sounded far away.

"Have we been sleeping long?"

She shrugged, and rubbed her eye with the heel of her hand, a casual, relaxed movement. I sat up. The bed was much too narrow to accommodate us both. Our shoulders pressed against each other.

"What's the matter?" But I was asking this of myself. An odd feeling had come over me, a brown, not-right feeling, time out-of-joint. I felt almost panicked for a moment because I was sleepy and confused when I wanted to be alert and awake. I rubbed my face in my hands. My sweat, dried, flaked away with my fingers. The feeling grew louder, like an alarm sounding.

"Vidya," she said, softly, and then she said again, "Vidya."

I got up without speaking and went outside. I knew I had to be outside for the feeling to pass, and it did, roaring past with tremendous, ugly force, then ebbing. There were some small stars out there. Now that the panic had passed I felt around at the space curiously, with a different kind of fear. I leaned against the rough trunk of my mango tree.

"Vidya!" Farnaz was returning from the library, her arms loaded with books. All rose-colored her face and arms, the pink stood out in her cheeks. "What are you doing out here? It's almost curfew."

"It's too hot inside," I said.

"You look strange," she said, coming closer to me and peering at my face. "Are you alright?"

I nodded.

"You really don't look alright, joon," she said and then, looking at me hard and very closely, she whispered, "You're not in trouble, are you?"

"I think I am," I said.

"I didn't even know you had a beau; you and Radha are so secretive. Listen, joon, it's okay, Sita was in trouble last year but we helped her, we'll help you too."

I nodded again. Then I said, "I don't have a beau."

"I'm not the Assistant Warden," said Farnaz, "you don't have to lie to me."

"I'm not."

"Well, what happened then?" her face darkening with worry. "How did you get in trouble?"

"I'm just . . . I think I'm losing focus a little bit. I don't think it's my dance, but I think I'm losing focus. I just need to try harder, really."

"Losing focus!" said Farnaz. "What on earth are you talking about? Your exams?"

"Yes," I said. "What were you talking about?"

"I thought you were *pregnant*," she whispered. We could have laughed, both of us, but didn't. We just stood, slightly bewildered and relieved, out there on the lawn.

"What would give you that crazy idea?"

"You just looked," she said, frowning, "like a girl in trouble."

Then I was alone. I stood in front of Radha's door but didn't knock; when I saw her from a distance, I went the other way. Her figure, slight, upright, and proud, seemed to burn a hole in the middle of my vision—a white pain flared so brightly I had to avert my eyes. Behind her door she was silent; the movements of her pencil against her notebook and the thoughts against her mind were so quiet I could not detect them. Once, I passed her in the corridor—her face opened in a smile and she began to speak, and the sound of her voice caused a feeling of alarm to flood me so utterly that I had no choice but to walk past as if I hadn't seen her. From then on she did the same. So simple—it didn't seem to trouble her at all—I just vanished from her face. The version of me who teased, listened, goaded, admired, and advised, all the hours of our lives together—they were simply gone from her: I could not detect any hurt. I came away from each encounter trying to reason with myself. Exams were looming, not so far in the future that they had shifted the hostel schedule into frenzy, but close enough that one could not afford to fall behind, or to lose their place ahead,

a place that required an almost superhuman level of vigi-
lance. So I returned, reluctantly, to my own studies.

There were two ways to learn: one was to be curious,
to offer the hungry mind a question and patiently let it
seek the answers out. For many months my curiosity had
found an object outside my studies, and the information I
gathered on this subject only made me hungrier for more:
what were her home-days like, her family and especially
her sisters, which foods did she prefer, and which songs,
what did she pray for, and why at all did she pray—but
though this curiosity threatened my studies, another, fed
by Radha, aided them. Without Radha's curiosity my own
faltered. Therefore I turned to the second mode of learning,
which was anger.

You gathered every *no* you had ever heard in your life
that had to do with the capacity of your mind, and you
held the freshest insults closest—the credit men took for
your work or your ideas in groups, the voices so many
used to speak to you, not just with scorn, which was tol-
erable, which was naked and therefore bearable, but also
the impatience and amusement that they never used when
they spoke to each other, the voice of a husband explaining politics to his empty-headed wife, or politely tolerating
the fizzy ideas of a younger sister—you took that anger
and pressed your mind to the hot, sharp point of it when
it was tired, and the little jolt of pain drove you awake,
drove you forward, yes, you could sit for hours with your

anger, not piercing the surface of the subject as you might with curiosity, but smashing the subject open with brute force, destroying it and dulling it with no pleasure, and not even total understanding, but mastering it. You were aiming yourself for the moment that the sheet of your silence would drop, and behind it, the lovely blazing tower you had built and built from your anger for hours or months would finally be revealed—not the meek woman who stopped raising her hand after nobody would ever call on her, though she always had the right answer, but the *you* who had been all this time coiled inside her.

We all studied this way from time to time, even Radha, I suspect, who might have drawn upon it only in her final hours, when her mind was at its most exhausted. In those weeks, I lifted myself out of my body for hours, studying, and came back to it famished, thirsty, needing to use the toilet, cramped in my back and in the backs of my legs, and triumphant, a feeling somewhat akin to happiness. I took some food in the mess hall alone, the simple rice and dhal of an ascetic, like an ascetic not wanting to speak, my mind humming with the silence of my hours. I could feel myself spreading out into my body again, occupying it again, affectionately. It was small and brown and soft, and young, I realize now, though I cannot remember whether I felt young then in my body—to feel youth in one's body, I think, means one's youth has nearly ended. I was impatient too, or, if not impatient, then conscious that my days as

a student would come one day to an end, and that there
was more ahead, blank but more, and lots of it, its very
blankness was a joy, for if I allowed myself to contem-
plate my future in its particulars, to write upon the blank
wall all the outsized dreams I had cooked up, my terror
was greater than my joy. To be a dancer, to never marry,
to live apart from my father, to live alone, even to cut off
my hair—the weight of these possibilities, of their logisti-
cal demands and the consternation and even outrage they
would inspire, brought up a panicky feeling. Sometimes,
instead of looking far down along the road it was better to
step and step into darkness, trusting your body to intuit the
safety of your steps. So often I turned my face toward that
darkness, that dazzling blankness, in which each possible
future described itself into a gleaming noise of white.

After the first time I saw Radha in the corridor, I took
pains to put as much distance between us as I could without calling attention to that distance, though doubtless it
was noticed by the other girls, a hurt so visible that they
did not bring it up with me, knowing better than to tease
or joke. Early morning, coming back from the bath, I saw
her leaving her room—morning so early only we two were
awake, still dark, the dreaming time that I loved best for
working, when I could walk straight from my dreaming
into my dance. I was unguarded in this moment, and the
sight of her face caused tears to spring to my eyes. Her face
was so soft, her cheek creased where it had been crushed

against the pillow, and she was wearing a plain yellow sari that made her look like a bird, a bright little bird—and in her eyes, the recognition of me that had only so recently died—had been suppressed—now flared back up. I was alive to her and she to me—what was all this nonsense?

"Good morning," she said.

"Good morning," I said.

She rubbed her eyes with her fist and I thought about the burn on her thigh. I thought about the smell of singed flesh, the fresh damage, and felt ill. Nonsense or not, I could not, after all, look at her.

"How are your preparations going, for exams?" I asked her, and then I said, "I know already, of course: they are perfect."

"I'm having a little trouble paying attention."

"You?"

"Yes, me. I'm only a person."

"No, Radha, you're the goddess of physics herself."

I could feel her eyes on my face, trying to read me. The tone of my voice was a little too sharp. I could not read myself.

"Vidya," she said, "what happened? Why don't you ever come to my room?"

"I don't want to distract you."

"You don't distract me."

"I do."

"Well, a little. But I don't mind."

"You *should* mind. You should forget about all this time-wasting we did."

"Forget about it?"

I met her eyes. They were brimming with hurt.

"It was nothing," I said, hurting her. "It was time-pass, it was nothing; better to forget it."

I started to feel it then, guilt. I had taken her solitude and turned it into loneliness by our friendship—I knew because I was lonely now too, now that I had finally tasted true kinship and had lost it, and, standing apart from her again, I could see just how tightly she held herself in the company of the others when, by necessity, she joined it. It seemed so plain now: what came off as cool aloofness, an absence of need, was actually a shyness that bordered on fear. What did it take to be so excellent? From everyone else she had hidden behind the dazzle of her ability, becoming just an outline: the genius, the number-one student, the proud one, the impervious one, flawless and hollow as a god: pristine. She had let me look behind—even just a little. And I had refused it.

So something was lost, had been lost, my Radha, and the feeling of loss pervaded me when I was not dancing or studying, or dreaming against the blank wall. Something else had been lost, many things had been lost, perhaps everything had been lost, the girl I had been felt far away, though I had come to school to be rid of her—the sad, motherless girl with dry ugly knees and a dark ugly face: that girl, I could not remember her as me, I could only remember her as though I watched her from somewhere outside her body; I could not remember what it felt to occupy her skin and her moods. But why should it be any other way? Why mourn those lost, painful hours, hours lonelier than the ones I spent now? Those that had been lost willingly, almost eagerly, unlike the afternoon hours with my friend? Oh, what a talent I had for sorrow! Or more perversely, it was this very feeling, of loss and melancholy, of *wanting*, the feeling I always had so acutely and still have so acutely, though the object might waver, that made me feel, if not quite happy, then at least comfortable, at least myself. It is in fact better, I think, when the feeling can be fixed—contained—on a single object. When it was Radha, she became the organizing principal of my sorrow, and I understood myself through my sorrow. That's why, when I try to put this time into words, I find I am not able to capture what I truly felt, for the words "happy" and even "melancholy" do not seem to hold the meanings I need. I need a shape, a taste, an essence, a pose, I need a stage and movement, I need bells, color, sound, light.

Still: what a pity, I thought, to not be able to see Radha in her final exams. Distraction or not, I knew she would not falter. Unlike my dance, hers was a feat that could not really be witnessed, for the drama unfurled silently on the stage of her mind, the only outward expression of such furious movement were the small gestures of the hands and eyes, all that was needed from the folded body, whose hungers and feelings were otherwise completely irrelevant and unfelt. I could see her sitting in the classroom, her hand moving quickly over the paper. She would finish an hour early, and then wait, not even checking over her answers, just trying to make the distance between herself and her nearest competitor not appear so unseemly, but after fifteen minutes, the tiredness and hunger of the previous days and months flood her and she cannot sit for any longer awake in that chair and so brings her exam to the proctor, who smiles, thinking she has thrown the test, and inviting the horrified looks of the boys, who know she hasn't. Later, in the violent sunshine, she meets me, I am waiting for her, her body exudes a soft pleasant stink that I breathe in standing close to her but not touching her. She's not joyous—the pleasure is already over—but she is calm. She would follow me upstairs, out of blinding sunshine into the frank dark of my room and our eyes would speak in the dark of my room, our mouths speak or perhaps only our quietness, the rich, vegetable understanding that surfaces in silence.

No. She would come out of the building alone, she would walk, alone, to her room, and in to that room I could not penetrate, even with the keen eye of my imagination.

"There's a boy for you," Farnaz announced at my door, unnecessarily, as the watchman was already shouting from his post, "Number forty-one, your man has arrived!"

"For me?" I said, already blushing under my dark. "Who?"

"I've never seen him before," she said, then laughing, "would you like to tell me something after all?"

I thought briefly of the pale-faced man I had seen from my window, but that had been many months ago: why would he come now? Yet who else could it be? Against Farnaz's obvious, gossipy pleasure, I felt a confused revulsion: when someone makes their want for you evident, they put themselves in your power; you almost feel sorry for them, I thought then, though later I felt differently: I did not *not* feel pity, later, but I felt something else too. I followed Farnaz hangdog down the stairs, where indeed there was a boy waiting for me, halted at the office of the Assistant Warden, where all visiting men were detained: not a suitor at all, but my brother. It was a Sunday and the campus was mostly empty, and those that were around were studying in the library. My brother stuck his hands in his pockets, American pockets, they seemed, in his thin, bellbottom jeans. The pockets were not deep enough to contain his fingers past the first knuckle, yet he was so proud that there were pockets at all he could not seem to stop himself from bringing attention to them. "What are you doing here?" I said instead of hello.

"Can't I come visit my own sister?"

The Assistant Warden, for we were standing in her office, frowned; too many couples had already tried this lie: as far as she was concerned, the relation of brother to sister had ceased to exist.

"Oh, it's your brother?" asked Farnaz, disappointed, who still believed in siblings.

"Yes," I said, and then, "has something happened?"

"No."

"You're not allowed to come up."

"Take him to the visitor's room," said Farnaz, who had sat many times in that dim, stuffy room, holding herself flirtatiously apart from the man across from her, increasing his desire for her by holding herself away from him: she could, after all, have taken him out, they could have walked together in the forest and had a little more privacy, away from the punishing gaze of the Assistant Warden and the curious glances of passing women: like a dancer, she knew the power of spectacle, and used it.

I took him out, my false suitor. It was still quite hot outside but it was worse to be inside with him, where someone might see us, so I took him on the illicit path that lovers took, curving past my window, then disappearing into the trees, out of sight. Except if Radha could have seen us together, not knowing his true relation, I would have been pleased; if she had, at the right instant, happened to have been looking out the window. I knew if she saw us she would mark the question in her mind without ever asking anyone about it, though what feeling the sight would provoke, if any, I could not guess. I looked up at her window as we passed, but it revealed nothing of its interior. My brother had a high, agitated step he tried to cool and match to my slow one and thrust his hands deeper into the thin pockets of his pants. Maybe Radha would see us returning.

"Can't I come live with you?"

"Me? Here?"

"Yes," he said, "why not, Farnaz likes me."

"Are you joking?"

"Yes. But I think Farnaz does like me."

"She thought you were my beau."

The trees were not bunched here; there were gaps between them, where light fell around their fingers. There was a feeling of spaciousness on the path, and it was as cool as a room, with a light breeze like a thread that wove itself through the large and small gaps. I liked looking at him from the side, as he seemed not to notice being observed. He walked with an upright bearing, his shoulders squared instead of slouched: light slid down his neck. "You could come here yourself if your grades were better."

"I did well on my exams," he said.

"How well?"

"Well enough."

"For here?"

"Well—no. Maybe not."

"That's a shame," I said, trying to hide my relief. "You'd like it here."

I could imagine it. He had intelligence but no will, so he would never distinguish himself unless provoked to do so, but he could pass his exams with only some effort, and could spend his days arguing with the Marxists at the tea stall near the physics building, or wooing the girls, who, in a few years, would occupy the rooms my classmates and I absented. Because he was a boy, he wouldn't have to *try*—not as hard as me anyway—though the thought of him, grown, healthy, grinning, twisted up in me a feeling almost like pleasure. What then? He could do anything: find a subject he liked and study it, get a good enough job to afford a car and a flat and a good doctor for our father, he could travel and teach, go to an American university— the world was waiting for men like this: skinny, smart, and charming, with a mouth full of crooked teeth.

"I can't believe how quiet it is here."

"It's not quiet," I said. "Listen."

Between the beats of our rubber sandals slapping the soles of our feet and against the soft, thick earth, there were so many birds in the trees of the college, so many birds whose names I did not know, but who never let the air grow too still, trilling and chattering and flapping their wings to make always a comfortable noise that was easy to ignore except in the silence lapsing between two people, for alone, you were always engaged in your own thoughts.

"You remember those games we used to play when we were young?"

"Yes."

"I used to imagine it like this. But with more rivers."

"More tigers."

"Just one tiger," he said. Then he said, "We had a fight, me and Dad."

"So apologize."

"I hit him."

"You *what*?" I stopped walking.

"Not—hard—I was—*angry*." Heat came up from his neck to his cheeks, he wiped his forehead with his hankie.

"Is he okay?"

"Yes, I didn't hurt him. I just got angry. You know Dad—he wants to force you into his way of not just doing, but *thinking*. I can't tolerate it."

"I've never seen him that way."

"It was different with you. He doesn't expect anything from you."

"No, nothing—except to cook and clean and run the house and make sure you'd done your schoolwork."

"It's different."

"Yes," I said, "very different. Were you drinking?"

"What?"

"When you hit him, were you drinking?"

"Why does it matter if I was or wasn't?"

"Rishi, listen. You're smart, you'll go far in this world,

you can attain whatever you want to achieve, you've had so many opportunities, a good education, and the benefit of your gender, but you'll ruin yourself—"

"I didn't come here for a lecture."

"I'm not lecturing you. You asked me for my opinion—"

"I didn't ask. I haven't asked for anything from you for a long time."

I made an unkind noise, a snort. "Well then, I don't understand why we're arguing."

"When are you coming home?" he said. When I looked at him, the mahua tree had cast across his face a continent-shadow, but the eyes that looked out at me from that shadow seemed bright.

"What do you mean?"

"When are you coming home? To live?"

"When school is over."

"And you'll stay? You won't go back again?"

"I'll stay until school starts again. Then I'll go."

"What about after?"

"After? I don't quite know about after. I'll work, I think."

"And where will you stay?"

"I don't know. Maybe I'll go abroad."

"Abroad? Abroad where?"

"I don't know," I said again.

"But will you come home?"

"Of course not," I said, exasperated. "Not forever."

There was a strange cast to his face. I could feel him

suppressing whatever he was feeling from showing in his face, which seemed almost clenched in its concentration to do so: a tightness around the eyes and mouth. The expression produced an eerie feeling in me. Because I could not see my father's features on his face, I think he must have looked like my mother, though I could not, not quite, remember her face, not clearly, only the ones captured in photographs. Myself I could not see in there, either, neither in feature nor movement: we were separate creatures. Yet he had always reached for me and not for her, the one that wore a version of his face; he had always reached for me as though he could sense our directions, the two mothers returned, but one pointing south, away from him.

"Rishi," I said gently, more gently than I felt. "You'll have to apologize to Father. You've hurt him; if not his body then his pride. But you must apologize to him and apply yourself to your studies. Then all will be set right."

"Yes," he said, in a strange, cold English. "Of course. I'm sorry I came here and disturbed you before exams."

As the date of the play grew nearer, I confess that it slipped to the back of my mind, while to the other participants it had barreled into the feverish front, and when I rejoined the practice of the boys, I saw an idea realized: lines had been memorized, costumes obtained, lights arranged, and they had even found another girl to be their audience, once I had stopped being theirs—a girl I didn't know and who might have been procured from another college, or perhaps was someone's teenaged sister; a perfect, silent girl, who performed her attention so naturally it had to be genuine, and whose voice, when I finally heard it, was pitched only slightly above a whisper, and very sweet. The play was polished now if not expert, and that I couldn't help but admire. They had made it with care. Quiet, quiet everyone. Can we have the sailors take their places? And here, Vidya, here you will come, you will enter from the left here, and you will come to center stage, and stand in your first pose until the lights change, they'll go from yellow to a sort of blue—Chuffy, can you show her?—see, like this, and when that happens the music will start too, you'll do your dance and hold your final pose, the lights will change back, and I want you to exit quietly from stage right, not my right but your right you understand?

Of course, but quietly? My legs were heavy with bells. I had already shown him the dance a few weeks prior, though I had made some embellishments and improvements since then—to be honest, I had changed it radically since he had last seen it, and I had a small fear now that Anand would not like what I had done, but he watched distractedly and said yes fine when I was finished, yes, yes, that will do fine, and though weeks ago I had worked hard to make it, I now felt so melancholy and distracted as I danced that his mild response seemed fitting. I exited the stage loudly, doing nothing to soften my step or muffle my ghungroos.

Though the days were brutally hot, the evenings were violet and gentle, the clouds gathered and swollen with light, diffusing it without bursting with rain. It was the last of the weeks before the heat of exams would start; already the most serious, like Radha, had buckled themselves to their studies, but the lovers became more romantic, and friends more social, like farmers working hard to pull in the abundance of wheat to last the bitter months of dust. I practiced my stage makeup in the mirror. I had gotten good at drawing on new eyes around the eyes I already possessed, such broad strokes did not require a skilled hand, eyes that were meant to be seen from far away, and from far away they could strike you dead. I did not own lipstick and had to borrow from Farnaz to give myself a carmine mouth. I did not have foundation so didn't bother with it. I asked Anand to get me some flowers to braid into my hair. He showed up at my hostel with a useless bouquet of red roses, long-stemmed, heavy, and expensive, tied with a long, silly ribbon printed with teddy bears. "Anand, what am I supposed to do with these?"

"Girls love roses."

"But I told you, Anand, it's for my hair."

He shrugged. "What do I know about hair?"

No man had given me flowers before, let alone such velvet roses. I snapped the heads off the flowers and pinned them down my braid, wet-ink black punctuated by drops of blood. They were too heavy for the turns I would make onstage; they would weigh me down and throw me off balance when I made my quick and final turns. No matter. My mirror showed me the mask of my face and I was pleased. I walked across the soft grass to the auditorium already dressed in my white costume, a cotton salwar kameez, and my alarming face visible to all who passed me, and backstage I sat down to tie the ghungroos. The boys, my boys—for they were mine, suddenly, I felt for them the affection a mother must feel, watching her children from a distance—they gave off the pleasant stink of nervous energy, ribbing one another until it was time to be quiet and take their places. I stood half-watching from the velvet wing, the boys on stage, the ripple of the audience, illuminated only by reflected light, light vaguely outlining noses and lips and the gleam of glasses in the dark. But I wasn't watching anything, I was listening to the poem, which was read first by Anand very seriously in English, slowly and a little too theatrically if you asked me for the poem by itself was enough; still, the poem, which I hadn't truly listened to in months, had an odd effect on me: it dampened the light, it softened my breath, it lifted me out of myself. The texture and the tone of the words, the rise and fall of them, felt as familiar, at that moment, as my own breath: like something sprung out of my own mind or from my own dream, long ago dreamt and only half forgotten, existing like a ghost at the periphery of my consciousness, not a terrible ghost but a sweet one. For many minutes after Anand finished reading, and the actors were onstage, speaking their Hindi lines, I was not conscious of the play at all, even where I was standing. I felt like I was on the edge of something and I wanted to reach it. Before an idea becomes an articulation it hangs before you like a cloud: you cannot grasp it. It was Anand who shook me out of this reverie, and pushed me onstage, for I had nearly missed my cue.

The actors were slumped onstage, dreaming. They had chewed their lotos and made a dream: I was that dream in white. The light changed, but the music didn't start. Between the time I lifted my foot and set it down I realized I needed no music, the first blow of my foot against the stage drove me hard into my dance, it nearly crushed me into it. I was a dream, beautiful at first, but of my own accord I grew angry, I was not a good dream: I was not a good wife, content forever to wait. I was not a good woman but a rageful one, and my rage was terrible. I gathered it and thrust it up between my eyes. I was crossing the stage to look and look against the sea for my lost husband, I was nursing my son into a man, feeding and dressing him, growing him into a warrior. Again and again my hands shaped a lotus at my breast, but each time they did so the lotus became sharper, like a star-pointed blade. So much time was passing: I grew older, but the intensity of my dancing increased with my age instead of lessening. It was against everything I had been taught, to dance like this, so wildly, not building the column of energy up from the cool center, not filling the limbs with remote movement, practiced to the point of sleepwalk perfection, and then infused with the subtle emotions of the eyes and brows and mouth. My dance teacher was right to be shocked. The movements my body made were almost out of my control: the body wanted to vibrate out of its shell. Since there was no one there to speak the bols, I spoke them. It was a shock to hear my voice so rough out of my mouth: at another time I might have felt embarrassed. For this rough anger-filled voice was my true voice, I knew as soon as I had heard it, the one I had strove to disguise from everyone, and from myself. My legs hurt with the force of their exertion, and I felt it even as I pressed onward. I turned, the huge, heavy braid wrapped around my neck like a rope. I turned: I grew older. The beat of my heart was quick, subdivided into fifths and eighths by my feet. From the rafters a soft snow fell, white petals that stuck to my skin where they touched me, glued by sweat. I had not known it would happen, and for a moment I was startled, as though I had myself conjured it from the force of my dancing. The white petals looked blue in the light, as I did. Again I felt myself close to something, very close, but not enough to grasp. I could not push myself over the brink. Then it was over, I stood posed on the stage. Panting. I had not been on a stage with the eyes of the audience on me in several years, and when I returned to myself and the room that held me I could make out individual faces in the crowd. I saw the black muzzle of a camera, and when it was lowered, I saw the face I had half-looked for since I had seen it last so many months ago from my window, the pale face of the man who walked with Anand. One row behind him, and slightly to the right, was another face I had looked for, the dark face whose familiar contours I had long gazed at, these weeks, in the privacy of my memory. When I lifted my eyes to her, her eyes looked back. And was it my eyes, the cold light, or were her cheeks wet with tears?

# IV

❊❊❊

We lived then in Versova, in a small cottage by the sea. We couldn't see the ocean from our window, but with the window open we could hear its dull noise, the terrible crying of the gulls, and the calls of the coconut vendors, along with the conversation of the sophisticated kitty-parties of the neighborhood ladies leaking out through their windows or wafting, on mild days, from their verandahs, the sounds of the neighbors' servants chatting, or sometimes singing to themselves as they worked, the shouts of children playing in twos and threes instead of tens and dozens like the chaali of my childhood, and, very distantly, the traffic noises of the arterial road where I bought my vegetables and caught the bus that I took to reach my dance students' houses, and to the theaters in which I performed. I did not particularly like teaching, for none of my students were very good; they were all rich, which is why they could afford an individual lesson, the space to host it, and a tabla player to score

it. Their homes were vast, lavish, and gleaming, like the
sprawling sets of movies, almost as opulent as the home in
which my husband had been raised, and these surroundings made me drive the girls quite hard, I wanted to scar
their feet with thick, black calluses they could never erase.
Oh, they were good girls, their bodies were soft and fresh,
but they did move them into the proper shapes, without
feeling but with the desire for feeling, their eyes looking
almost alarmed out of their faces, wanting me to smile. I
never smiled, because none of them were very good. But
I myself danced alone in the mornings when my husband
had left for work, and I danced too in some festivals and in
some small shows in some ordinary halls, small and ordinary, but I danced, and once my picture appeared in the
Gujarati newspaper (the caption identified me under my
married name, Mrs. Rustom B, which displeased me but
would have horrified the Bs—though of course they had
neither the will nor the ability to read the Gujarati newspaper). I was never paid more than it cost to pay the tabla
player, but it made no difference to me, for my true payment was the chance to perform itself, which often, though
not always, left my body pounded and sweet, as though
filled with honey.

Versova was an odd choice for a young couple—aside
from the fisherfolk who had been, it was said, Bombay's
original inhabitants, few people lived in the village year-
round. Instead they kept their second homes entirely for

their pleasure, deciding on a whim to escape the heat of the city some weekends or weeks, a private calendar I seemed to have no access to and could never predict. Being so far north, and rather isolated, it felt apart from the city, though it lay within its limits, and therefore apart from my own history, and my husband's: out of reach from my mother-in-law's influence, clean and new, where we could be the people we were only to each other and not to anybody else. I was determined to preserve the girl I had presented to my husband in my letters during the first two years of our courtship, and later, our meetings, a girl slim, dark, intense, driven, and free, determined not just to preserve this girl to my husband but also to myself. It was not a dishonest portrait, but, of course, a selective one, or perhaps I should say a hopeful one: my husband made me hopeful.

But why not, we asked each other in our letters, why did we have to be the people who the world expected of us? Why could not a union between a man and a woman contain their lives as artists and equals, instead of only lust, breadwinning, housework, and slow-growing affection? He wrote to me from England, where he was finishing his schooling—it was only by chance he had seen me leaning out my window at the college, and again dancing in the play, for once he had been on holiday, and the other called back to India by the death of a distant relative, and both times taking advantage of his stay to visit his friend Anand, who had been his dearest friend in his boarding school days, and continued to be despite their distance. In my letters, the reader was unhitched from his physical form, which lay sprawled across his university bed, separated first from me by a vast expanse of sea, time, and culture, conveyed in the *sky* by a vast roaring metal machine whose movements and velocities I studied even as I struggled to grasp its existence in reality, the tones and feelings of a body in flight. When we met on his visits home, and after he had completed his studies and come back to India to live, he was in flesh a stranger whom I knew well, who knew me well, a shock in flesh, always a little different than I had remembered, taller, softer. We did not touch, like lovers, or how girls touch, so easily looping one's arm around another's shoulder or linking hands as they walked across the courtyard to class, and so my body, charged with his presence, at times nearly buzzed with the pressure of our not-touching, a sensation that felt at times superior to me than the sensations of flesh, though I often felt a shame as I returned to the hostel, not at my impropriety, but at my lack of it.

Only once we had breached the limits we had tacitly imposed, having stranded ourselves at the desolate Parle station after a concert gone late—so late that the trains had stopped running for a few hours, forcing us to wait in that liminal purple hour that was neither night nor morning. The station was empty but for two yellow and black dogs that loved each other extravagantly, almost frighteningly, curling up against the other's mangy body, nipping at the other's throat. They would explode into motion running down the platform for the joy of their speed, doubling back, barking in fits of ecstatic communication, ugly dogs that stirred in me a strange feeling—embarrassment, perhaps, or pleasure. Very suddenly he took my hand, then bent his face to mine and kissed me. His lips were warm, dry, as subtle as paper, and through them I sipped the surprising air issued in exhales, almost sighs, that were colored by his mouth, his tongue, tasting faintly of the crumpled taste of tobacco, and of a warm and distinctly animal scent. I wanted to be kissed again and again—and not at all, for I wanted too to remain the mind he loved: so pure, unsullied by the realities of the body.

What of my husband's mind? I had it in my letters. As I held those letters, densely inked with his confident, angular hand, I felt as though I was holding his mind, it somehow never occurring to me that his "I" in the letters could have been as hopeful as my own. He talked often of his homesickness, which made him lyrical about the city he so missed, a city very different from the one I lived in, though we shared a knowledge of its streets and landmarks. I was fascinated by the ease with which he moved within the world, which was apparent from both our meetings and our letters, not in the least because with his native charm he gave the impression that it was not he who caused the world to be so pliant but rather, that he was revealing its natural state, which had all my life eluded me, turning toward me an indifferent face. Once he had taken me to the cinema—extravagant enough—and then he had suggested a stroll along the beach, and I had agreed, knowing that each step we took now together took me a step further from my life at the chaali, and even at the college, and deeper into the shared life we seemed to be inventing, in speech as well as silently, privately, through a subterranean understanding or perhaps simply a mutual longing, a knowing that grew against reason, or at least beside it. If I had followed my usual course, we would not have even met, he would have passed beneath the window of another girl as he visited his friend Anand during his holidays, and would have taken another photograph at the play, the frame empty of me, and this knowledge was electric to us; our opposites, my dark and his fair, my poverty and his wealth, my femaleness and his maleness, seemed to make our shared understanding of the other more intense, more destined, or blessed: to look in the eyes of another so different from one's self, and find a friendly soul there, one whose path you never should have crossed, was to feel the hand of destiny itself bending the universe toward you. The breeze from the sea was lovely, so cool, in the leopard-light. If I looked at him, it was only dartingly, through the corners of my eyes, but he didn't care to disguise his gaze and I didn't mind. I wanted him to look and be sure. (But I had never asked myself if I was sure, as I walked farther and farther out, passing by many familiar things, and leaving them behind.)

"Are you hungry?" he asked me, and I said no, but he asked me again and then I said I was, a little. He stopped then at a fried-snacks vendor and asked, "What would you like?"

Looking at the vendor, and the four or five options laid out before me, I was again silent. I didn't know. I was incredibly hungry and I felt baffled. Each was delicious, each I seemed to have developed a special fondness for. But he had already paid for the movie, though there I had successfully evaded his offer of snacks during the interval, saying that I had just eaten. I was used to managing my hunger and would not have minded waiting to eat until I was back at the hostel, but there, with the smell of food and the possibility of food right in front of me, oil and fat and salt, the wet, green-licked chutney, potatoes in a sighing, perfect gold, I could not help but feel my hunger in a crazy, almost unspeakable form and I thought almost that I would cry.

"What's the matter? You don't like?"

"No, I—"

"Brother, we'll have one of each," he said to the vendor, who had been watching me curiously.

"No, no," I said, horrified. "I'm not even hungry."

"Have a bite of each, then, and throw the rest away." He handed the vendor some small, crushed bills. Then I did start to cry. I was embarrassed and I tried to wipe my tears from my face discretely. But he noticed.

"Have I done something wrong?"

"No."

Not wanting to embarrass me, I think, he didn't say anything more, and he didn't try to take my hand or touch my shoulder. He took very lightly the end of my pallu and held it in his hand.

IN OUR HOME I lived free, no portrait of my mother hung upon my walls, and almost no vestige of any of my former possessions, for my textbooks had all been sold, my clothes all discarded in favor of a new wardrobe, austere but tasteful (so I hoped), which I purchased at the urging of my husband. Instead, there were tasteful decorations, framed concert posters and prints of his photographs, including, despite my protests, the portrait he had taken of me after I finished my lotos dance. Two rooms in the house, both laid with marble tile that was cool against the soles as one walked or danced, and arched doorways that separated the rooms from one another, from which we hung sheets of printed cloth, as there were no doors, and a window from which I could look out at the garden that separated our little cottage from the landlord's large bungalow between us and the sea. Our landlords were an Anglo-Indian family who lived in the modern fashion, free from in-laws or parents or extended families, only themselves and their three children, and their staff of ayahs, butlers, chauffeurs, and housemaids. Knowing my husband from his childhood, they had offered the cottage for a modest fee, therefore siding with us and against my in-laws in accordance with their modern values. "It's all too, too *romantic*," said Mrs. Kelly as she handed us the keys, nearly spoiling her kindness with the repetition of such pronouncements, but then she was gone and we shut the door and were alone in our marriage.

Versova was small. I was nervous to run into my dance teacher now that we lived in the same neighborhood, and took pains to avoid the same small lanes and alleys she might use to reach the commercial road where vegetables were sold. Once or twice I did see her, always at a distance, and I was always able to remain out of her line of sight, all the time watching her as she went about her daily tasks, testing the weight of a turai in her palm, or bringing a bunch of fenugreek up to her face to smell, laughing with the vendor as they parried good-naturedly over the price of ginger, and walking down the road with her small basket now filled with fresh vegetables, which seemed brighter in her care than they had at the stall. I had never before seen her outside her home, and it brought me a strange comfort to see her move. She didn't walk as a dancer, walked maybe like the leopard I had once seen at dusk at the edge of my grandmother's village, whose body seemed to express movements both deliberate and unconscious, and with an equal awareness of its power and the threats that might be posed to it: a body wholly in accordance with itself.

One afternoon she was wearing a fresh cream–colored sari with a green-and-gold border that seemed untouched by the dirt of the road or the diesel-blackened air, a deliberately austere choice that stood her out among the colorful clothes of the other shoppers, as perhaps it was intended to. Each time my eye lapped against the pale cloth, it produced in me a soft, wistful calm, and I followed her. Down the lane that led to her house there were fewer people, in fact the street was nearly empty, but she took no notice of the ghost that trailed her or at least gave no indication of an awareness of its presence. Had she forgotten me? All those afternoons we spent together. My action against her had been so odd and so unconscious, the words I spoke coming out of my mouth as though from a dream; I could not regret them. They felt destined. But watching her walk I almost started to cry. When she reached her door I called her name and she turned around in a fluid movement, but I could tell she had been startled.

"Vidya?" she said. Before an expression hardened on her face it was just as I had remembered it, soft and open.

"Yes," I said. The smile was tight on my lips. She was not smiling at all.

"So, you're married now." For I wore, dutifully, red in the part of my hair, red between my brows like a good wife. I liked the look it gave me, though I still didn't fully believe it, one of bold, adult modesty, a woman whose eyes may be lowered not out of shame but as a trick, to disguise her thoughts, her self, from the looker. Sometimes—though not always—my married aspect parted men like a blade: no one touched me.

"Yes."

"And dancing?"

"Yes," I said, feeling careful, not wanting to break the spell of her not-anger with me.

"Well?"

"I saw you perform. At the summer festival."

"What did you think?"

"Oh," I said. I stepped closer. "For days afterwards I almost didn't feel like speaking."

"Why?"

"I'm not sure. I felt like you had made something so delicate I didn't want to disturb it."

"Who are you studying with?"

"No one."

"In fact, I saw you perform too, at the festival. I came early to see you. I was curious."

"You did?" It left me almost breathless. I had not seen her, sitting simply, her face. Not felt her, as I imagined I would.

"You did it justice," she said, "But I never gave you that piece."

"I taught it to myself, remembering you."

"You made a clay idol of me and practiced before it," she said, "is that it?" She was, finally, faintly smiling. "Shall I ask you to cut off your thumb?"

"Is there another student you love better?"

"No," not joking now, almost sad. "Come in, Eklavya." She opened the door. Her birds began to cry as soon as they became aware of her presence, and she spoke to them soothingly as she put away her groceries, and began to tear up a stale roti to feed them. She filled a small dish with water and placed it in their cage along with the roti. "Do you want tea?"

"Yes," I said. "I'll make it."

She was satisfied with this, and sat at her small table at the corner of her kitchen where she could watch the love-birds and me as well, and the jade-colored sea. She seemed just the same, all but her eyes, darker and a little more worn. "The tea-leaves are in that red tin," she said, when she saw me looking for it. "Make it strong, na?"

"I've been practicing."

"Making tea?"

"No, dance."

"You'd be better off with tea," she said. "Your husband lets you dance?"

I put the cup of tea before her without answering and she cooled it a little and drank. The birds, now sated on their food, were drinking too, dipping their small orange beaks in and out of the water. Their black and yellow eyes seemed flushed with a shared, alien knowledge. "I was wrong, didi."

"Oh?"

"I've never loved more the way that anyone has moved." I sat at her elbow with my own cup, so we were not facing, but very near.

"You're a strange girl," she said. "It's funny that you showed up today. I was thinking of sad things."

"What sad things?"

She looked at me, appraising me. "Nothing. I was thinking of time, time passing."

"That's not so sad." It had been a long while since I had sat with any woman at all and talked. Not once, not really, since I married my husband, for I had lost touch easily with all of my schoolmates, all but Farnaz, who had returned to Iran and was very diligent about responding to letters; as for the others, some had stayed in Bombay and found jobs, some had married and quit their careers, and some had gone abroad like Radha to continue their studies or seek better employment. Radha and I—we did not speak, we had not written, or at least, the letters I wrote to her I never sent—after her graduation ceremony she had all but vanished from my life, though, strangely, had maintained her presence—in some ways her presence grew only stronger. For as she vanished from my life, she appeared more and more naturally in my imagination, where she took on more color, shape, and depth than she might have acquired from the faint polite words of her letters. Still there remained that smear of shame, but this feeling deepened the others around it, a bitter note that added complexity to a good dish.

"You're too young to know it is."

"Yes, maybe," I said. "I live here now, you know. With my husband."

"In Versova?"

"Yes."

"It's a long way from the city."

"I don't mind. I like it. I like being so close to the sea."

"Yes, you like the sea, don't you. I do too. It's good for humans to live near it. It keeps us closer to our natures."

"Didi, what you danced in the summer festival—I want to move like that. It's like nothing I've ever seen."

"You want to study with me again?"

"Yes."

"Your turns, my dear. That's just to start. Without a teacher you've lost some good years of study."

"I'll make it up."

"And then what, leave again?"

"Not this time."

"Do you want to learn kathak just to break it?"

"You didn't break it. What you danced, that was kathak. It was just . . . more . . . deeper . . ."

She wiped her eyes quickly against the back of her

hand, gently enough so as not to disturb the lines of kohl that delineated the sharp edges of her eyelids. Then she said, "My own teacher would never have taken me back."

"I know." It was good strong tea that I had made, sweetened very thickly with sugar, although after I burned my tongue I sipped it slowly. Exasperated, she picked up my cup and saucer and cooled the tea between the vessels herself. There were strands of gray at her temples; perhaps there had always been. "Finish your tea and let me see them."

I drank the tea she cooled. I could feel its warm drive downward, the way it made my eyes more open. But I didn't need it: my body was like a coiled spring in those days, always ready to leap into motion. I remember the way my hands sometimes rested on my thighs as I watched my husband eat, the fingers unconsciously expressing lotus mudras. And I dreamed hard of dance, waking damp and ready, as Radha had dreamed her maths. Through the years of my practice I had come to understand my body, its limits and its pleasures. The "I" did not burst upon me anymore in a terrible dazzle, it lay soft in me, alive to the surface of the world as my own flesh. I put my cup down. I didn't hesitate. I turned. I turned. I turned.

That night I lay awake in bed thinking about the summer festival: a vanity. A vanity, but I could not help myself from taking the memory out of my pocket like a candy and placing it again and again into my mouth: tasting then a double sweetness, of time passed but also of time promised—the festivals I had been invited to and that would come after, and later, the performances I would carry on my own. All the stages of the world, sleeping and awake, lit for a performance, blazing with music, or resting, quiet, silent with the unspoken desire to be occupied by voice and bells, to be slapped awake by quick and merciless feet; they seemed to me, in those nights, mine, as I looked out through the eyes of memory from the stage constructed for the summer festival at Azad Maidan, I was looking out at the audience as I did so, running my eyes over their faces just as a tea-seller counts his coins: with a detached, professional pleasure. Ah, they still leaned toward one another, heedless of me, one laughing at her companion's remark, another openly reading a book, glancing only from time to time up at the stage, there, my husband, with a camera propped on his knee, yes, I had him, but none of the others: I would have to win them, for they had not come to see me, a junior artist performing so early in the evening, before the sun had even set.

It was a grave honor to be so young a dancer and to perform at the summer festival at any time slot, even one so early, which I had secured by performing well in the Shining Stars of Youth concert. From seventy performers they selected ten to dance in the summer festival, one young artiste—"star"—to open each night of the ten nights of the festival, and with payment enough to secure accompaniment. By coincidence, the night I performed was the night my teacher was scheduled to dance too, though as I looked for her in the audience almost despite myself, I could not locate her, nor did I really expect to. I was dancing a traditional piece, one taught to me by my teacher—not taught, or not quite given, but one absorbed through the afternoons when I sat through her practice, carefully watching her movements and the way she instructed the tabla player, which I had begun to practice in earnest in the years of our absence. It was the dance I had first seen flickering in black-and-white on the screen of the campus movie theater—the one that had called me to her, and bound me.

I stepped into the dance as I had once stepped into the lengths of soft, dry cotton she had offered me in exchange for my wet garments. When I had been her student, the feeling had been one of borrowed elegance; now the feeling acquired a new dimension, one of sorrow, though the dance itself was a joyful one: I was honoring her, as if she were dead. As though dead, but sometimes too I had the feeling that from far away my mother watched me, from very far away, and still I dared, committing all sorts of actions she was sure to dislike. I could feel the crowd begin to pay attention to me, but as my awareness of this feeling grew, I realized that I was not dancing for them at all. I was dancing for her.

When I was finished, the sky had darkened with evening, and some lights had come in. I had won the audience, most of them: I could feel their attention and accepted their applause with a small, short bow. The makeup was smothering, I seemed to be sweating underneath it, without that sweat being able to express itself to the surface, and when backstage I tried with a washcloth to remove the mask that had been painted on me without complete success, and left the tent mortal, a mess. With this face I reluctantly met my husband who was waiting for me at the entrance. "You danced well."

"Thank you." The sight of him could make me shiver— as though in fright, or recognition. Today in a printed cotton shirt and bell bottoms, both better versions of the outfits my brother wore, having been purchased in London, instead of stammered out by the local tailor.

"You looked happy up there."

"Of course," I said.

We walked together to the lawn. I was thirsty, but didn't have anything to drink; he went and returned with two soft drinks without my asking. Licking, burping fizz, electric, sugar light on the tongue, he would not hear my protestations, "Already bought," he said, and when I was finished he went to take the bottles back. I was hungry too, cooling slightly in the slightly cooling air, returning to my civilian body after wearing another's. Pouring myself back into my body, or drifting back into it. We were listening to the

next performer, a Hindustani singer whose voice held an
appealing textural roughness, almost a dirtiness, which, as
she stretched one note to the length of her breath, smooth-
ened and cleared. It was a dusk-raga and matched the light
and air: indigo and gold, and I was aware of my husband's
proximity to me, the big messy bow of his long legs folded,
and his long, gleaming arms, and just the very edge of his
scent—man's sweat, and a kind of spicy perfume that I had
never before known any man to wear. If, when I danced, he
looked at me with the camera's eye, in life it was a glancing
look, softer and more gentle, the kind of look one caught
only as it moved away, having already touched its object
softly and thus briefly satisfied its desire. I looked at him
like this too, in pieces: whorl of ear, hump of nose, soft
ridge of lower lip.

"She's not so good," my husband whispered. "You were
better."

"You can't compare," I said, blushing. Not displeased.

She was finished now. A new audience was beginning
to arrive, a fashionable crowd. Two women in silk: one in
black and white, one in a blue-green, both with tall hair,
came and spread a dhurrie in the space in front of us and
tucked themselves into beautiful shapes upon it. The lift
of their hair left their napes clear, their cholis cut low in
the back so their white necks looked long in the last of the
light, soft and long, like panes of moonlight. The tones in
which they spoke their English resembled my husband's,

warm, but formal, and with only the barest traces of an Indian accent, which expressed itself more in the cadence than in the vowels.

Black and white: "Yes, the next one's her. You've never seen her dance?"

Blue-green: "No, dance or otherwise. Is she very good?"

"*Very* good dancing and otherwise, if the gossip is to be believed. You know Sachin keeps her out there in Versova all year."

Tongue click. "But she doesn't mind Versova? What am I saying, doesn't his *wife* mind?"

"She must, but what can she do? Even still, Sachin is so possessive, you know, she used to have a very handsome tabla player and he made her change to someone older."

"Well, perhaps he was right to; women like that can't be trusted around any man."

It was then that my teacher took the stage, and the women fell silent, as if she could hear them. I felt full as I watched her luminous body cross the stage to its center: full of what precisely I could not say, tenderness or sympathy for the years of gossip that drifted wherever she appeared: but it was more than just that. She was dressed in gold silk. Through her makeup I could see her face—in fact, the thick makeup she wore seemed to clarify it rather than obscure it, its elegance and the softness of its features, the characteristic girlishness I imagined she'd wear long into old age. The program began in the traditional manner: she passed through the vandana and then the slow, expressive movements of the nikas, using, as she always did, her face as an instrument to capture interest, her eyes especially, bright as they tracked the movement of her hands or kept them fixed in front of her. It seemed then that she danced out of her eyes, that her gaze served a double purpose, capturing the audience with its liveliness, but also capturing her own interest, as she fed herself on the crowd's delight. She had it, like she had had me, from the moment she arrived on the stage. The rhythm quickened with the aamad, then grew even more complex with the chakradar: her eyes didn't waver, and her face seemed to grow more serene the more complex the workings of her feet, seemed to soften with her body's love. Then the music ceased. The singer, who had thus far been articulating the bols that the feet followed, came now to join the dancer at the center of the stage. She held in her hand a strip of black cloth with which she bound my teacher's eyes, erasing them, and erasing us from her, and returned to her seat. Thus the kavita commenced, explaining the strange action through the words of the poem the singer spoke: my teacher was dancing as Gandhari, the wife of the blind Dhritarashtra, who willingly took blindness into her healthy eyes and wore a blindfold until her death. It was a story I did not care for, valorizing as it did women's sacrifice, one-sided, for no one would ask Dhritarashtra to bind his sighted eyes for Gandhari's blind ones.

Yet, though the piece was supposed to be narrative, enacting the stanzas of the kavita, my dance teacher's movements grew abstracted, and she began to incorporate the complex sequence she had danced with sight during the chakradar. Without her gaze, the meaning of her body shifted, what had at first seemed opulent, almost voluptuous, now became austere—her body moved with a strange tenderness, following the tabla as the rhythm raced forward, time itself speeding forward. There she danced, her gaze gone and us vanished, in a world built wholly of movement: instead of serenity what lay across her brow was something even more difficult to articulate. Her arms whirled around her, conscious, now, of the substance of air. She was stripped clean: free: no desire, no wanting, not for anything she did not have, only a reaching out with her strange dance to whatever lay beyond it, a vision that the dance reflected like an imperfect mirror. To be a mirror—to be—nothing—

For all my desire for a clean, new life, I crossed often into the territory of my old life—not the chaali that I had fled, but the theaters in which I performed, and the concert halls I had begun to frequent with my husband, and the homes of the rich girls to whom I taught dance. I had had trouble finding an engineering job: my prospective employers were startled, even offended to see that the *V.* on my resume obscured a woman's name. They were sure that I would quit as soon as I married, and, upon learning I already was, that I would soon leave to have a child. I was tired of the interviews where comfortable men sat behind desks, not even pretending to look at my qualifications, but openly examining my breasts instead. So I went another way.

Like a needle I slipped not only back into my own life but into the old life of my husband, for every Wednesday I would take the long journey to Malabar Hill to give lessons to the daughter of the Ghoshs, whose house was in the same neighborhood and even on the very same street as my in-laws' mansion, mutually shaded from the other's gaze by their respective walls topped with high glass, crushed, over which mango and guava trees spread casually their branches, and dropped their fruit into each other's gardens, and onto the road. This house was difficult to get to from our cottage, a journey that required a three-kilometer walk and three buses each way, but one I quite stubbornly refused to give up despite my husband's entreaties. From where the last bus dropped me off, I began to climb up the hill, and it seemed, though my effort increased, that the air became cooler and more pleasant, scented with the many unseen flowers of the neighbor's private gardens. From the rooftop of my childhood I had gazed at this green hill: it stood to reason that the reverse would be possible too, but so shaded was the street I walked, by the trees and walls, that I could not make out anything more distinct than the haze of the city, its chatter and stink very distant from this serene place.

As the door of the Ghoshs' residence opened to me and I was shown inside by a servant, I would try to imagine myself the daughter of the house, returning home from some pleasant activity—horse riding, swimming at the club, or an afternoon at the cinema—being greeted affectionately as "baby" by the servant, instead of the infinitely more distant "madam." My clothes would be western, my hair cut short, my face neatened and made coherent—made fairer and luminous—by the makeup I would expertly apply, the everyday makeup so different from what I wore onstage, and subtle enough to require an artist's hand, though in its own way very theatrical. "Some nimbu-pani, please, Madhu, it's beastly hot outside"—it was not just the words they used with their servants, but the tone; though when they issued commands they did so without the severity or even the formality the women in the chaali used to address their bais—there was almost an affection to it: for being so far above their servants in station, there was no need to forcefully assert their superiority, and their address was genial and relaxed, unless a mistake had been committed that required a scolding. My imagination was too thin to fully inhabit this other-self or, perhaps, there was something that stopped me from imagining an alternate life too fully, a feeling I thought might be disgust, though its object—whether it was myself or my surroundings, or the Ghoshs themselves—I could not discern.

Susheela, my student, would often be waiting for me in what I came to think of as the Music Room; in it, various instruments were kept in specially made glass cabinets— two sitars for the elder daughter, and a collection of violins Mrs. Ghosh had played in her youth, hung by their necks. The furniture in this room was heavy, darkly carved, unlike the modern furnishings of the downstairs parlor where sometimes after the lesson I was served tea, but the windows let in enough brightness to make the room feel spacious instead of oppressive. Susheela reminded me of saffron, if not the color, then the scent and texture, the luxury of its flavor. Her eyes were large and dark, wounded eyes that doubtless captured many hearts, and sometimes I wondered in idle moments if one of those hearts might once have been my husband, or at least, his mother. It was easy to be charmed by a girl like Susheela, to whom, like my husband, the world had been so kind, and who therefore had the ability to approach any person with the friendliness of one who doesn't anticipate hurt. Sometimes, as she danced, my eye traveled to the window, where, past the border wall and through the many branches of trees, the top of my in-laws' home could be glimpsed, blinding in the late morning sunlight, white, and crusted with orna- ment. Now and then a figure could be seen on the balcony, a servant shaking out and beating a brightly patterned rug, or someone leaning over to water the potted flowers that lined the balustrade in great profusion—a woman whose face was too distant to make out, but which, through her bearing, I could only assume to be my mother-in-law Mrs. B herself. My hand still slapping my thigh in the beat of Susheela's lesson, or even chanting simple bols, but I was calling Mrs. B with my gaze, wanting her to straighten for a moment and shield her eyes to look out across the wall into her neighbor's window. From such distance, I could still see the sheen of silk her saris gave; the way even light touched her was gentle. Then she would disappear again behind the glass doors, polished by the sun into mirrors, and I would turn my dazzled eyes back to my student.

Why my husband wanted me to give up these lessons was obvious: he had grown up with Susheela's elder brother, and he had liked the Ghoshs, whose motives were unclear. Had they employed me in order to show him their support or to anger his mother? It seemed to me the former, for Mrs. Ghosh would take tea with me from time to time in the air-conditioned parlor, asking after my husband and after Susheela's progress, but she could scarcely be ignorant of my mother-in-law's displeasure. No matter how respected, I was, after all, simply another employee on the family payroll, which opened a third possibility—that this position was intended as a slight to my husband himself. And why did I so fiercely defend my right? He was protective of me, of my dignity, wanting me to enter these houses as his wife or not at all—he wanted all rooms to be open to me, and all the paths of the gardens, as they were for the daughters of the neighborhood, as they would have been for me if we had been correctly married. He would have liked to show me the neem tree whose branches had held him in boyhood many evenings aloft, and to bring me to the cool inner rooms of the family home, from which there was a pure, seemingly endless view of the sea. But he did not want me there, on these terms, alone. I had jammed my foot in the door but could not quite kick it open; I had stuck my finger in the wound—why did I do this?

We fought about it. Once uncapped, my anger was immense and surprised us both, for what did I even have to be angry about—wasn't he the injured party? I could feel myself using my face like I used it onstage, putting all of my burning feeling into my eyes. In contrast, my husband's anger was cold, so much so it was hard to even recognize as anger, and he had on his side a powerful command of English, his mother tongue, in which he could express many logical statements with a particularly wounding edge. The language I reached for was Gujarati, but I never let it pass my lips. What more did I want? I couldn't say. Not in English, nor the language of my body, for it was bitterness that moved me, a bitterness I did not want to express. When I left the Ghoshs' house, walking back along the mostly empty streets, descending, it felt, into the heat, chaos, and stink of the city, the city's many grasping hands,

I had a taste in my mouth like the aftertaste of sugar. I was looking again, in vain, for Mrs. B, wanting her to not only know but to witness my successful infiltration, wanting to see in her eyes some measure of the humiliation she had dealt to me. For it was she who had shown me so clearly how I could never assimilate into my husband's life, her cutting words delivered with such a serene countenance that they were doubly destabilizing. That I could not hold a fork and knife properly, that I had failed to present myself to her in the appropriate attire: these were just small things that showed the bigger problem, a problem, surely, I had to see too; I could recognize that this marriage would be the cause of my own unhappiness. I was dark, overeducated, unpedigreed, and worse, unskilled at the tasks that a daughter-in-law would have to fulfill, tasks that could not be studied for and could not even be taught or learned, as they depended on her native grace, beauty, and unfailing poise. "But it's done," I had said in slight wonder, "we're already married." She had not yelled, the beautiful Mrs. B, though color had rushed into her fair cheeks, nor did Mr. B, a neat little man in a stoic gray suit, make any sort of angry declaration, he had only called to the servant to get his lawyer on the phone, first for the purpose of having the marriage annulled, and then, when my husband made it plain in his parting words that he would not consent, to make an update to his will, a conversation that, I can only assume, happened shortly after we left with the same odd calm in which the entire conversation had been conducted.

And yet I had nearly separated this woman, Mrs. B, whose face was held tightly and who wielded her English with frightening precision, from the loving and indulgent woman who featured in my husband's childhood stories; I still, somehow, loved *that* woman, and enjoyed hearing about her. Through the transitive property of marriage, she was mine in memory. Many days, as I walked, I could see her in my mind's eye standing on the verandah, calling out to her son across the neighborhood, past the distance her voice could penetrate, but which nonetheless reached his ears and sent him running toward it, and, scaling the slope that led to his parents' home, he could see the outline of her before the particulars, the dusk-pink of her sari in its immaculate folds, and the softness of her face. I'm coming, I'm coming, he'd call back to her in dreams, running and running up that hill but not able to reach the top where she stood, still calling, unaware that he was right there, and trying, but unable to reach her.

"Have you ever been to Delhi?"

"No." I had never been anywhere. Sometimes I realized, as I dreamed of Paris or New York, that my own country could offer many escapes that I did not allow my imagination to explore. Why was I so occupied with getting all the way out? I thought it might have something to do with my body, the way, in public, I so often felt vulnerable, wilting under the eyes of men, who were emboldened, I think, by my dark skin, and by my modesty, moved to make ever more lewd comments outside the presence of my husband. But it was not quite that; it might have been even more than that, a desire to leave the rest of my history, to become so anonymous under the public's gaze that no one would be able to read me: my dark face and my plain sari would be a mask instead of a tell—that they would therefore approach me warmly and kindly, as they approached a man. But of course this position was naive to the extreme: surely no place in life offered that. "Is it beautiful?"

"Yes," said my dance teacher. "The most beautiful gardens in the world are there. Would you like to go?"

I WAS RAPIDLY progressing at my dance. And so the world seemed full, made of movement, offering something secret that I could almost understand. I felt very close to understanding. The way the sea rippled in the evenings along the shore, adding variation to the lines it cast on the sand, following a pattern, but elaborating on it; the various poses of trees, some curled, bent, as though old, some standing broadly with their arms thrown up, some gripping both the earth and the sky, and one immense banyan growing between my teacher's house and my own, whose movement was stillness, draped in its own concentration; the running of dogs along the shore, wild and barking at one another and the waves; the crows' bodies in flight, moving with an almost brutal power; and, of course, the movements of people, which defined their bodies, bent or upstanding, soft or hard, feminine, graceless, or like water, so gentle, the way children would throw their bodies forward, even the girls, the shy gesture of a student's hand brushing the hair from her forehead—more graceful than her pained mudras—the arms of the neighbor's servant as she hung light-dripping clothes on the line. All these were not scored by music, or even rhythm, yet they were coordinated, as though by infinite and subtle concert, each communicating *something*, alone, and in relation to one another they gained even more meaning—meaning that I could not, not quite yet, grasp. In my dance there was a ceiling, a limit: I came close, I could brush my fingers if I reached, but I could not reach it, straining, straining, pulling the string of my body tighter. And afterward, sweating and almost crying, not because I was frustrated or even sad, but from sheer effort. *Close*. To what, I could not say. Not quite say. What was on the other side? It was a field of unbroken light.

My husband showed me a poem he had written. He wrote in English, privately, in the evenings when he got home from work. He wrote longhand and then typed what he had written on a typewriter, a big beautiful machine that filled the flat with its noise. The rhythm was erratic, but not, it seemed, random; at times, I unconsciously marked its syncopation as I went about my evening tasks, the noise

marking these tasks as the tabla marked my dancing, or
the sound of my teacher's voice. I always looked, reflexively, for women in the poems he wrote, though often there
weren't any: his poems were populated with animals, as
this one was, a poem about a dog we had seen walking
along on the shore. His dog was very alone, dark black
and wet, lost; it was a plain poem that spoke of a loneliness
that frightened me. I handed it back. Are you so alone? I
wanted to ask him. Did he miss so terribly his old life, and
the people who had populated it? His face seemed pensive
as always, carrying the melancholy air that I had noticed
so long ago from my hostel window—yet this air was what
made his face so tricky, for often it opened to a smile very
suddenly, like a door burst open, and the sweetness of the
smile was sharpened by the distance the face seemed to
have traveled to arrive at it. His eyes too—*green*—as my
schoolmate Ruchi's, her most prized possession, and I had
imagined she slept with her hands cupped over her sockets
so no one would steal them. Born rich, my husband was
more careless with precious things. "Well?"

"You know I don't know anything about poetry."

"That means you don't like it."

"No, I like it. It just—makes me feel . . . empty."

"Empty?" he said, not displeased.

"What's it called?"

"I'm thinking 'The Dog.' They're going to publish it in
*damn you*."

"Is that good?"

"Yes," he said. "I know—that name. They're trying to be cheeky."

"You only show me your poems when they're going to be published."

"Well, you don't like to practice in front of me."

"That's true."

We went outside. It was evening. The beach-houses were all full this weekend, due perhaps to the city's unseasonable heat, and the shore was littered with the children of film producers and bankers, building sand structures with small shovels and small hands. Farther out, the fishermen were pulling their boats in from the day's harvest, brightly painted boats bestowed with the eyes of gods to spot the shoals of fish; dark, lean bodies pulling these boats through the mist that gathered there along the curve of the bay, but still visible, the bodies and the eyes, and the boats heaped with silver. Women came to meet them at the edge of the water. Only movement, no sound, for the sea swallowed the words they spoke to one another. My husband lit a cigarette. "Why is it," he said, after a while, "that you only ever wear the same three saris? You never wear the blue one for example."

"What's wrong with that?"

"Nothing," he said, "it's odd, only. I have more clothes than you do."

I began to blush. "Well, it's just that . . . I'm saving them."

"For what—your funeral? Don't you like them?"

"Yes."

"So if you like them, wear them."

It was so simple for him. Sometimes I would pull the blue one out when I was alone, and open it across the bed, and spread my hands along its length. There was a subtle undulating variance in color I thought I could feel, the way the sky might feel at dusk under the palms. Another thing Radha would laugh at. But with pleasure.

"Anyway I have something to tell you. My teacher is performing in three months in Delhi. And she wants me to go with her."

"Tell me or ask me?" my husband said.

"Tell you," I said. "I thought you'd be pleased."

"I can't get the time off to go to Delhi."

"That's okay."

"So you'll be alone there."

"I'll be with my teacher."

"She's a woman."

"I thought you would be pleased. I'm performing too."

"I'm pleased."

"You don't seem pleased."

He looked at me. When his face wasn't smiling, it could be so cool, almost unreadable. He had thick eyelids and long lashes; the hooded eyes, I thought then, of a bird of prey. But it was perhaps just that I didn't understand men. There was something you had to do with them I had not learned, a kind of surface deference you must perform, smiling like a mask, as you enacted your own will. My father had not required this.

"What's in Delhi anyway? And who's paying for it?"

"The festival's paying. Train fare, hotels, meals, everything. And we'll have a dinner with the president of the arts council."

"It looks like you've already decided."

"What's there to decide?"

He exhaled, turning his face away from me to blow out the smoke. When he turned his face toward me again he was smiling. In his face, in his eyes, I saw my friend, the one who had sung to me a love song at the empty train station in the early hours of the morning, the one who had looked with his camera eyes not just *at* me but *in* me as I danced. The one I too had seen, shy and lovely, openhearted as a boy. "Good," he said, "very good. My wife the famous dancer."

One evening we had a party. Many men and fewer women arrived at our flat, bemused by the length of their journeys but in good spirits, claiming that the air was fresher out here. Some poets, some musicians, a screenwriter, the artists all men, and the women all girlfriends, no dancers, no wives, bearing bottles of beer and whiskey that clinked together cheerfully in the jute bags that they were carried in. Everyone was dressed in Western clothes, the women in trousers or a long skirt, and so though it was my party I felt silly and wrongly dressed in my blue-dusk sari. "Come have a drink!" my husband said to me, and I demurred as I always did. We had a record player, a fine and beautiful instrument I cared for like a child, and though we had precious few records, we listened to them often, Ravi Shankar especially in the evenings, which many times reminded me of evenings on the roof of the chaali, where I could watch blue fall over the city before all the electric lights buzzed on, watching the activity of the children from a great height as I began my change into a night-creature who had no need for companions; a blue feeling in which the music seemed to shape itself to the fresh, living moment. On this night someone had brought a record of the Beatles, of whose music we only had a single album, and whose English I had trouble understanding, and so absorbed was I in making out the words of a particularly beautiful song that I did not at first notice that the eyes of the party were on me, all of them, and that someone had said something that had turned their eyes to me and made them laugh. What it was I will never know but my husband said, "Come, come, Vidya, have a little sip, celebrate with me."

I put a hand over my mouth to block the glass he was trying to press to my lips. The smell of whiskey smarted my eyes, making me desirous and sad. "Women don't drink whiskey."

"Since when were you worried about what women did or did not do?"

"You married the satya savitri, yaar," said another poet, the red of whose eyes seemed to burn against the whites. "Now you can't expect her to behave like these . . . *girlfriends*."

Under this blow none of the women winced, though some of the smiles on their mouths hardened. I understood English very well, but had the feeling that another language was being spoken under the words they used, one for which I had no textbook or tutor, and whose meaning was so slippery it evaded my grasp. Tonight it had a hard quality to it, the quality of metal being struck.

"She'll have a drink for me," my husband said, and poured the glass, still speaking the under-language, which darkened his face. "Just for me, Vidya. The liberated woman, free from conventions."

"What about the convention that a wife must obey her husband?"

"Obey? No, indulge." He took me by the wrist, hard, but his voice was still playful. "Not even my wife will celebrate with me? What will all these people think?"

"They don't mind."

"They'll think you think you're better than them."

"I don't."

"But they'll think that and I'll think that too."

"I'm not better than anyone." My voice became more and more quiet.

"Look at the way you're standing here, in your nun's sari, always frowning frowning frowning, so proper and middle class and correct."

I put my hands to my face. And it was true, I had been frowning. I saw myself all at once the way he showed me, small, serious, dark, in old-fashioned clothes, sitting silently as I always did at the edge of the conversation, trying hard to follow it or dipping for a few moments into my own thoughts, and looking—yes, bored. They were all wondering why my husband had married her.

"Such a *good* wife, such a *good* woman—"

I lifted the glass to my lips and took it all in one swallow. It was bitter, and burned all the way down. A few laughed at the face I made when I was finished, but the drama was over, and the focus of the party shifted away. A cheerful song played on the flipped record, but the layers of instruments seemed now to clash with one another, and the hollow sitar was played by a hideously inexpert hand. I dreaded the feeling that was beginning to build, and the pleasure I took from it: all at once like a room opening: a bright utterly spacious and friendly room filled with delightful objects. Was this how my brother felt? I would have liked to be alone with it, but there were people covering every surface of the apartment, leaning against the wall, seated on the bed, and some even on the floor, for we had only one rickety wooden chair where Rustom wrote his poems, and where he sat now, lush and triumphant if not quite handsome, for the drink made his features come slightly off kilter from their sober axis. He was not a big man, I noticed as though for the first time; his frame was only slightly larger than mine, and, I thought now, if I ever were to pull on a pair of his bell-bottom jeans they would surely fit me. He looked quite young sitting there, almost on the verge of tears, I thought I saw just the edge of it, the gleam around his eye.

He drank and drank. I stumbled through a conversation with a girl whose eyelids were painted a soft white-blue; under her adult makeup she revealed herself to be quite young, with the chaste shyness of a village-cousin, speaking in a slight, breathy voice that she seemed unused to using. She wanted to be an actress, and her boyfriend, the screenwriter, had gotten her a few background roles in three recent films. Had I seen them? I had seen two of them, and to please her, I said, "I thought you looked familiar." She beamed. "It all comes down to who you know. Some of these people," she lowered her voice, "could make your entire career with just one snap.

"I'm happy to talk to you, didi. You're famous to us."

"Famous?" They could not have known about Delhi, but had, perhaps, seen me dance.

"Yes, he *married* you."

"Oh—" Well, of course. They had other dreams too.

"If Rohit would marry me, I'd give it up, acting."

"I still dance."

"Yes, yes," she said, "but you'll give it up once you have children, won't you?"

"No, we don't want children. We're happy like this."

She looked at me with surprise. "You never want to be a mother?"

"Do you?"

"Yes, of course," she said. "But you? How else do you plan to return to his family's good graces?"

"I don't care about their good graces."

She was looking at me strangely. "You are very idealistic aren't you? Well, you're still newly wed. You'll change your mind. And be practical," she said, "how much longer can a boy who grew up with so much money content himself with so much less? It would be good," she said, she the older one now, her voice growing more sure with her advice, "for you to have a child. He would never leave you, the parents would have you back, you would have money, your husband would write more poems, you would all be very happy."

"We're happy right now."

"Yes, yes," she said. "Now is one thing. Tomorrow is another."

Soon our flat was too small for the party to continue: they were visiting someone else's beach bungalow farther down the shore, where another larger party awaited. But my husband would not go, and after much protestation the party left him still seated on his chair. I lifted the bedspread and shook it out in the doorway. It was smudged here and there with ash, and one black spot where a lit cigarette had briefly pressed. But we did not have another. Where was Radha on this night? Awake, for it was late morning in Saint Louis Missouri. Did she now wear blue jeans? I could picture her only in a yellow sari, not even in the jacket that she would need to wear against the snow and cold.

"Make me one cup of strong coffee, will you?"

I clicked on the stove. Could marriage be a dance? I thought: no. You never really dance with someone else. You only dance with yourself. I burned my finger and sucked it, but even that pain felt distant. I brought my husband his coffee and he sat me on his lap while he drank it. "What is it you want?" he said.

"Nothing," I said. He was petting my arm. His hands were rough from his boy-years gripping a cricket bat.

"Go be a sannyasi then, if you want nothing."

"I want to be your wife," I said, cautiously—his voice had a bitter edge. I should have been irritated because of his behavior all evening, even angry, but I wasn't. I felt small and plain, a little sick from the alcohol: someone easy to leave. When he didn't offer anything else I said, "Those women your friends brought. Will they marry them?"

"Not likely."

"What will happen to them when their boyfriends get tired?"

"They'll find another man, probably a richer man, in fact they might find him before the boyfriend gets tired."

"What if they get pregnant?"

"They take care of it. No one wants to get married. Not the men and not the girls either."

I touched his rough cheek. He was sweating in his kurta, brightly patterned, but cotton as always to announce his poverty. His arms smelled faintly of roses, having picked up some ambient perfume. "I'm sorry I was frowning. Why didn't you go with them? It's good for you to get out of the flat."

"You want me out of the flat?"

"No," I said, "it's not that. It's for your sake."

"Am I a bad man, am I a worthless man?"

"How could you say that?"

"You want me to be nothing—well, I am!"

I wiped the tears from his cheeks. I could not see into his eyes, they were odd and glassy, almost angry. "What are you saying?"

"I don't—love it, like you."

"Love it? Love what?"

He shook his head. It was distressing him greatly but he could not bring himself to say it.

"Love what?" I said again, trying not to be alarmed, stroking his cheeks with my fingers. "Our life? Love me?"

"No, no," he said. "Not that." I held him and listened to him cry. It was an aching, plaintive sound that wet the front of my blouse. Was it just the alcohol? I took him to bed, undressed him, as though I were the experienced one. I led him to me and I surrendered.

But then I fell terribly ill. I could keep nothing down except for salt biscuits and softdrink both brought to me by my penitent and anxious husband. I had strange cravings that inspired in me dread: I desired many of the sweets and snacks that I craved in my childhood, their broad and subtle flavors, which I had spent hours and hours as a girl reconstructing, dry, flaky, drenched with honey, dusted with silver foil and some glittering, precise crumbs of salt, and had been infused in my memory with such longing that the memory had outmatched the sweets themselves, and each time I tasted one now it was with a bitter tongue. There seemed to be nothing in my stomach but bile that burned my throat, my tongue, and even my teeth. And yet beside the nausea there was a horrible hunger.

I cannot logically explain how or why those days became so close around me, except perhaps that it was that I was too sick to dance: thus closed the aperture of the world: I felt it slipping from me. Afternoons alone in the cottage the light pierced my eyes, giving me headaches of an intensity I had never experienced before, but which I remember afflicting my mother. Between the bouts of pain and nausea, I experienced some clearings of not-pain and not-nausea, during which my soul hesitantly peered into my body and even experimentally crawled, for a few moments, inside. The body the soul entered was drenched, for I sweated now more than I ever had, and braided into my usual smell was a new odor, one stinking, metallic note that disturbed me, and suddenly the air passed cool over the skin, I could feel the wet sea air in my lungs and against my palms in a stunning pleasure that carried with it no joy: it was simply the body's response to certain soft stimulus and the absence of pain. At the heart of the small cottage I lay, prone, sweating, breathing, my life whittled down to the relief of my body, and then charging back into my body's pain, and the soul fled. When my husband came home, he would wipe my forehead, tenderly but grimly, with a cool rag. "It's time to see the doctor, my darling."

"No."

"It's been weeks of this. I'm worried."

"You're not worried."

"Of course I am," he said. "How could you say that?"

I turned my face away from him. I didn't want to see a doctor; I was afraid what he would say. Beside my fear was my husband's eagerness for the same news, an eagerness I could not bear. Delhi was in a month: I would not go, for I had not been able to practice, I had sent word to my teacher through my husband, who softened the news of her disappointment. How much could she guess? With her regard she sent some herbal water she had prepared, muddy brown and bitter and cool against the throat, which soothed my body and made it drowsy: then it would sleep. She sent this water but she would not come herself. If she had come to the door I may have refused her, from shame.

An appointment was made; we took a taxi, which we could not afford, but which I did not have the will to protest. I shut my eyes and opened them in the clinic. The doctor was looking at me through his gleaming glasses. His touch, equally impersonal and intimate, produced in me a long, ugly feeling, almost in itself a kind of nausea, and I sat for some moments reeling at the table after he was finished. I did not like to be touched there. "You're with child, my dear. I'm sure your husband will be pleased."

The words were not surprising, not blinding. They felt like alcohol, stinging and sweet. A baby, with my husband's dear, green eyes? And what of me—my hands, my smile? And yet, if one arm held the child, the other would not be free to dance. My body and his body had conspired.

"I'll call him in then, while you dress."

"Wait—!"

His head had a crust of hair, white as ice. He looked amused. "Yes?"

"Is there—well—can there be some way—that is—is there anything to be done?"

"Be done?" he said, not yet sternly.

"Yes," I said, looking down at my lap, draped in a green cloth that had been provided to me, and below it, my own nakedness. We had driven for a long time to get to this clinic—a long time in a taxi, so an expensive ride—and the clinic itself, so clean and quiet, with its green cloths and offers to my husband to provide him a soft drink—must be expensive too. I tried again, "Is there something I can *do*—"

"I don't think I understand you," he said. "You're quite healthy, you need rest, eat lots of dhal and eat greens—mustard greens are good—and you must avoid at all costs papaya. Your mother-in-law will be happy to prepare some special foods for you, I'm sure, so you can enjoy your rest."

"No," I said. "If a woman is not quite—ah—*ready*—to be . . . Once my friend got into trouble and she told me there was a procedure. Something you could do. To fix the problem."

"You're not in trouble," said the doctor now very stern. His hair so white but his face was smooth, but for the folded brow my vexing request had caused. His hands too were unlined and smooth, and on his left he wore a wedding ring like a Christian. "You're married, you're healthy, your child, as far as we can tell, will be healthy, you're at a good age for your first baby, and there's nothing to fear, these days, there is so much to be done for a woman in labor, I'm speaking medically, especially a difficult labor. As for the sex of the child, well, we just can't know that, so you must pray to god for a boy."

"I can pay you," I said.

"I'm being well paid my dear by your in-laws right now."

"They're paying you?" I blurted out, before I could think to disguise my ignorance.

"My fee is not inexpensive," he said proudly. "Don't you love your husband?"

"Of course I do. But—"

"Well, then," he said. "That's all there is to the matter, isn't it?"

"You could just say—it was an accident, that I was never pregnant—or that something happened—something naturally—"

"Put this nonsense out of your head," the doctor said almost angrily, and then he softened his tone. "It's natural to be afraid of birth. But you'll find that modern medicine—and you will have the best, you understand, you must have some sense of how lucky you are—modern medicine offers much to the expectant mother. So you see there is no reason to be frightened. You might find the pregnancy does pleasing things to your figure. I've seen it often with women so skinny like you. The figure . . . comes into bloom. You will be pleased, and your husband also will be pleased, I think." His look then was not so hard to read, and I cast my eyes to the flecked green tiles of the floor trying to keep the sick-feeling down. When he got no response from me he called in my husband. "Everything's looking too good," said the doctor. "You'll have a healthy child."

"A boy?" said my husband. He looked young, flushed, pleased in his suit; he had come from work.

"Well of course we can't know. I know your parents are quite keen."

"Yes," my husband said. "Well, we just want a healthy child, isn't it, Vidya?"

And then another taxi home. The money should have been no mystery. He couldn't help telling the driver, "Brother, today is a good day, we've got some good news!" which the driver, understanding the euphemism, met with many effusive congratulations, angling for a bigger tip upon our arrival. I was so embarrassed I pulled my pallu over my head and sat in its private shade as though a bride. If I met the driver's eyes in the rearview mirror I knew I would see his knowledge of what had been done to me to make me pregnant, euphemism or no, and he wouldn't be able to help thinking about it himself. My husband took my hand in his and kissed it, and set it back down in my lap.

"Why is your family paying for my doctor's visits?"

"Why, they want to!"

"But you didn't ask me, Rustom."

"What was there to ask? I want the best for you. You've been so sick."

"The doctor didn't do anything to change that."

"Don't be cross," he said. "Today's a good day."

We were curving along Marine Drive; it looked serene from the vantage of the car, the hard afternoon light softened by the whitish haze of the ocean. Seeing it through the window of a car was almost like seeing it through the screen of the cinema, or through the hazy generalities of a dream, midday there was not much traffic, and we moved quickly enough that the eye could not hunt out the particularities of trash and stink that were apparent both to a walking body or a face on the bus. This unnerved me. The city from the car was the beautiful city of the rich, who dulled their eyes by ignoring the city of the poor that the car's vantage could not erase, the other city that rapped against the glass at the traffic lights: skinny girls always with a child balanced on their hip and wild, dirty hair and dirty threadbare dress walking calmly through traffic, always the girl with a baby on her hip and another bare-bottomed baby trailing behind, who needed no words to express their plight, only a hand lifted to an open mouth, I too turned my face away from them as they came to rap upon the glass. Would the doctor tell my in-laws what I had asked? Perhaps it would not serve him to give them such a report, lest they deem me unfit and decide to stop paying for my medical expenses. He had not, in any case, told my husband.

At home, I was so fragile to my husband he practically wanted to carry me into the house. It's true I was tired, I had a pleasant heaviness in my body that tugged me easily under the surface of a dream, in which I was back at the hospital where I had had my appointment, and the doctor offered me a deal: he could not remove the baby from my body, but he could ensure that it never grew any bigger, and that I would never give birth, it would stay in me always the size of a child's thumb, the only concession I had to make was to feed it, I would have to insert my pointer finger, I would have to jam this finger hard into my lady's part where the baby would lean down and suck my finger, drinking each day a few small drops of blood. "Shall I show you?" said the doctor, stretching out his hand. I woke before I could reply. It was dark and the flat was empty. I went to the bathroom and washed out the dank taste of my mouth. I was incredibly hungry, with a pure clean hunger I had not felt in weeks. Almost as soon as I switched on the lights my husband returned with hot pakoras greasy in newsprint, so fresh they burned my fingertips as I grasped them, and I ate them quickly saving none for my husband, conscious of nothing at all except the salt and oil I ate and the wash of spice against my mouth. When I was finished I looked at him and his eyes were on me. He was smiling. "Hungry?"

"I'm sorry, I didn't leave any for you."

"They were all for you."

"How long was I asleep?"

"Three four hours. You must have been tired. You were snoring."

"I've been so hungry," I said, sighing, I was still hungry, but would have to make food for myself if I wanted it, and I didn't quite yet feel like moving.

"Oh, I'd almost forgot." And he brought a little news-paper wrapped bundle and placed it in my lap. Inside were the bitter, warty, green vegetables I had asked for days ago.

"Karela!"

"Yes. They're good for you, aren't they? I thought they'd balance out."

"How much did you pay for these?"

"I won't tell you," he laughed.

"How much? One rupee?"

He shook his head.

"*More?*"

"Don't send a man vegetable shopping."

"I'll cut them," I said. He gave me a knife and I sliced rounds into the newspaper. Inside, the flesh was turning yellow and the seeds were hard—the vegetable seller had known to pawn off his worst wares on this unsuspect-ing fish—but the raw smell was still so bitter my mouth began to water confusedly. "Ugh," he said, "how can you stand it?"

"After all, what's more bitter than whiskey?" I said. "Here, you press."

He took his task seriously, and squeezed out the pale juice between his palms, catching it in a steel cup, which I immediately drank, undiluted by water. There was a slight salt taste that was, I think, the sweat of his palms. I licked his palm. It was an animal action my animal body did, and surprised us both. He had not been allowed near in weeks.

His skin was smooth from the bitter green and hot under my tongue. He looked at me. Who didn't want to be the object of such a gaze? Not I, but my body did. Now there was nothing left to lose it went dumb to my anger. What did it want? My husband put his damp hand on my breast I let him. It was yes my body said my legs opened. He was gentle at first and it hurt only a little. Too gentle my body wanted it to hurt a lot. It wanted to be thrust into so hard it tore open and the soul poured out. I gripped his shoulders. Both of us were still dressed. My body made some horrible grunting noise I gritted my teeth. Even through his pleasure he looked at me with a damp alarm. Should I stop? I didn't say anything and he didn't stop. My body thrust its animal hips up to meet him deeper where he knelt hot inside me. What it felt was not a sweet feeling, it was dirty-good, like scratching the scalp until it bleeds. Or: better. Or: worse. This time, he pulled himself out from my body's socket before releasing his white-pearl-mucus against its thigh (as he had neglected to before), perhaps out of some primal superstition to protect the unborn child. Something released too inside my body and charged forth, starting from my core and flushing through my groin, a wild, hot, scary movement of blood that made me cry out with raw fear and sent soft needles through my limbs. I had never been so tired before. I pushed him up.

"Where are you going?"

"To wash."

"Wait," he said, "don't." I think he wanted me this way: marked, smelling of him: his. So I let him lay with his head on my breast. Under his ear my heart slowed and my breath became more normal, though, slumped against the wall, I soon developed a cramp in the small of my back. I touched his hair. Down at the root his scalp was sweating, and there was one single white hair that sprung out against the black. "I've never been so happy," he said. "And you?"

"Yes," I said.

It was the body I had always dreamed of inhabiting just like the doctor had warned. Though the nausea did not ebb, beside it grew a terrible hunger, one that seemed never able to be sated. I could deny myself nothing, my desire for food became pressing and singular until it was attained. Sweets: yogurt: milk: cream: milk: milk: milk, glass after glass, until I was sick. Not only my breasts grew—the nipples themselves grew and darkened almost to black—but my hips took on substance, and my thighs thickened and touched: my whole body was rushed with blood and with it a lust for itself, its own fertility and abundance, it wanted to spread and spread, to be rubbed with oil or ghee until it was polished to the apex of its dark shine. In my belly she was still no larger than an idea, and my belly revealed her not at all in her particulars, though all in all I was transformed, lush, suddenly, as a cinema star whose glittering face adorned the city's colorful hoardings. A stranger might not have guessed my condition, unless he smelled its slight fecund stink. Alone in the cottage, I wound the ghungroos around my ankles. I had never spent as much time away from my work as these difficult weeks, and I felt even before I stood up that something had been eroded, in my feet and legs especially, in my body's tautness. I asked my customary blessing from my guru and forgiveness from the floor, but when I straightened up to begin the simplest of movements I felt almost panic—had it all been lost? Years and years of work lost, just slid out the body? My body was so heavy, it wanted to move slowly as though through thick water. I thought: and then? My in-laws would not want a girl, but they would suffer one, if another child was promised, and then, if that one was not a boy, another. If it was not lost—and it was not, not yet, my feet, though heavy, remembered their rhythms, the spine its posture, the hands still bent—how long would it remain in my custody? It needed daily attention and care, it needed time to express itself through its long embroidered thoughts and phrases. And those soft, empty, evening moments, and a strong, free body.

In fact, my husband didn't want me dancing at all, and I did so only in secret. If we had been living already at his parents' house I wouldn't have dared—the walls have ears in such places—and even the chaali would have frowned at my behavior, hearing, as they would, the distinct, gold-textured noise of the bells. Here, no one marked me. In our neighborhood, screenwriters, bankers, high-level civil servants, and their wives spent their weeks and weekends in unpredictable bursts. Their fellowship was more casual, though no less competitive, than that of the chaali, if I could glean anything from the murmuring and laughter of the kitty-parties that drifted up some afternoons into our open window. I was never invited, which was a relief to me, the pleasant scorn they regarded me with was the most comfortable thing they could offer for us both, and this indifference emboldened me: I even danced with the accompaniment of the record player, a record of Zakir Hussain, and sometimes, a record of the Beatles, especially "Here Comes the Sun," whose crenellated rhythm was a pleasure to pass around and elaborate with my feet. I lifted the needle and placed it at the beginning of the song. Here I played, softly and desperately, letting myself off kathak's swift track, and instead putting my feet in pursuit of the music I heard and the movements I had, through the week, accumulated. I felt as though I had crept up to my own balcony and called to myself, and I had come to myself when I was called, letting myself be held, quick and sorrowful, in my own arms.

Then my body was tired and I drove it forward. The sweet feeling had passed. My body didn't want to move so quickly and finely, but I halved the beat, quartered it, dancing in silence now, but for the ghungroos. I parceled time into its smallest slivers with each of my feet, and each time

the foot hit the floor, it sent time ringing through me, hard
as a knife I hoped. I had a half-thought I might dislodge
it, and my body and my future would come again into my
possession. It would be a secret I folded and ate. If, god (no
god, god-habit), I was free of this burden I would be more
careful next time. I didn't like to say no to my husband, he
who had once accused me of feeling no desire, but if on
some dangerous nights I refused him, then on other safe
nights I could become doubly pliant. (Farnaz had taught
me the method of accounting, though, at the time, I had
accepted her knowledge with only academic interest, sure
I would never have a husband or a lover.) I danced against
myself like this until my head began to have that curious
floating-up feeling that told me I must stop, and after this
I washed very quickly and heated my lunch. I had, I knew,
about a half an hour before my headache would obliterate
me, for now the lightness was becoming tinged with the
beginning of pain: I could feel it touching its cold fingers
against the ball of my skull. Still, my body had a tired feeling that was earned, and the food tasted very good to me,
though very simple, so as not to turn my stomach, bland
dhal with only a little ginger and haldi and some plain
rice. I sat down on the floor and ate it quickly, before the
headache came. Then I lay down on the bed and closed
my eyes.

She stuck fast.

"You've returned, Eklavya," said my dance teacher, and looked me down. "I guessed as much. I should offer you my congratulations."

By her voice I could not guess the sincerity of her words: her tone was dry. How she stood in her doorway—just stood—so simple and neat, her sari the palest yellow.

"I've disappointed you again."

"Yes and no," she said. But she caught me as I knelt to take the dust from her feet—she held me in her arms as she never had before, close, and kissed my head, and my body responded like water to her touch. Oh. I had needed to be touched like this, with the softness and gentleness of a woman's body—a touch that didn't ask anything, only offered itself. She smelled of rose at her neck, and let me go.

Inside, her house seemed spacious in a way it never had before: large, light-filled and gracious, clean and free of sordidness, the site of a good life. I thought of the branch Radha had given me, which I had thrown away after the semester had finished, but which I should have kept, I realized now, for it was such an object that could make a room feel large, open, or deep: it could make a room feel possible. I would never find another branch like that, for each fallen branch to my eye was the same, equally unlovely. It took a special eye to pick one up and say *look*. It took a life lived for oneself only to keep such an object in a room, an object that might cause only its owner pleasure. My flat, so

tasteful, though it never before felt small, felt so now: there
was no room for such objects.

"Have some tea," she said, "nice and strong. It always
makes me feel better," and her face, like her house, was
clean, simple, and beautiful, though, I saw now, undergo-
ing a kind of translation, somewhat belatedly, from youth
to middle age, especially around the kohl-dark eyes, where
kindness had creased the skin with its own history. Onstage
she would retain her youth forever; it was a gift of intimacy
to receive a close look, to allow a loving eye to track the
changes time brought. Her face showed age as my mother's
never had—and as I crossed this birthday into another year
of life I too would stride forward into the vast field of time
from which my mother had vanished, and the unknown
years would mark my face as they had never touched hers.

"I was pregnant too," she said. Pouring milk from a
metal bowl and she didn't look up.

"I didn't mean to—" I blurted, and then, absorbing her
words, "You were?"

"Yes."

"What happened?"

"I had it taken care of," she said. "I wasn't married."

"I—I can't. It's too late."

"I know."

"I tried." And I had. But after the doctor had refused
me, I had not sought another: I had not eaten the quantities
of papaya he had warned me against—I had not written

to Farnaz and asked what had happened to Sita, all those years ago when she was in trouble. Shame—and my husband, so happy, bursting in each evening to the cottage with a smile.

"I know."

"How?"

With a bright hiss, the tea fizzed up the sides of the vessel. She clicked off the stove.

"You so wanted to come to Delhi." She came to me where I sat at her small table and wiped my cheek. "You wanted to come to New York too."

"New York?"

"Yes, darling," she said, "I'm leaving. I've been invited to perform at a dance festival in New York—not in the city, but in the country, north, very green, I'm told, and dancers come from all over the world. Then I'm going to New York City itself to start a company and to live, I've been offered a residency. It's for two years, but who knows. Maybe I'll like it too much to leave."

"And you were going to ask me to come with you?"

"Yes, though I knew it was going to be tricky with your husband."

I was silent. Her birds were singing. It was not a music you could dance to, it was not even beautiful. She went to the cage, opened the door, and offered them her finger, one hopped out easily, and then the other, she brought them close to her mouth and said something to them quietly. I had never seen them out of their cage before: they looked brighter, greener, almost wet with their color, and they threw themselves into the air and began to fly, chattering happily, filling the space as easily as the silence, with a kind of joy. After a while they seemed to grow tired and returned to her finger. Back in the cage they groomed themselves as luxuriously as cats.

"You said you'd dance in your mind if you couldn't dance with your body."

"Yes."

"Do you?"

I shook my head. "Yes. But it's difficult."

"Difficult," she said. "More difficult than not dancing?"

"I don't know. No."

"You know, no one understands the story of Eklavya."

"It's a story about the way the world is ordered," I said. "We use religion to justify why some people are advantaged and some have to suffer. We call it destiny."

"Not destiny, dharma."

"Dharma, even worse."

"You don't understand the story either. By submitting to the demand of his teacher, by cutting off his thumb, Eklavya *becomes* the arrow, the bow. The intensity of his desire and his devotion sharpens him into a weapon: an instrument. And then he fulfills his dharma—not his dharma to be less than Arjun, but to be the truest archer, the gift he was born to. Do you see?"

"No."

"You will," she said. "Come, I forgot our tea. I hope it's not cold." But it was still steaming as she poured it into cups. She set my cup in front of me, a cloud of scent, cooked milk and ginger, bloomed around me.

"It's a terrible mess," I said. "My husband—he wants to return to his family. Everything we had planned, it's different now. He wants to live with his family and let them raise our child and he wants me to come there and live like a good daughter-in-law who serves her family—not to perform, not to dance. He wants me to come and live there quietly my whole life like that. And what else can I do?"

"Drink your tea," she said and paused, considering her words carefully. "Don't hesitate. You keep moving forward. Don't look over your shoulder now. Keep moving forward."

"I don't know how."

She looked at me sternly. "Don't you?"

I felt small under her gaze. "When will you leave?"

"For New York? Only after the new year."

"Can I come again to see you?"

"Of course."

"I should be going."

"Vidya."

"Yes?"

She took my hand. I could feel the warmth of her blood through the palm. "Take care. Take care."

The monster grew: my body. When my condition was evident, I stopped leaving our cottage. Out the window the quiet streets grew even more still, and thus the sea seemed louder, dull and angry, occupying all the silence it had been given. What of the advice my dance teacher had given me? Perhaps I was not the kind of dancer I thought I would be, one who danced for her own pleasure only. Perhaps I was the kind of fickle dancer I had once scorned. For I could not, even in my mind, dance. I was not a mind: I was a body: my body would not dance. My body, who for so long had worked side by side with my will, as though horse and rider, working so closely as to be almost one as they raced forward, for the joy of racing, now became stubborn, oppositional in its lethargy. She wore *me*. She wanted to eat. She wanted to lie on the divan late afternoon after eating, stretching into a soft, dozing state, not quite asleep, porous to the noise of the outside, which poured into her open ears. She—my body—was not unhappy. The roiling unwellness of the last few months—what I had begun to think of as seasickness—began to ebb, a long wave pulling back from the shore. My body was sleepy and calm. In the afternoon she wanted to walk.

Around the apartment she walked and walked. Though my body no longer danced it still could not help but keep an even beat in its steps and its heavy gait: one-*two*, one-*two*, one-*two*, one-*two*, one-*two*. My *mind* did not like afternoon, it twitched inside the body, especially at this angle of light; if the body were to stray too close to the window and see the light flooding through the closed shutters she would wince. Outside, afternoon obliterated the streets, it turned the sea and the backs and bumpers of cars into unbreakable flats of blinding shine. In this high, terrible heat, there was no room for thought, only dread. Why should this light bother *me* if it did not bother the body? The body could simply narrow her eyes and look away from the window. Around and around, not looking where the feet were placed, only walking forward in a tight, endless circle.

It seemed to come from somewhere, the step and step. Slowly, over many afternoons, an image became clearer. I remembered a woman room-walking from end to end. The woman had a dark look and a swollen belly. As she walked she kneaded the belly and muttered in time to her walking. The movements and the words came from the body of a sleepwalker, I walked with her, following her motions, until I could see even deeper, to an earlier time, when I myself was rocked and rocked within an endless, wary walker, one whose body walked and walked without the mind, against the mind, long and long hours damp of afternoon, for no light would reach the room in which I slept, still the feeling of light—red light—

Walking, remembering, I felt a strange mixture of feeling: so close: seeing her, being within her, *being* her: my mother. I was frightened. It should have felt like sweetness.

My body was a house built by her, inhabited by her, and no matter where I made my home—Versova, Paris, the moon—I would not escape her. Yet, at the same time as I experienced this suffocating closeness, I felt the yawning gap. I could not ask her a single question. We shared a body but her mind I could not reach. Why was this. Why was any of it. Then I was tired, and slept.

When I awoke the sun had set, and my husband returned home. In those waking minutes, it took a long time for me to locate myself. It felt like much time had passed since I lay down to sleep, and that I was now old, possibly dead, while life continued on outside without me, with all its heartbreak and commerce. "Sleeping?" my husband said, amused, switching on the light. When he leaned down to kiss me I could smell the evidence of outside upon him, mixed with his sweat, and the deep green of his French cologne, one of the many extravagances of his old life he had carried into the new one, and with it, I could glean from his cheeks the scent of cigarette smoke and laughter, and the sharp smell of outside air. "Have you eaten, love?"

"Yes," I said.

"But you've been asleep."

"I'm not hungry."

"How are you feeling?"

"Oh fine," I said. And my body glowed: she *was* fine, large, beautiful, docile, calm. The belly humped beneath my petticoat held a creature whose movements I was beginning to discern, movements that felt arrhythmic and unsettling. I had the image of a creature in there with the gold-ringed, alien eyes of my dance teacher's birds. Had the soul come into the body? Almost willfully it had, rebelliously, she had come where she was not wanted—barged into my body. As I had too, I think, so sick my mother had been. How unlike me to come without being called. For my mother, seventeen, surely had not called.

"You're not suffering so much now? No headaches?"

"Not suffering so much now," I said.

"That's just smashing," he said. "Look what I have for you."

He had entered with a package, which I had not noticed, and he picked it up and placed it in my arms, watching me as I opened it, pulling off the brown paper to reveal a shining white box tied with a red ribbon. The lid of the box lifted to reveal a shock of violent color, and the faintest whiff of perfume: the single most beautiful sari I had ever seen: red as the marriage sari I had not worn at our courthouse wedding, shot through all over with gold thread, gold thread along the border inscribed dancing-girls and jungle birds, and men and women and birds danced together down the generous pallu: how such fine silk held the heavy gold thread I could not understand, and I could not keep my greedy hands from traveling over its length, which felt cool against my palms. "My mother wants to see you."

"Did she send me this?"

"Yes, she said it would suit you."

"She said that?"

"Yes, and she's right. Look. The colors suit you exactly. Will you put it on?" He sat down beside me on the bed.

"Maybe later," I said.

"She wrote you a letter," he said.

"I don't care. I don't want to read it."

"Don't be so unreasonable, Vidya."

"*I'm* being unreasonable? Not the woman who came to my father's house and slapped me and called me a whore? Why do you want me to read it?"

"It's all wrong, Vidya. It's not what she's like. It was a mistake—"

"A *mistake*?"

"Why can't we even discuss it? I'm never supposed to think about them again? The people who raised me and cared for me and gave me everything?" And he was up from the bed. He opened his hands helplessly. "I don't understand this about you. So many girls would trade anything to be in your position."

"Aren't you *glad* I didn't marry you for your money?"

"Well why didn't you?" he said lightly.

I made an exasperated noise. If anything, the ease with which he had spent money during our courtship discomfited me, physically—to see his money fly out of his pocket

and into so many open hands, and especially for my benefit, gave me a queasy feeling that I could not disguise: a new
shirt when your old one tore, or simply because it struck in
you desire; a taxi when you were tired; a watch for a girl
after she arrived late to your previous date—trace the wrist
before the watch is placed around it, and tell her, "See, now
you'll always be on time." I was glad when we lost the extra
income his family supplied before they learned of our relationship and we were forced by circumstance to stand on our
own feet.

Still, I consistently admired the gentle confidence that
shaped his stride and his dealings with the world, and that
was not quite money—as often as not, money could make
a person cruel—and he approached each person he met
with a democratic respect, almost a deference, regardless of
their station. No, he had been mothered sweetly, and well.
A mother had cleared the obstacles from his path with
a gentle hand, and presented the world to him as a toy
that existed for his pleasure: someone had lifted him while
he was crying and brushed the tears from his face. I had
imagined him as a boy in a hand-sewn costume, the stripes
of the child-sailor matched at the seams by his mother's
careful fingers, and I had imagined someone nearly as
lovely as Mrs. B brushing the tears from his cheeks and the
corners of his nose as he cried. In fact, I myself had brushed
my hands across the plains of his face, tracing the path of

those vanished fingers. Did I hope that his mother would see how wholly and excellently I loved her son, and open her arms to me? Ah, not even I was that naive.

"Even if you didn't care for money, what's wrong with enjoying it?"

"They wouldn't tolerate my dance."

"You never let yourself enjoy anything, Vidya." Having regained his patience, his voice was tender. "It's good to eat until you're full."

"I do. I have a different stomach."

"Yes," he couldn't help adding, though he knew the joke would hardly advance his cause, "a much larger one, in fact."

"Is this funny to you?"

"I wish it was funny to you. I wish anything was funny to you right now. I haven't seen a smile on that face for weeks."

"A smile?" I said, for a moment, stunned. What I had been trying to hold together was tearing irreparably: the husband that lived in my mind and the husband who stood before me. "We planned, Rustom. My career—your career—this house—"

"Life resists plans, I suppose," he said, I think, to the wife in his head, the wife he was struggling to hold together too with this mixture of desperation and cheer. "Accidents happen in love, and one just has to make the best of it. *I'm* happy," he said, "I wish you could be."

"Weren't you happy before?"

"How can a man be happy when his heart is being torn in two?"

"Torn in two? You're not making sense."

"I don't make sense to you," he flared finally, his voice raised, "because you have no family. You can't understand what you were asking of me."

"I have a family."

"You can throw yours away when it suits you. It doesn't cost you anything."

"Cost me. Only a rich person thinks like this."

"That's not what I meant."

"What did you mean?"

"I thought—" But then he stopped himself. Shrugged. My friend was gone. My husband lit a cigarette. His face was handsome and hard, a man's face. I began again to feel a sense of vertigo. Who, if not his family, would help me raise the child? For unlike the chaali, where children were largely left to their own devices, with a distracted eye of some mother glancing out from time to time over each child, and come suppertime a child could be fed in any house it visited, there was no group of women here to join and throw my lot into the communal pool, my hands help-ing some with their day's work as some hands would come help me with mine, and to contribute some little crumb to the afternoon's store of gossip. Some days I listened to my landlord's servant and the neighbor's exchanging small news over the wall as they hung up the washing: they were sisters, I later learned, who had managed to find such proximate employment, and their words to each other, irritated or sweet, and their dry, teasing laughter, seemed too humble a thing to be envious of. But I could protect myself from many things with my ability to sleep, deeply and vastly for hours on end, a sleep that didn't compromise my nighttime hours. Some animals did this, dreamed deeply, impervious for months to outside weather. I kicked myself back into sleep, and lay back into the vast dark pool of my dream.

Into the sleep-room came my brother. So much dreaming, though forgotten, robbed me of my surprise. I was not expecting him, but I let him in when he knocked on the door, then went to wash my face and my mouth. When I came out of the bathroom he was standing next to his shoes, having no idea where to sit: the unmade makeshift double bed (its scandalous width and my condition gave it a distasteful, seedy aura); the unsteady wooden chair where my husband, seated at the rolltop desk, wrote his poems by hand and then banged them out on his typewriter; or the floor, of which there was not much, the largest expanse being in the kitchen, where my husband and I ate our meals. I went to the kitchen and he followed me and sat. His shoes. I took a second look. Then I moved my eyes away as though I had seen something illicit. Deep brown leather, worn, they looked too small for his feet. And.

"Aren't you going to ask why I'm here?"

"Yes, when I wake up all the way."

"So the wife of a rich man spends all day sleeping?"

I moved slowly about the kitchen, fixing some tea. I had some dry bhakhari I kept in a tin only for myself, as my husband didn't care for it, and this I set down in front of him with only a bit of irony. It had been months—maybe longer—since I'd seen him, and his body startled me: it was long and thin, the color of amber, and it glowed with a false health, almost a feverishness. His hair was too long, and unkempt, it kept falling into his eyes as he spoke and he brushed it away with a distracted irritation. "So this is where the wife of a rich man lives?"

"He's not a rich man."

"Tell that to the ladies at the chaali. They can't stop talking about it."

"I'm not worried about what they think."

"Yes, the troubles of petty mortals do not penetrate such lofty heights."

So long had it been since I had spoken Gujarati with anyone—months, or longer—that despite my brother's bitter words, or perhaps because of them, the language seemed almost unbearably sweet. And it was as though a door opened through time, stepping into the language as one stepped into a city inhabited by long-vanished creatures; I was my brother's sister, my father's daughter, even my mother's—the act of feeding my brother even this small snack returned something also to me: time that I had felt careless in, those afternoons returned from school, a mother in the other room, and my itchy mind straining toward something, to be free of chores so that I could spend some small time with my little knotted rag-doll, or with my sums, or browsing through the day's many miscellaneous thoughts: the way names, for instance, could doom or save someone's nature, like how a naturally bitter person, given the name Mitthoo, would through some mysterious alchemical process reconfigure herself to the sweetness of her moniker, or how Kacharo's parents succeeded in warding off the evil eye by naming their beloved son after garbage, and thus he survived his infancy while all his elder and nobler-named siblings had perished, or even I, fulfilling the destiny of the original Vidya, the dancer whose image had so enchanted my mother through the black-and-white grain of the newspaper—so many thoughts I had, so eager was I to think them, that it felt to me my mind was a large blooming tree whose many branches I longed to scamper around and explore. I had wanted those days to be over quickly, over so that I could be free to explore them. Alone. Yes, and they had gone from me willingly, while I had been like a girl racing back from the well, so eager to reach her destination, and so sure of abundance of water in her jar, that she does not choose her steps and is heedless of the water she spills against her dark braid and in the dust of the road, believing she will never be thirsty. Those days in which my mother had still been alive.

"Where did you get those shoes?"

"The old man gave them to me," he said. He took the tea from me, and the bhakhari. "I never thought I'd see you like this."

"What 'like this'?"

"*With child*," he said in English with a smirk.

"Why not?" I asked, and when he shrugged I said, "Have you grown taller?"

"I've been at this height for several years. You might get used to me this way if you came more often to visit."

"You too could visit." I sat on the floor of the kitchen. My lap was occupied by the bulge of my belly.

"Well here I am."

"Yes, here you are."

He looked perfectly natural in my kitchen, though this was the first time he'd been in it, and though the image of him sitting there so naturally troubled me, wearing rougher versions of the refined clothes my husband often wore, thin bell-bottoms a little bare at the knees, a red-and-purple printed cotton shirt open at the throat. On his upper lip there was a nice thick and carefully kept moustache. When people saw this young man walk down the street, did they see the boy's eyes in the man's face? They were bright, slightly yellow around the core, and some fine tracery of veins marked the edges: eyes that held a direct, almost accusing gaze that could not disguise their hurt, even a stranger could see it.

"You came here to tell me something."

"I wanted . . ." he said, and his demeanor started to shift, almost despite himself, into something a little more boyishly shy. "I wanted your advice, or actually, I think I wanted to ask you a favor."

"What's the matter?"

"Well, the old man's told you, I'm sure, that he's fixed my engagement?"

"Of course." The engagement ceremony had been only a week prior, but I had been too sick to go, or so I'd said. I'd sent a letter to my future sister, a young girl I had never met before but who I was told was fair, along with a present of a small gold bangle. The reply I'd received was exceedingly polite. She had asked to meet me some afternoon in the coming weeks, but I had demurred, citing my illness; in truth, I did not want to be met like this, especially not for the first time, and had promised to receive her gladly once the baby was born.

"I won't marry her, Vidya."

"What do you mean?"

"Just that. I won't marry her." He couldn't help but smile a proud smile.

"Why did you agree to?"

"I don't know—I was—confused. I thought it would be nice—to have a girl in the house—again."

"And now?"

"And now I love someone else and want to marry her instead."

If there was a fault in the boy it was, in part, mine. I had not brought him up with a thought to the next day, to the grown man, only to the boy wailing or quiet in my arms, hungry or sleepy or needing to be washed. "Why is it you only come to me with trouble?"

He didn't say anything.

"Have you told father?"

"No. I was hoping you would."

"Me?"

"Yes, I think he'll take it better coming from you."

"I won't help you with this. You'll ruin that girl's life. The engagement has already been announced."

"But I could just explain—I mean, you, and I, and the old man, we could all just explain that the fault wasn't hers. We'll say she's a very good girl from a good family. We would tell everybody. We would say that I am to blame."

"Why didn't you fall in love before you got engaged?"

"You're hardly one to lecture me about proper marriages."

"My marriage didn't ruin anyone's life."

"Except mine!"

"Yours?" I looked at him, surprised. "Don't be ridiculous, how did I ruin yours?"

"You left me," he said. I could see his cheeks flush dark with blood. But how long would it be until I could no longer find the child's eyes in the man's face? How long until he would be grown? He looked away, wiping at his eyes. Looking very small for all his leggy length, and very alone. And how did I look to him? My body was already reflected in a warped mirror. But the eyes that looked at him were unknowable to me, my eyes and what he saw in them.

"Your tea's getting cold," I said, and then I asked again, "Where did you get those shoes?"

"I told you, the old man gave them to me. Well, I found them, and I asked to have them."

"Where did you find them?"

"In the almirah, where else?"

"Did he tell you whose they were?"

"Yes, my mother's. And before that they were her father's."

"Her father's?"

"Yes."

"He died when she was young."

"She was seven." But I hadn't known that all those years my mother wore her father's shoes. I longed to turn them over in my hands, even to smell them. At the same time I had the perverse instinct to hurl them out the window, throwing with such force they landed in the sea. "Couldn't you marry Alopa?"

"No."

"Who is this girl you love?"

"You know Urveshi from the third floor?"

"You mean the Kapadias' girl? Isn't she very young?"

"Well, so am I, aren't I?"

"What a mess," I said. I got up, again very heavily, to take his empty cup and rinse it in the sink. "Do you want some more tea?"

"No, this is enough. Are you angry with me?"

"I don't know," I said. "I think you should talk to Father about it."

"I'm talking to you about it. Don't you care at all?"

"I don't understand why he gave you those shoes. It's bad luck twice over. You shouldn't have brought them here."

"You've really changed," he said, scornfully. "You never used to believe in superstitions."

It was not superstition, not quite. The shoes were exactly parallel to each other, pointing away from us, toward the door, or beyond it, their ancient dust-gray laces untied. Each shoe suggested a foot, two shoes two feet, and those two feet two ankles, bared as the wearer lifted her sari slightly, the lifted sari suggested hands to pull up the fabric and then to reach down to tie the laces, and a golden back fully bent, and the slip of a thick braid over a shoulder, dangling like the loose end of a rope, and then there she was, just from the shoes, not whole, in pieces, turned away from me as she put them on. And so the shoes must have been for her, suggesting other feet, other legs, a father's rare brown hands, the shocking vulnerability of his old-man neck, and the thin curve of a spine through white cotton.

"You don't know, do you, how Mother died?" He brandished this question at me in a sly way, the way the robber shows the knife. We had always known how dangerous questions were. He was angry, that made him ask it: his anger made him brave, to pick up and wield the weapon.

But I did know, for all at once, I did know, in fact I had always known; it was not the feeling of a memory freed from the dark reaches of the mind and floating up to burst like a bubble of air in water, fully fresh and intact, but a thing as dull and steadily known as my own name. "She jumped off the roof of our building, and when she hit her head, she died."

"You knew?" he said.

And how could I explain it, even to myself, but I did. I remembered shutting my eyes on the bed, trying hard to sleep, but I had heard a sound—a scream, and then a long wail—and I had gone to the window and looked behind the shade. My mother was on the ground. Her leg was bent back at a weird angle. There was a deep color around her head, almost black, which it took me a long time to understand as blood. Her eyes, were they closed or open? This I could not remember.

"You know she had me with her when she jumped?"

"What?"

"She wanted to kill me too."

"No."

But he was right. I had been alone in the room. The scream must not have been my mother's—maybe a neighbor's. And the wail was his. Someone had run down to pick him up as I stood there watching. She rocked him back and forth. I don't know why, but I thought of Radha then, of our last afternoon. Somehow the two memories had knotted up together in my confused mind, and now they played together in tandem. A body in a bed, a body on the ground. Pleasure twisting through, and a cold distance. I don't know why.

"You remember?"

"The old man told me."

"You *asked* him?"

"Yes."

"But you weren't hurt. When she fell."

"No. Because of how she landed, you see. She could have survived the fall. If she fell another way she wouldn't have died. But she hit her head on that step. The old man says she must have changed her mind. From the way she fell she was protecting me. But I don't know."

"She didn't want to be apart from you."

"No," he said, "she wanted to kill me."

"She wanted to take you with her."

"I guess we can't know."

"I know, I was there. She loved you." I was very far away from myself, from my brother and from my body. Distantly, I felt something like envy. Even in this, the last, she had loved him more, and thought nothing of me: she had left me and kept him. Then she had died for him, instead of living for me. I felt an emotion like fear as I looked at my brother. There it was, the moment had come so quickly—I had lost the child in him. He looked— even old, very much like our father in the gritted cast of his face.

"Are you—okay? You look—ill—" He didn't want to look at me either, shifted his eyes away from me. He had wanted something else. But what? I couldn't give it. Now the true story had been spoken we couldn't have another one.

"Yes, yes, I'm fine," I said, pulling hard at the words until more of them came. "You know, I've been so sick, the first weeks I couldn't keep anything in my stomach. I felt sick all the time, and I was so worried I was going to be sick for nine full months but luckily I can eat now. I don't feel sick except sometimes I get headaches."

"Like mother."

"Yes," I said. And then the words dried up again and I could only manage to say, "Please, take the shoes away from here. You should—destroy them."

"Are you sure you're alright?"

"Yes."

"I shouldn't have come."

"No," I said. "I'm—glad—"

"Well, I'll be going then."

"Yes," I said. I sat down on the bed and turned my face away from him. When he left, I shut the door and latched it. I felt—I think—cold. It was a strange feeling that visited my limbs first, then my groin then racing up to my head. All the hairs standing up and almost a pain—I think it was cold. I just stood there looking at my furred arm. After a while I began to shiver and my teeth were chattering. Yes: I had been cold once: on a night-train: sleeper's class with dark air streaming in from the window: I wrapped only in a shawl: dozing against my mother. Now the feeling came over me I remembered it. I took a sheet from the bed and wrapped it around myself. It was not enough to staunch the cold. I remembered how I thought being cold would be a clean feeling, a white feeling, like ice. I had been wrong. No, it was a dirty feeling. I realized I was a little dizzy because the breaths my body was taking were so small, only like little sips. I could not expand my lungs quite enough to take a good deep breath, but I could make my breaths a little longer. Curiously I felt fine. It was like listening to something underwater. My husband had said it was easy for me to throw my family away. Not easy—but I had. After a while I was warmer and I took off the sheet.

Of the following days, the less said the better. They were not very good days, hot days, days—pardon me—of hell, where I lived in a dark room, shades drawn in a flimsy attempt to keep the heat at bay, neglecting the housework so badly that my husband hired two bais to pick up all the work I had left, and which he must have paid for at least partially with his parents' money. These two women punctured the cottage's silence—they opened the windows to let the air in, and they talked to each other and tried to talk to me, but they could not puncture the strange, oblong state in which I lay, egg-shaped, oblivious, in the vast and strong reaches of the afternoon, which seemed, each day, endless, simply punctuated by the arrival of my husband, and therefore of night, and the departure of my husband, and therefore the arrival of day. Through these day-long afternoons my mind traveled endless spirals of thought, no, one circle of thought, like the snake eating its own tail, or a lost, baffled explorer traversing the same small section of forest, unable to point himself in another direction. I can say that the circle of thought began and ended in the death of my body, and that death aroused no fear in me, as it had those days of the top-step at the Bhavan, a thrilling fear that was in its own way like joy, but only seemed at the time a logical end and a logical beginning. Once, through the dullness, I felt the recovered knowledge come up in me, come up like bile in my throat. No, like electricity, a scorching feeling. My eyes flared very suddenly open and I began to sweat, and the child, feeling my alarm, started banging against my body, wanting to be let out. The surface of me rippled with its hardness, fists and knees: it was angry. Or, I was. It would have felt good to scream or to cry, to beat myself against something as it beat against me, blind and rageful. I could not do it. No sound came through my mouth. I started to hit my thigh with my palm, keeping a violent taal. It was hypnotic, the feeling of the thigh against the palm. Both stung: the thigh and the palm, the palm I could see becoming red. I began to calm. I let the room glaze. Then I could breathe again. The child was coming, though I had not wanted it, though surely there was no one less fit to mother it than me? Mrs. B could have her, and if she loved her with one tenth the love she reserved for a boy, well, even that would be enough to raise her in the infinite rooms of her elegant home, hire one man to teach her how to ride a horse and another man to teach her how to swim in the Parsi Gymkhana's jewel-colored pool. Would be enough—would do. Would be more than I had.

No. I had no mother, and neither would she.

"Here, you must eat this, in your condition, you need to eat and keep up your strength," said the kind voice of the younger bai, truly they were kind, I could see this from far away, and I accepted their food into my body knowing the child needed it, and that the body would need it to expel the child, but I could not taste the food or maybe didn't try to register it. Then I lay back down.

When my husband came he greeted me with affection and went to bathe, then he put on a record that we both liked to listen to. I wasn't listening. He said something to me, and then he said it again. I said, "What?"

"Can you please tell me what's happening to you?"

"Nothing."

"Nothing," he said. He was angry. "*Nothing*. Look at you."

What difference did the body make, let alone its appearance? He would have paid the bais to bathe me and dress me if he could. But the next day he came home and told me that he'd spoken to the doctor and that everything was normal. The doctor said that sometimes women become erratic and odd in the last week or two of pregnancy—the hormones. Just as long as I didn't have a fever, which, my husband confirmed, putting his hand against my forehead, I didn't, I felt completely normal. Yes. Long ago I had visited a woman in a room who turned her face away and whose words, if she spoke in the room at all, carried no sound. She was just tucked inside her egg, I knew now, as I was. "Yes, normal," he said, and then, thinking I needed some reassurance he continued, "You'll have the best care, my love, the best medicine, there's no need to be afraid. And look, you've seen how nice it is to have a little help, at my parents' house, you won't have to lift a little finger. You can rest, recover, and then *enjoy*, have a cold drink, learn how to swim, meet my mother's friends, my family's friends, they're quite—well, some of them—are quite—"

"Okay," I said.

"Okay, what?"

"Okay, let's shift to their place."

"Really?"

"Yes, really."

He looked so pleased, solved, as though someone had just popped a dislocated shoulder back into its socket. "That's just wonderful, Vidya—you'll be—I promise—so happy—"

Happy. A word didn't hurt more than any other. That was the odd part. There was no hurt, no ache at all. It was like sweat, it just stayed on me. Might pain be better? Where was it going? I almost couldn't feel my body, except in its heaviness, its lethargy, so swollen that I was unable to take deep breaths all the way to their apex.

On that night, as I lay awake, listening to my husband's breathing, and to my own, which was soft and lapping, not quite in concert with my husband's, I could feel that though I was ready for sleep, my child was awake, and I could feel this not from her movements but from the wide-openness of her eyes, black, and lashed, lidded, open inside me. Looking. I was being looked *through*, and because the seeing was so deep I looked in and out of myself at once: through my own consciousness and through a consciousness so intimate that it was a surprise to realize that it was not actually mine. The look of my body, its humped casing dampened by the blue-purple light, and the feel of it, of the her, the other I, the not-me, pushing out through me, all came oddly and exquisitely together. Instead of fear it was an animal calm, like those dreams where you remember you can fly.

The contractions started in the morning, shortly after my husband had left for work, and in the afternoon I decided it was time to go to the hospital. We didn't have a phone in the cottage, so when the latest contraction abated, I went around to my landlord's house, knocking a little too urgently on the door, which was answered by the maid who conversed over the wall with her sister—it being the middle of the week, the family was away. Without hesitation she sent a houseboy out on the main road to call for a taxi, and asked if I would like to come inside and telephone my husband, but I told her I would call him from the hospital. Between the pains of the contractions I felt fine, almost giddy, and I did not want to walk across the vast and gleaming parquet floor, which looked both treacherous and easily spoiled. Anyway, the taxi came quickly, and bringing nothing but my purse, I sat in the back seat. The driver was none too pleased with his charge, once he saw my condition and learned our destination, but I was already inside his car. We drove: too quickly. I was fine for a time until I wasn't: it was difficult to breathe. I gripped the armrest and made no sound. The pain passed. Pain—not just. It was strange and deep, the movements that originated inside. Already in the center of their hot moments, time had begun to change around me, I lost the thread of it, so fully occupied in the intensity of the sensation until it let me go. We had arrived at the shining white building I had seen all those years from the roof of my house, built for British ladies to deliver their babies, fashioned of rose-blushed marble, shining white against the green hill, seeming to pick up some dazzle from the ocean below. The taxi driver had glanced at my face during the pain and softened toward me, and perhaps he was grateful that I didn't soil his car: he got out, opened the door for me, and then walked me to the entrance, leaving me in the charge of the admitting nurse.

I loved the smell of the stairway, cool and mineral as rain. I clutched the banister as I climbed, slowly, feeling the full weight of my body—for the last time, I thought, not savoring it, but soon I would be, again, alone, and light. Down the long yellow hallway, pale yellow with mint-green trim, the floor clean and smelling of disinfectant, but my room was painted a melancholy blue I liked, and I was on the bed before the next contraction came, knocking the breath out of me as the indifferent nurse took my blood pressure. Then I was left alone in the room, alone, for I still had not yet called my husband, and didn't want to. (I had told the nurse when she asked that he was in an important meeting and not to be disturbed, and that he would come to the hospital when his work was finished—it was not at all strange for him to not be in attendance, though it was odd that none of my family was there: no sister, or mother, or brother-and-wife, or anxious mother-in-law.) There were bars on my window but my room had a door that led out to a balcony, all mine, that looked not onto the sea but onto the continuation of the hill's green slope. The sight of so many trees, dark-branched, stocked with crows and smaller birds, some bunched with small yellow flowers whose overwhelmingly sweet fragrance, when I heaved myself off the bed to open the door to the balcony, mingled with the strong, harsh smell of disinfectant, reminded me of the edge feeling of the college campus, and I missed, wildly, desperately, Radha. I wanted her here next to me on the hospital bed, scolding me for making such a fuss, though she could see the depth and breadth of the pain I was in from the way I held my body and the length of my breaths, and so her scolding would only be to comfort me, to remind me of the other world, the one that existed outside the violence happening to my body, the one I would reenter when the pain left. How did you get yourself into this mess, she said to me, sitting on the edge of my bed and smoothing the hair from my forehead, very damp, you said you would never marry.

So did you.

I didn't.

But you will.

Don't accuse me of your sins.

I didn't think anyone would ever love me.

I loved you, she said very simply. But even then I could not say it to her.

I don't want to die.

You won't.

I'm frightened.

First you want to die, now you don't. You claimed you'd never give up dance, then you did. You said you'd become an engineer, then you didn't. You swore you'd never marry, then you married. You didn't want to live with your in-laws, now your husband *this very minute* is moving your things to their place. You said you loved this man, now you want to leave him. You didn't believe in your mother until she was dead, then you wanted her back. You didn't want to be a mother, and you're having a child. You're having a child now, and you're going to be a mother. You're not going to die, but what are you going to do now? What kind of way is this to live?

I covered my face with my hands so I wouldn't have to look at her, to look down at my alarming body, flushed and distended in its soiled sari, pink and smelling darkly of its seeping odor. Soon, blood, they'd part the legs, push up the skirt, and bare a wound stretching open. I didn't want it; I just didn't want anymore to die.

Why not, if you've lived your life so badly?

Because, I said, the pain was so terrible that I could

feel death, I could feel it the way my mother felt it: not peering down from the ledge, but an inch from the earth, and it was not right, it was not comfort, the body did not want to release me, the body remembered pleasure in that inch more desperately than ever before; remembered the silky days of childhood in grandmother's garden, whose soil was watered daily with the water in which we washed, and whose black perfume was sharpened by the acres of dust that surrounded it, stirred when the surface was broken; remembered my mother's fingers in my hair, the strong smell of hair oil and the intelligence of her hands rubbing at my scalp; remembered the specific weight and heft of the brother I had failed, before I had failed him, the warmth of his small fingers around my ear; remembered you, Radha, your eyes closed and your lips slightly parted, and the cadence of your quickened breath, so sweet, sharing the body's capacity for pleasure, the knowledge that pleasure meant something, it could be the opening to the soul—

I'm just babbling, I said, I'm frightened, for pain had come again and I was afraid I could not stand it, no, I was certain I could not: there was no way to reach the logical mind and assure it of its continuance, though the stern nurses made no attempt, just came in to note the frequency of my contractions, conferring with one another as though I myself were not in the room—in a way I wasn't, in those moments of pain, yet I heard their distant voices with mounting anger—look how this one screams, and she's not even at the worst part yet, the whole city will know when it comes time for her to deliver. They shut the door to the balcony and scolded me—this whole time, the air conditioning was escaping out the door, and when they closed it, I felt the full weight of it against my skin, white women gave birth like this—in ice-boxes—

It was evening now, and my husband arrived. He was still dressed from work and looked quite angry, his anger, enacted by a resident of the world-without-pain, looked almost comical to me and his words came from very far away. "I was worried," he said, "I was so worried when I got home, why didn't you call me?"

"I—*oh*." Gripped and gripped, one hand in the other.

"Why are you sitting alone in this freezing cold room? Where is your doctor?"

Seeing I could give him no answers he left; I could hear his footsteps down the hall. When he returned, he was shouting at my stern nurses, who followed him into the room, "Sir, air-con is a feature, sir, cool air is very good for the mothers-to-be—look, still she's sweating, sir, the doctor has been called, but the case is not urgent, she has not yet even halfway dilated, sir, please lower your voice, we don't have control over the temperature, sir—"

Their voices, angry, kept in time with my pain—pain, a word for which there is no good substitute, but now seems so empty when I set it down, almost completely devoid of meaning, when the experience of it dominated every inch of me, it defined my body in the bounds of the room fully and made my mind so utterly singular: no room for the thought *stop*, or *no*, or *help*—and I began to panic, I started screaming, not out of pain but of fear, cries that alarmed my husband, whose face went strangely white—and as I did so I could feel my body closing up, holding on to its spectacular pain and the baby folded inside it. Drawn perhaps by the voices, which, all raised, were surely attracting attention, for there was nothing unusual about my cries alone—these walls had heard worse, and would, even throughout the course of the night, still hear worse from my lips—another nurse came, one I had not yet seen. This nurse spoke quietly to the other two, who then left the room, and then she spoke very gently to my husband, "This is no place for men, sir. The doctor will be here soon, and in the meantime, your wife is doing very well, she's quite strong, she's young and healthy—"

"I've never heard her scream like this," he said almost in awe.

"To me it's the most ordinary sound in the world," she said. "Come now, have you informed your family? Are there any preparations to be made? There's a phone in our waiting room, available for just this purpose. We'll inform you, of course, when the doctor arrives and of what he says."

With a mixture of relief and anxiety my husband let himself be led out of the room. "Let's take a look," the nurse said when she returned, and pushed my sari up past my knees—I so far gone that her gaze *there* did not bother me, nor did it bother me when she pulled the lips open with her fingers and clicked her tongue. "They shouldn't have let him in here. But he's handsome, your husband, isn't he? Sort of a big shot?"

I nodded. When the doctor came I *did* mind, I gazed at him with hatred, I resented his fingers on my body, returning to the places he had already dispassionately charted. "It will be a while yet," he said, "You were dilating nicely, but you stopped, you just squeezed shut as it were. You need to relax—

*"Relax—*

"—and just let mother nature do her work."

But the nurse, when the doctor left, spoke more kindly, "It *is* quite cold in here, isn't it. Let me see if I can turn it down—" disappeared, and moments later the arctic rush ceased. The absence of cold rendered warmth pleasant—I was *glad* to be warm again, feeling my skin loosen, my face and my thighs. The contractions beat against my body like waves. Would I die here? Or worse—I would live like this, suspended, I and the child, between this place and the next not for hours but for days—not for days but for years, for ever? This was not like death, there was no nothing in it: each moment was filled with sensation, pain, then no pain, pain, then no pain, and the violent inrush of breath.

"Come on now, sister," said the nurse, in a soft, almost incantatory voice, "your body wants to open and you must let it open, more and more your body wants to open, and now listen to me, it won't be easy—"

"—won't be easy," I repeated,

"—it won't be easy but women have done this, your mother, her mother, and her mother—"

"—and her mother—" And the pain, ebbing for a moment as though to allow me to catch my breath. "But my mother died."

She frowned, "God jesus, in birth?"

"No, later." Where was my mother now? She was gone, dispersed, slipped into another body, or spread, her atoms, back into the earth. Not my mother anymore, I had no illusions about that, the poor Christians' mistake about the afterlife. But I had never, not once, cried for her. I had never marked her absence in any way. I had never even named it.

"Well see, your mother, her mother, and hers. Don't you see? Women have to be braver than men. Up you go, we're going for a walk now, come on." She came close to me and helped me shift my huge body off the bed by sliding her shoulder under my arm and dragging my legs toward the ground, almost as though she would lift me—and though she was very slight, this nurse, and young, younger, even, than me—her arms held a surprising strength as she got me to my feet. Walking up and down the hall in a slow, painful shuffle, I could see the pores across her cheeks—she smelled faintly of jasmine, and faintly of sweat, her voice was a practiced murmur of comforting near-nonsense: "You won't remember this pain when it's over, you'll be so happy, you'll see, this pain will pass and then it will be forgotten."

"I'll remember," I said. The tiles in the hall were large, and red—why red—and still damp from being scrubbed—further down a woman in smarting turquoise crouched with her rag. My shadow trembled twice, against the tile and against the bare white walls. Did other women, then, have holes torn in their memory, torn by pain? Now I remembered everything, and, no matter how awful, I did not want to forget.

"You'll remember that it hurt but not what it felt like."

"I'll remember," I said, and then the pain rushed back and I curled my hand into a fist so my nails bit against my palm, my body was incandescent, it was a magnificent horror, I began to shiver, oh god, I would be torn open, "I'll remember—"

# V

✖✖✖

For a time I had not had a child, I had only the idea of a child: imaginary but real in the same way god was. For the months in me, though her presence became more and more physical, she remained distant, abstract: I could not from her movements deduce her face, the reality of her body outside my body, held in my arms. I could not imagine her hands, her needs, her slate-colored eyes, newborn and unsettled—I could not believe they existed. It was as though her birth had been the end point rather than the beginning, the precipice from which I would fall—and die.

I went to live at my father's house. My brother, hell-bent on his elopement, had left the flat: my father still worked as hard as he ever did, traveling all around the city to give his tuitions: I passed day after day in the dream-state that mirrored my daughter's, never quite awake, never fully sleeping, my body always listening for hers. When my eyes were open, I studied her with curiosity—the mobility of her face, over which many expressions passed effortlessly and seemingly without meaning. Meaningless, the folded brow, the flickering smile that lived only for a second on her lips—and gestures of her tiny arms and legs too carrying no meaning, just a random and inelegant jerking of limbs. This perfect marvel of creation was badly made. Her hands, exquisitely shaped, with the slender, tapering fingers I immediately recognized as my mother's, could not even grasp their own movements, whether they flared into lotus shapes or knitted together as though in prayer when she was at my breast. Her eyes were hazy, unable to focus, her body dark and scrawny, the wild strand of darkness that ran through my family barely tempered by the other side's pink-rose fairness.

And yet, how much better was I? My body was big and dark and heavy and dumb—it was stunned from the pain it had walked through, even as it had lost the physical memory of the pain. It had forgotten how to express itself through the language it had so doggedly acquired, and so become mute. Worse yet, it had nothing to say. If I looked down I saw the deflated body of a stranger. I dried myself and put my sari on quickly.

When my husband visited, I didn't know what to say to him. He held the child badly, and she cried, not because she wanted me, but because she could feel his nervousness and it unsettled her. We could not look at each other, yet our hands touched as we passed her between us, and we spoke to each other easily about the shape of her eyes and her tiny random movements, the way her fist wrapped around an offered finger. I did not have the time or courage to study him, to absorb the hurt that radiated from him. To study his face or the posture of his shoulders would be to read the position of one's stars at birth, and then to orient one's life around the reading—I had no desire, no patience for his influence. I wanted only to put one foot in front of the other until I could understand the path my feet were making.

"You're looking well," he said.

"Am I?"

"Yes," he said, glancing away from me after our eyes brushed. Still, after everything, it thrilled me, his gaze.

"I find that hard to believe."

"You've softened," he said.

The baby—Kalki—had begun to doze in my arms. She loved nothing more than being held. Put her down in the cradle and she screamed, refused to be soothed by the rocking motion, screamed until she gagged, but nearly anyone could hold her—my father, the bai, a visiting neighbor—and she would begin to coo and often her eyes half-closed in pleasure.

"You look well too. Maybe it's just that we've returned to where we should be—this is where we look most right."

"You think you belong here?"

"Why not?"

"You never thought you did."

"I was too arrogant."

"I liked your arrogance."

I clicked my tongue. "Is 'well' the same as happy?"

"No," he said.

He put his empty cup down and stood up. In his beautiful clothes, he looked like a visiting celebrity, and people came out of their apartments to gawk as he left. He put on his sunglasses, strengthening that impression, but I knew it was because the attention made him feel ashamed, and he wanted to deflect it without communicating his shame. I watched him go like everyone else, so small now he looked like a toy-husband, disappearing into the toy-car with dark windows that waited for him just outside the gate. Back to his toy-life: wifeless, childless, and filled again with the ease of toy-money: toy-work, toy-parties, toy-women willing to gamble their reputations for a slightly tarnished prize.

But she was real: the child: my Kalki. Her needs were intense but simple, and I met them all; I fed her, I fed and fed her, I cleaned her, I rocked her to sleep. When she cried I held her until she was soothed. She was real, the butter-smooth length of her. But still her face did not settle into its future. It was trying on aspects, rushed with ancestors, and so changed like the shifting of a kaleidoscope's colors from angle to angle, mood to mood. A tilt of her chin: she was my infant brother; my husband's mother broke over her face as she laughed; my grandmother in her ears with their fat lobes, and in her long arms; my husband in the whorl of her darkening eyes, greenish flecks appearing in the outer rim of the iris; my mother in the look of concentration, as her body began to learn itself, as consciousness began to spread out in her, from the direction her eyes looked, to the expressions of her mouth, then out through the arms and hands, which learned how to wave and grasp their fingers.

Kalki cried: I lifted her to my breast. Her mouth fit neatly over the nipple, her eyes closed in nearly a swoon, her breath falling soft and hot against my skin. Alone in the flat, I didn't mind it. I had begun to cultivate a sort of affection for my breasts, the left one slightly larger than the right, and fuller with milk. If not beautiful, they were useful. I had not been instructed in the hospital of their use, the nurses preferring to feed the baby with formula, and anyway I had not been there long: I left long before they would have allowed me to, not wanting to keep spending my in-laws' money, not wanting to owe them anything else. But mere hours upon my return to the chaali, the chaali's women had come into the flat, had come thundering like water into the flat and washed away any resistance with sheer force, shooing my father out, swooping up the baby, surrounding me on the divan, opening my blouse, clucking at the hard breasts, at the hungry crying child angry in her hunger, who had seemed then like my opponent—a mother had taken my hot breast in her cool palms and kneaded it, another mother had settled the child in the crook of my arm and put her mouth to my nipple. I was nearly whimpering in pain. They had come because pity had called them; I didn't want their pity but I didn't care anymore: I was too tired to be embarrassed by my nudity, the breast that blared out of the blouse. They adjusted me and tried again, firmly and without sympathy. Then the milk began to flow through us. The relief was so intense that at some point it passed into pleasure.

"You're hungry, aren't you?" I said to Kalki now. I had begun talking to her just to say something to someone and for her to hear my voice. "I ate so many chilies yesterday I hope your milk isn't too spicy."

Her eyes were open, and she was looking at me. I wonder if we had been like this, me and my mother, if my mother had looked into my eyes with curiosity about the self that flickered inside them, trying to extrapolate the fixed future from the malleable present. It seemed impossible to me—even once—that she hadn't. Kalki came away from the breast with a sigh. I walked to the window and looked out with her—I was always looking for Mrs. B out that window, imagining her striding through the chaali to pluck her granddaughter out of what she would call its filth. I would have fought her—I wanted to—snarling like a beast, but she never came. They wanted nothing more than to forget us, the Bs, who had never laid eyes upon their son's child. Kalki would never have a grandmother, someone who loved her indulgently, and best. She would never have so many things. I propped her up on my knees. Her bright eyes tracked my fingers as they unhooked my anklet, and then dangled it within her reach. I saw something pass over her face: pleasure, from the sight and sound of the bells and the bright silver, then curious desire—she reached out and brushed her fingers against the silver, and made a crow of joy as it chimed.

I put her down. There was no music in the empty flat, just the mid-afternoon noises of the chaali: children returning from school, afternoon tea being prepared and served, cars on the road, dogs barking: noise. No music, but so outlined were her movements with her purpose, they stood out, gleaming, luminous; like dance. She kicked her dark leg, then kicked it again. I remembered the days in Versova where I leaned out the window, watching the movements the world had offered, so close to understanding them. I had promised my teacher I would dance in my mind if I couldn't with my body, but I had not understood my promise. I thought it meant remembering the movements, to rehearse mentally the sequence of steps and poses so that I would not have to reach for them when I danced, something I used to do often, filling idle moments on the bus or in bed with these thoughts. And I had thought that it was the poor substitute, the lesser thing. But I now understood I had been wrong. By watching, by listening, your body could pay attention. Then the movements, gleaming in their shapes, the kicking of a child's leg, the running of dogs in the waves, were like holes punched in the wall sealing us from that unbroken field of light, the places from which that light entered us. As the eyes and ears became more subtle, the more radiance they observed, admitted, until, infinite, the wall was smashed, broken, gone: you stood bare in front of it. To move one's body with purpose was to communicate some knowledge of this shining field, but one could not ever truly express it with mortal muscle, skin. The greatest of us could just become a dim mirror, a reminder to look. Eklavya arrowed with his body. I would dance with my life.

Kalki was laughing. I picked her up. The smell of her was of the red sweet oil I rubbed in her skin after her bath, was of milk, and the gentle musk of a clean little animal. I could feel her breath against my neck, her body as it responded to mine, resting her cheek against my shoulder. I carried her up to the roof. It was early dusk. I stood as my mother would have, if she had lived through the afternoon, watching evening fall over the city with a child in her arms. The city was so beautiful. Kalki reached out her hands to grab it, as though to stuff it in her mouth.

# ACKNOWLEDGMENTS

Thank you to my mother, Asha Pandya, who made herself an invaluable resource during the writing of this book, and who read the first forty pages and told me to keep going.

I'm indebted to the kathak artists Akram Khan, Roshan Kumari, Quincy Kendall Charles, and the dancers of the Chitresh Das Dance Company. Their work provokes, inspires, and sustains me.

Vivian Gornick's *Fierce Attachments*, Philip Pullman's *His Dark Materials* trilogy, and the documentary *Raga* all were foundational to the ideas about art, intention, and consciousness explored in the book.

Gratitude to the many people who gave this book much care at Algonquin: Brunson Hoole, Michael McKenzie, Lauren Moseley, Mae Zhang McCauley, Kelly Doyle, Stephanie Mendoza, Steve Godwin, and Christopher Moisan. Sasha Tropp for the copyedits and one brilliant ellipsis. Shyama Golden for the cover. My editor, Betsy Gleick, for her keen eye, sharp edits, and advocacy. My agent Samantha Shea for representing my vision of this book, for her savvy, and for a slightly embarrassing amount of hand-holding.

Thank you to Rachel Khong and Claire Calderón at the Ruby. To the San Francisco Public Library. To Hedgebrook, Willapa Bay AiR, and the Elizabeth George Foundation. To Kundiman and my Kundi-fam.

Thank you to my family, especially Asha Pandya, Sanjay Iyer, Bharathendu Swamy, Merylee Smith Bingham, Ed Bingham, Josh Bingham, Hansa Bhaskar, and Beena Sharma. Deep gratitude to Kavita's Nana and Nani who took such good care of her while I wrote. To the mothers and caregivers who I have learned from and beside.

In loving memory of Ila Mami, who lit up every room she was in. In loving memory of my Baa, the strongest person I've ever known. In memory of those who have passed into ancestor.

Thank you to my friends who read this book with beautiful attention, intelligence and depth: Sunisa Manning, Susanna Kwan, Mimi Lok, Shamala Gallagher, Rebekah Pickard, Rhea St. Julian, Abhay Shetty; Meng Jin, Meng Jin again for the second reading, Meng Jin a third time for the title and epigraph; thank you to C. Pam Zhang, Rachel Khong, Asako Serizawa, Peter Orner, and Megha Majumdar.

To Catherine Epstein, Chris Freimuth, and Shamala Gallagher. My kin.

To Kavita, for that kiss on my shoulder. To beloved Abe for the hours and the years.